"Rose, Rose..." a voice crooned in her ear. "Beautiful Rose..."

Go away, Mr. Wolfe. I'm sleeping.

Smooth, warm hands caressed her bare shoulders, spreading a strange heat through her chest, and warm breath fanned the side of her face. She tried to pull away but seemed paralyzed with lassitude.

Don't touch me.

"Rose, do you see the candle at the end of the corridor? I want you to go toward the light."

I don't want to go back there again.

"You don't want to learn the truth?" Warm hands slid around her torso and cupped both breasts. Rose felt herself rise up slowly, her skin tingling and aching. She shouldn't allow herself to feel pleasure at the hands of a stranger.

No, I—

"Once you learn the truth, we can be together. Then I will show you the glory of being touched by a man, really touched...."

Dear Reader,

We're really out to spook you this month—but then, October is the traditional month for ghoulies and ghosties and things that go bump in the night.

Start off your chilling reading experience with Patricia Simpson's *The Haunting of Brier Rose*. This eerie tale is set in the darkly forested Pacific Northwest and features a villain for whom time itself means nothing, a villain who has come from the past to destroy the heroine's future, unless she and the man she loves—the man she has always loved—can find a way to save themselves and preserve their love.

Maggie Shayne is a relatively new author but an extremely talented one, and *Twilight Phantasies* is the first of her "Wings in the Night" duo. You'll love this inside look at the life—and loves—of a man who walks by night and shows his love in a most spine-tingling way.

Next month, keep your eyes open for "New for November," when Shadows will feature two brand-new authors whose way with a spooky tale will impress you just as much as it impressed us. As always, turn on all the lights, draw the shades and lock the doors, then join us for a walk where only Shadows can lead you—to the dark side of love.

Enjoy!

Leslie Wainger
Senior Editor and Editorial Coordinator

PATRICIA SIMPSON

THE HAUNTING OF BRIER ROSE

Published by Silhouette Books New York

America's Publisher of Contemporary Romance

SILHOUETTE BOOKS
300 East 42nd St., New York, N.Y. 10017

THE HAUNTING OF BRIER ROSE

Copyright © 1993 by Patricia Simpson

ISBN: 0-373-27017-8

First Silhouette Books printing October 1993

All the characters in this book have no existence outside the
imagination of the author and have no relation whatsoever to
anyone bearing the same name or names. They are not even
distantly inspired by any individual known or unknown to the
author, and all incidents are pure invention.

® and ™:Trademarks used with authorization. Trademarks
indicated with ® are registered in the United States Patent and
Trademark Office, the Canada Trade Mark Office and in other
countries.

Printed in U.S.A.

PATRICIA SIMPSON

hails from the misty, moody shores of Puget Sound in the Pacific Northwest, the setting for most of her novels of paranormal and romantic suspense.

Though she has written stories since grade school, Patricia opted for a degree in art from the University of Washington and has worked there as a graphic designer for eleven years. She is an expert in desktop publishing and likes to create works in exotic paper for her friends.

Patricia lives in the Seattle area. Her family recycles and gardens organically in the hope that soon everyone will see the value of preventive health care for Mother Earth.

To Noreen,
for your special friendship & your knowledge
of secret worlds within and without

Then Tiny wept, and said she would not marry the dis-
agreeable mole. "Nonsense," replied the field-mouse.
"Now don't be obstinate, or I shall bite you with my
white teeth."

—*Thumbelina*
Hans Christian Andersen

PROLOGUE

Massachusetts Bay Colony, 1670

"Hurry!" Constance called. "We haven't much time!"

Nathaniel stumbled up the trail, half-blind in the twilight, but too worried about being discovered to carry a
lantern. In the dwindling light, he could just make out the
white oval of Constance's face as she waited for him near the
sundial, her shawl and dress wafting around her in the late
September breeze, a small satchel at her feet. For a year he
had courted her, suffering the silent scrutiny of the Bastyr
family, always conscious of their watchfulness, their censure, their severe morality. And now for the first time since
he had spoken for her hand, he was meeting her alone. He
broke through the ring of oak trees that surrounded the
small clearing and ran across the grass, grateful for the full
moon that illuminated his path.

"They didn't see you go?" he asked.

"I don't think so. But they'll soon miss me and come
looking. We've only a few minutes, Nathaniel."

He paused, suddenly unsure of himself. He had never
embraced Constance, never touched her hand, never kissed
her. She had always held herself back from him, worried
that one little slip would bring down the wrath of Seth Bas-

tyr. Nathaniel knew she would rather die than lose him to the Bastyrs' strict code of ethics.

"Connie!" A smile of welcome pulled at the corners of his mouth. His gaze swept across her lovely pale face, made more pale by the light of the moon and her fear of being discovered in her tryst with Nathaniel. Fright widened her cerulean eyes, parted her full lips, showing the barest ridge of her flawless white teeth. Nathaniel stared at the mouth he had longed to taste for the past year and the skin he had longed to caress for what seemed like an eternity. He had lost count of the evenings spent sitting at the Bastyr hearth, pretending to listen to Seth's sermons about colonial politics and the moral decline in the New World, when all the while his every sense was trained on twenty-year-old Constance Meybridge, the English bond servant and distant relative of widower Seth Bastyr.

Now she was here alone, willing to cut every tie and run away with him to Jamaica, to become the bride of a man she had never even kissed.

"Is everything ready?" she asked.

"Aye. We sail at dawn."

"Oh, Nathaniel, I'm frightened!" she exclaimed.

"Frightened? Why?"

"I'm afraid that it will never come to pass." She looked over her shoulder and back at Nathaniel. "No matter what I do, Seth seems to be watching, always watching!"

"Well, he isn't here now."

"How do you know? He could have followed me. Sometimes I swear he can read my mind."

"No one can read your mind, Connie. Don't worry." He grabbed her hands to reassure her. The contact of her warm fingers in his sent a bolt of sensation through him, as it must have for her, because she glanced up at him sharply, her eyes darkening as her pupils widened. Was it her feelings for him that darkened her eyes? Or alarm?

For a moment Nathaniel was at a loss for words, overcome by the heady closeness, the sudden possibilities of being alone with her. He drew her hands to his lips and kissed her fingers. "It will happen. We will be man and wife tomorrow, Connie. Joined forever."

"I only wish tomorrow were here!" She closed her eyes and lifted her face, her auburn lashes dark against her porcelain skin. God, she was beautiful. How could he have found a woman so beautiful and yet so innocent of the power of her beauty?

The chill wind blew through the oaks, singing softly in the brittle leaves, lulling Nathaniel into a special world where the Bastyrs did not exist, where contracts and duty had no place, where the declining morality of the New World had no business interfering. All Nathaniel could see was the surrender of her upturned face and the rise and fall of her breasts, and all he could feel was the burning, undeniable hunger for her in his heart and loins.

"Connie!" He choked on the effort it took to speak.

Suddenly, after the long year of dreaming about her, aching for her, living for her, she was in his arms, her soft woman's body pressed against his hard male frame.

Like an untutored schoolboy, Nathaniel lost control of himself. The response to her was instantaneous, overwhelming, a swelling of need so great that he moaned in painful surprise. He had wanted a woman before, but he had never waited this long to slake his desire. And with Constance, there was so much more than simple desire. His feelings for her were like circles that wound around each other, spiraling upward into glorious rapture, threatening to set his heart to bursting.

"Connie!" he said against her lips, unable to put his feelings into words. Nothing he could say would ever do justice to the way he felt about her. He could say he loved her a million times, and he *had* declared his love in previous encounters, but words could never convey what his body longed to shout to her. He backed her against the edge of the huge granite slab of the rustic sundial, pinning her between the stone and the undeniable flag of his desire. He only hoped the raw honesty of his body would not scare her away and send her running back to the Bastyr house.

As if to allay his fears, she wrapped her arms around his neck, pulling him down to her sweet lips for a kiss that was so innocent and yet so ardent that he melted inside, like a candle set too near the flame. His hat fell off, but he paid it no mind. She wasn't afraid! He had known in his heart that she shared his love. And her hesitant mouth and small trembling hands upon his shoulders were proof of it.

"I've wanted to touch you for months," he breathed.

"And I you, Nathaniel!"

"Ah, love!" Nathaniel swept his hands down her back and over her hips, fanning his hands over her skirt to press her into him. He forced her back against the stone while she gasped, spreading her hands upon his chest. "I want to touch you everywhere, know every inch of you."

He could not deny the truth of his love for her, nor would he hide the fact that he wanted her as a man wants a woman. How he wanted her! His blood roared through his ears, his mouth went dry, and his skin felt as if it were aflame. All he could do to keep himself in check was to kiss her, deeply and passionately, showing her with his tongue what he longed to do to the innermost reaches of her.

"Nathaniel!" she cried, breaking away from his mouth. Her lips were swollen, her eyes cloudy with passion, and her nipples hard and erect, quite visible through the woolen homespun dress she wore. His body surged anew at the sight of her. "We must stop! The Bastyrs—"

"They don't know you're here, love." His voice was hoarse; his mouth felt as if it were stuffed with cotton. "And we'll have no privacy on the ship."

"But—"

"Connie, I've waited more than a year just to touch you, to kiss you. I can't wait any longer."

"We've got to go to the ship—"

He silenced her protests with his mouth, kissing her lips and then her throat and ear. Her head rolled back, and she let out a moan of pleasure as he put his hand on her sensitive breast and kneaded the firm rounded flesh. He moved against her belly until he thought he would explode with longing.

"I'm to be your husband, Connie, and you're to be my wife. The captain on board will make us so. But we'll have no chance to be alone like this. Not for weeks!"

"But, Nathaniel, what if Seth finds us?"

"He won't!"

She closed her eyes, moaning again when he pushed aside the shawl and her fichu, exposing most of her left breast. Then he slipped his hand into the furnace of her bodice and encompassed her breast with his hand.

"Nathaniel!" she gasped, her voice queerly constricted.

"I shall die of wanting you," he murmured, amazed at the desperation he heard in his voice. "Let me come into you, Connie. Let me."

He stepped into the apex of her legs, making his intentions even more blatant than his verbal request. She raised her knee to accommodate him, angling it alongside his thigh, and he growled with hunger as she presented the more intimate position to him. Clutching her slender thigh with his left hand, he dipped slightly and came up against the heat of her most guarded flesh for the very first time. The contact, even through the layers of their clothing, galvanized both of them.

"Yes, Nathaniel," she mouthed against his feverish kisses. "Oh—"

He was barely conscious of rational thought. All the months she had tempted him beyond reason without the slightest intention on her part, driven him crazy simply by her gaze, were about to come to a screeching, glorious halt. Tomorrow she would be his wife. But tonight she would be his lover. He reached for the skirt of her dress, yanking it upward. He had to strip away all barriers until he felt her hot, moist flesh enclosing his own.

"Please..." Her voice trailed off as he cupped her with his hand and found that she was ready for him.

He fumbled with the buttons of his breeches. The mere touch of his own hand as he unfastened the flap nearly sent him over the brink. He was breathing heavily in anticipation before he even freed himself.

Constance's hands pushed into his hair, capturing him as she kissed him in answer. He felt the surrender in her slender frame, in the press of her thumbs at his temples, her fingers behind his ears. His tongue met hers as he lifted her off the ground and let her slide over the hard planes of his body in a rehearsal of the moment to come.

Then he felt for the ties of her bodice and unfastened them as he showered desperate kisses on her throat. She moved beneath him, all fragile warmth and softness, as he peeled away her somber layers of homespun to reveal the ivory perfection of her body.

He could hear the rush of blood in his ears over their tortured breathing, and was barely aware of an echo behind him, as if the wind and leaves were chanting in time with his heart. Constance stood before him in her chemise, her head thrown back, her eyes closed, as he reached for her. But something caught his arms, stayed his hands, and then he was jerked unceremoniously away.

Nathaniel twisted around, shocked to see figures in black robes standing in a semicircle around them, chanting.

Constance saw a tall robed figure stride up to the sundial. She grabbed her discarded skirt and held it to her breasts, mortified that she had been caught nearly naked, while Nathaniel buttoned his breeches.

"Seducer!" the robed figure hissed. "Fornicator!"

Constance recognized the dry tone of Seth Bastyr's voice and felt another flush of mortification tinged with fear. He *had* known she had left the house. He *had* been watching her. Swallowing her fear, she stared at him, willing her hands to remain steady, her eyes to remain clear of fright. She hated Seth Bastyr and wouldn't allow him the satisfaction of seeing her cower in his presence. But why he was dressed in the strange black robe?

Nathaniel, unarmed and defenseless, tried to shake off his captors, but the two men only yanked back his arms.

"Leave him be!" Constance cried, seeing pain flare in his face. "He meant no harm!"

"Meant no harm? He nearly took thy virginity!"

She flung back her hair. "I'm not a child, Seth Bastyr, I'm a woman. And I have chosen Nathaniel as my husband."

"'Tis not a choice for thee to make!" Seth thundered. His black eyes were wild. She had never seen him so agitated. His cold glance raked her from her toes up to her tousled head, where her red hair had come undone in the throes of passion. Constance felt a blush creep up her neck.

He smiled knowingly, which increased her embarrassment.

"I have gone to great lengths for thee, Constance," he said, stepping closer. "And thou art mine to command."

"You have no legal hold on Connie," Nathaniel retorted. "Her contract is fulfilled."

"'Tis not fulfilled yet." Seth turned on Nathaniel. "There remains one night before she is free."

"A night cannot matter overmuch." Nathaniel pulled away from his captors. "Come, Connie."

With a metallic swish, Seth drew a saber from the folds of his woolen robe and held it out to block Nathaniel. "Not so quickly, Nathaniel Cooper. Constance is not leaving with thee."

"Yes she is. We have made plans to marry."

"Constance will become a bride tonight, but not to thee."

Shocked, Constance turned to stare at Seth. The Bastyrs expected her to marry someone? Seth had not mentioned the fact. The Bastyrs rarely discussed anything. In fact, they rarely spoke at all.

"Wh-what are you saying?" Constance stammered. "That you intend to keep me here against my will?"

"Against thy will, dear Constance?" He smiled again, a smile that echoed his humorless voice. "Where did thee get the notion that thee would be dissatisfied?"

"I will never be happy here. Not without Nathaniel!"

"Nathaniel?" He laughed mirthlessly. "Nathaniel is but a pawn, a tool to get thee ready."

"Ready for what?"

"For thy role as wife and helpmeet. To me."

She gaped at Seth in utter disbelief, stunned.

"No!" Nathaniel exploded. He grabbed a branch from the ground. "Never!"

Seth lunged for him, glancing a powerful blow off the oak branch. Constance staggered backward against the cold stone, watching in horror as Seth closed in upon Nathaniel, slashing the air.

"Nathaniel!" she cried, realizing that Seth meant to hurt Nathaniel, not just drive him away.

"Run!" Nathaniel yelled, holding up the branch to ward off a blow.

For a moment Constance hesitated, frozen with worry. What if Nathaniel was struck by the saber? What if Seth meant to kill him? What could she do? Run for help? She hadn't the faintest idea how far away Nathaniel's ship was anchored, and whether or not he had come ashore with any of the crew.

"For God's sake, run!" Nathaniel yelled, just as the saber broke through the branch, splintering it with a loud crack. Before Nathaniel could recover, Seth struck again, slicing through Nathaniel's leg, laying the flesh open clean to the bone. In agony, Nathaniel toppled to the ground, holding his leg while blood gushed over his hand.

"Nathaniel!" she screamed, dashing to his side.

Seth barked commands to two of the other robed men. They grabbed Constance's arms and pulled her away.

"Don't kill him!" she cried. "Please, don't kill him!"

"No need," Seth replied. "He'll bleed to death before long. Besides, 'twill be better should he be forced to watch."

"Connie, go!" Nathaniel moaned, struggling to get up. He slipped on his own blood and fell back to the damp matted grass.

Seth surveyed him while he untied the robe at his throat. His eyes held neither compassion nor concern. Constance watched in horror, unable to help Nathaniel, who lay panting with pain, in too much agony to speak except with his eyes, which pleaded to her to do something to save herself.

She writhed, but the two Bastyr men held her fast.

"Dost thou love him?" Seth demanded.

"Yes." She raised her chin in defiance.

"All the better." His eyes narrowed. "Then thou will give thyself to me to save him?"

"Yes."

"No, Connie!" rasped Nathaniel. She could tell by the weak sound of his voice that his strength was flowing out of his body as surely as his blood.

She swung back to face Seth. "Spare him and I will do anything you ask."

"Anything? How generous." The corners of his mouth twitched. He turned to his daughter, a bloated, prematurely gray matron who was years older than Constance. "Fetch me the cloth, Patience," he instructed. Patience walked forward, holding a folded garment in her outstretched hands, as if offering up a sacred object. Constance glanced at her, wondering if the woman was in some kind of trance. She made no eye contact, and her face held no expression in the shadow of her hooded robe.

What was Seth going to do to her? Rape her in front of everyone? It couldn't be possible, not after the pious speeches she had heard from his own lips in which he damned fornication and all the other sins that took people down the wrong path. Yet he had asked that she give herself to him. Did he mean spiritually? If so, why had he untied his robe?

The thought of Seth touching her in any way, spiritually or sexually, made her stomach flop over with dread. Constance tried to yank herself loose, but the men gripped her firmly and ordered her to be quiet.

Patience gave the bundle to Seth. He took it, putting it under his arm. Then he turned to Constance, pulled away the dress she clutched to her breasts and ripped off her thin chemise. Flushing with embarrassment, she stood completely nude before the Bastyrs, her only covering the cloak of her unbound russet hair, which rippled around her in the autumn breeze.

She couldn't run. Pleas would be useless. All she could do was stand there, a prisoner. Her only hope was that her humiliation might save Nathaniel. Waves of shame and helplessness washed over her as she felt the eyes of every man and woman present feeding on the sight of her naked flesh.

"Hoist her up," Seth said, nodding to the men who held her.

They lifted her off her feet while a third man pulled her to the flat surface of the sundial, dragging her across the rough edge of the stone slab and scraping her thigh.

"On your knees," Seth commanded.

Were they going to pray? Perhaps he planned to humiliate her as some sort of penance? A small hope flickered in her chest that she might yet escape physical harm.

At first Constance refused to obey him and looked him directly in the eyes as he came to a standstill a few feet from her. His eyes glittered up at her, lit by the moon. For a moment he stared deeply at her face, and then his gaze traveled downward, over her neck, her breasts, her belly and her thighs. Constance felt a new flush of shame course through her. But to save Nathaniel, she would have to submit to anything Seth asked of her.

"Ye are lovely," he remarked in a dry voice. "Now, down on thy knees. 'Tis long past time."

Constance shot a glance at Nathaniel. His eyelids fluttered as he tried not to succumb to his injury. For Nathaniel, she must be strong. Choking back tears, she sank to her knees.

Another robed figure lashed her wrists with a leather thong to the crude iron gnomon of the sundial. Constance watched him, realizing in an offhand way that the moon cast a shadow much like the sun, and that the time on the dial showed midnight. She had reached the evening of her twenty-first birthday and the end of her servitude, only to be lashed to a sundial for purposes she didn't even want to contemplate. Pockets of gloom ringed the dial, where strange angular symbols had been carved in the stone long ago.

"Lift me," Seth demanded. Out of the corner of her eye, she saw him being raised to the flat surface of the rock. He walked to the center of the dial and gazed down at her.

"Lean over," Seth commanded. "And present thyself to thy master."

She placed her palms on the stone. The shame of the position was nearly too much to bear. Tears of fright clung in her throat while she stared at the rough stone beneath her, too ashamed to look at Nathaniel.

Terror sped like wildfire through Constance's veins. What was going on? How could Patience let her be treated this way? How could another woman just stand there like that and watch?

Suddenly she realized the people in the robes had begun to chant in a soft drone that blended with the rustling breeze in the oaks. She couldn't understand the words, whether because they were spoken in a strange tongue or were sung too softly to be heard, she couldn't tell. Unnerved, Constance craned her neck in an effort to look behind her. The moonlight silvered the pale skin of Seth's bare feet and legs and cast a sheen on the cloth in which he had wrapped himself.

For a moment he regarded her from above while the chanting increased. Someone hit a small drum as if to mimic the sound of a heartbeat, although Constance's heart raced far more quickly than the *thump-thump, thump-thump* of the drum. Through eyes wild with horror, she watched Seth step up behind her.

"And so it begins in the New World," he said. "A new world, a new family, a new bride."

New bride. The words resounded in her ears as if a thunderclap had boomed overhead. His hands clutched the shining cloth around his shoulders, and she suddenly realized the cloth was the very same fabric she had been weaving on her loom, and that he was stark naked beneath the shining cloak.

She watched him smile and knew that he had seen the recognition in her face. The smile sickened her. His bride? Was this why they had sent for her two years ago—to be his bride? That hadn't been part of the contract! She wrenched at the thong that bound her wrists but she couldn't break free. There was no escape. No hope.

The drum suddenly stopped beating.

"This union shall strengthen us," Seth declared to the sky. "And this woman's love for Nathaniel Cooper shall nourish us."

With a flourish, Seth opened his robe. Moonlight poured over him, highlighting the front of his body. Horrified, Constance gaped at him, for she had never seen a naked man before, and certainly not one in full arousal. The sight terrified her. She cried out and yanked on the thongs as Seth knelt down. The drum began to beat furiously, again echoing the hammering of her heart. He draped the shining cloth over her, covering her entirely, as if he did not want to see her body or her face. Beneath the cloth she felt as if she would suffocate from the musky smell of him and the heat of his body. The cloth turned her skin to fire and then to ice. She tried to hold on to the image of Nathaniel, tried to convince herself that this would be over soon and she would be saved. But she couldn't think over the thundering sound of the drum. Then Seth's cold hands imprisoned her hips, and as he clutched her, the image of Nathaniel faded, became a blur and disappeared forever.

Through a shimmering haze, Nathaniel watched Seth Bastyr thrust himself against Constance. "No!" Nathaniel wailed. "No!" He tried to get up, rallied all his remaining strength, but it wasn't enough. He couldn't even get to his knees. He never should have lingered in the clearing. He should have taken Constance to the ship at once, just as she had asked him to do. Why hadn't he listened to her? Why had he let his lust dictate to him? Now they were both paying the price for his foolhardiness. His Connie—ah, God, his Connie—was paying the highest price of all.

The chanting droned through the buzzing in Nathaniel's ears as he struggled once more to stand. He stumbled to the sundial. "Connie!" he gasped, sliding on the wet grass. He fell to the ground near her satchel, mouthing her name, and knew that he had failed her. Panting in frustration and helplessness, he laid his head on the ground and closed his eyes, trying to fight the heavy lassitude that weighted his limbs. He was so tired—so tired. For a moment he closed his eyes. Then blackness swept up in a wave and devoured him.

CHAPTER ONE

Brierwood, outside Seattle. the Present

"Bea!"

Twenty-year-old Rose Quennel rushed down the stairs. She had just heard the strangest noise—something akin to a chord on an organ, with deep ominous notes. The sound had come from the gardens behind the house and had been loud enough to reach her workroom on the third floor. Perhaps Bea had heard it, too, and would be able to identify the sound.

Rose called again and searched the gardens to the rear of the mansion, thinking she would find her guardian in the vegetable patch weeding in the cool of the evening. Mrs. Jacoby was not there. Perplexed, Rose stood near a clump of poppies, her light cotton dress wafting against her shins. The summer evening breeze suddenly felt chilly. Rose shuddered and glanced around. Where was Bea? Her guardian, the housekeeper of Brierwood, was old and not one to wander too far when daylight began to fade.

Suspecting that something was wrong, Rose broke into a trot. She ran past the sundial to the herb garden, which was enclosed by an old stone wall, and pushed through the wooden gate. There stood Bea, staring at the still figure of her husband, who lay facedown, his arms and legs splayed like that of a tragic scarecrow. All around him, the pennyroyal and lady slippers were withered and brown, as if a killing frost had struck both the plants and Mr. Jacoby, toppling him into the garden.

"Bea, what happened?" Rose dashed to the old woman's side.

"I don't know, Rose! I heard an awful noise and came out and found my Donald lying dead!" She turned to face Rose, her wrinkled face gray with shock. "He's dead, Rose! He's dead!"

Rose dropped to her knees beside the man who had been her surrogate father and her friend, while shock dammed a flood of tears that sprang into her throat. She reached out to touch Donald Jacoby and instantly recoiled. His skin was cold, even though the summer night was balmy.

"Did you hear him cry out?" Rose asked.

"No. Nothing." Bea fingered the lace collar of her dress, and her hand trembled visibly. "Just that awful noise. Oh, Rose, my Donald's gone!"

What had happened to him? Rose surely would have heard him if he had cried out. Rose's workroom on the third floor of the house was directly above the garden, and she had been up there all day with the windows wide open. Had Donald come out to the garden and collapsed? Was it something as common as a heart attack, or had someone done him harm? Did the strange noise have something to do with his death?

Rose forced herself to reach out again. She eased Mr. Jacoby onto his back, a difficult feat because of the old man's bulk, and then glanced at his face, afraid that she would see a mask of terror and fear. But Mr. Jacoby's eyes were closed, and his wrinkled mouth was slightly parted, as if he slept. Rose inspected the rest of his ample frame. She could find no evidence of violence. Perhaps he *had* died of a heart attack out here in the garden. He was seventy-five years old and had never practiced healthy eating habits.

Yet why were the herbs withered? And what had made that horrible noise? She looked back at his body, at his outstretched right hand. It was then that she noticed the emerald was missing from his ring. Had a thief killed Donald Jacoby for the sake of the modest gem? Somehow, she didn't think so.

A movement near the garden wall caught Rose's eye. She searched the shadows and thought she saw the dark shapes of animals in the shrubbery. Dogs? There were no dogs at Brierwood. Perhaps she had seen the leaves of the rhododendrons shivering in the breeze. Rose stared at the shadows and felt an almost overwhelming urge to run for her life.

San Francisco, a month and a half later

"I'm afraid, Mr. Wolfe," the doctor said, "we don't know what's wrong with your eyes."

Taylor Wolfe's grip tightened on the handle of his cane. "What do you mean, you don't *know?*" He turned to face the doctor, and a sharp pain shot up his injured leg. "You're a specialist!"

"I know, I know, Mr. Wolfe. But we found no damage to the retina or optic nerve. No ocular trauma whatsoever."

"You're saying that these flashes of light I see have no medical explanation?"

"None that I or my colleagues are familiar with. However, there are one or two more tests—"

"No more tests!" Taylor waved him off with an impatient hand and turned back to the window of his hospital room. Just beyond the rooftops he could see the sparkle of San Francisco Bay and the orange span of the Golden Gate Bridge. He yearned to be out of the hospital and back on the water, where he belonged. No more hospital room for him. He couldn't stand another day cooped up in this sterile prison.

"Please, Taylor, listen to Dr. Bennidetto," his mother repeated. She clutched her purse and leaned forward. "There still may be some hope."

He slanted a dark look at his frail mother, sitting there in her rose-colored suit with her snow-white coif, not a hair out of place. He wished she had never come to the hospital. She meant well, just as she always did, but the sight of her kind and honest face always made him feel like a heel for the time he had spent avoiding his family and their wealth. She was not responsible for the shadow on his soul. She didn't know where the Wolfe fortune had come from and what it had cost a frightened young woman so long ago. Only he and his father knew about that. And now that his father was dead, the secret resided in Taylor's heart alone.

"I know this must be hard for you, Mr. Wolfe, being such an active man," the doctor said, coming up behind him. "If there's anything we—"

"You've done your best," Taylor put in.

"But what about the other tests?" Ruth Wolfe turned in her chair to look up at the balding doctor. "I want only the best for my son."

"Mom, don't. I've had enough." He reached for his worn leather jacket hanging on the back of a chair. "My insurance is topped out with medical expenses as it is."

"Taylor, you know you don't have to worry about that. I'll take care of it."

"No, you won't." He shrugged into his jacket and held his cane in his left hand while adjusting the collar with his right. Every time he came to San Francisco it was always the same. His mother tried to force the Wolfe money on him. And always he refused it. Blood money—that was how he saw the family fortune, and he would never spend a dime of it. Anything he possessed in the world—no matter how insignificant when compared to the Wolfe estate—he had earned with his own two hands. And that was the way it was going to be.

The car crash had left him with a scarred face, a crushed right leg and impaired vision. The doctors had told him he was lucky to be alive—many in the pileup had died—lucky to have retained the use of his leg—even though the wound wasn't healing properly—and lucky that his scars could be repaired with plastic surgery—over a period of time, of course. Lucky, hell. He was twenty-eight years old, disfigured and crippled. Sports were out of the question. Sailing his small schooner with impaired vision would be risky. Running, dancing, playing racquetball—all would be impossible. And his love life would be nonexistent. He could just imagine a woman tracing his scarred face and whispering sweet nothings in his ear. He could just imagine limping up to a woman and asking for a date. Some stud he was now.

Taylor squeezed off his dark thoughts and looked down at the drapes blowing in the breeze from the air conditioner. He had to get everyone off his back and be alone.

How would he tell his mother that he wanted to say good-bye right here in the hospital? No dinner at home, no coffee in the cafeteria downstairs, not even a ride to the dock.

"Perhaps if you rested your eyes—" the doctor said behind him.

"Rest? I've had enough of that."

"Yes, well—the human eye is slow to heal, Mr. Wolfe. Much slower than other parts of the body. I suggest you refrain from returning to your normal activities for a few weeks. Perhaps take a vacation—somewhere quiet."

"I've got to get back to work." Taylor had money socked away but refused to dip into his nest egg. And if he didn't return to his job at Jenson's Quality Boats, he would be out another paycheck, not to mention the hefty commissions he made with the company. People would come in to Jenson's just to talk to him about his voyages, get caught up by his love of the sea and end up purchasing a boat of their own. Taylor had intended to stay at Jenson's only long enough to fund a trip to New Zealand. But his accident and subsequent hospital stay had seriously impacted his traveling plans. Taylor limped to the nightstand and lifted his water glass.

"If you return to your active life-style, Mr. Wolfe, your eyes might not have a chance to heal at all."

"And what will that mean?" Taylor sipped the water. "Total blindness?"

"We don't know at this point. I am merely suggesting that you take time off. Find a peaceful retreat."

Taylor squeezed the glass. If he spent any more time surrounded by peace and quiet, he would go absolutely crazy. But the alternative was even worse. What if he should lose his sight altogether? That would mean losing his independence. Scars he could live with. A limp could be overcome. But blindness? He gulped the water, hoping to douse the burn of panic in his gut.

"Whatever you decide, Mr. Wolfe, I advise you to limit strenuous activity, long stretches of reading and exposure to bright light."

Taylor nodded, only half listening.

"Do you have any other questions, Mr. Wolfe?"

He shook his head and put the water glass down, noticing the red scar between his thumb and forefinger, another souvenir of his car wreck. He had sailed alone around the world. He had faced hurricanes and typhoons, had spent weeks adrift in the Sargasso sea with a burned-out engine, had been knocked overboard off the coast of Alaska. He had escaped all kinds of perils, only to come home to San Francisco and fall victim to a common fog bank.

"I'd just like to say what a pleasure it was to meet you, Mr. Wolfe." Dr. Bennidetto held out his hand, and Taylor shook it. "I've read about you in the papers. Must be something to live those adventures we mere mortals just dream about."

"Yes, well, thanks for your help, Doc."

"If you have any questions or concerns, please don't hesitate to call me."

"Right."

The doctor turned to the door. "Good luck, Mr. Wolfe."

Luck? As far as Taylor was concerned, his luck had run out.

After the doctor left, Taylor limped to the door, still frustrated with a body that did not perform in peak condition.

"You're not really going, are you, Taylor?" his mother asked, rising from her chair.

"Yes, I am. I'm getting the hell out of here."

"Do you think that's wise?"

"I don't care. If I stay here another minute, I'll go crazy."

"Wait a minute, Taylor. I'm coming with you."

He stepped into the hall, frowning. Instantly his vision shifted into a cacophony of color—technicolor tunnel vision that swirled around the periphery of his sight. Nurses blurred into moving blobs of green and lavender. Doctors disassembled into flashes of red and blue. Carts and gurneys shimmered into floating planes of pink. And from somewhere came a crazy quilt of tones—buzzing, chiming, clanging.

Taylor struggled to maintain his balance as the colors danced and flared in a dizzying array and the noise pressed in on his ears. He grabbed for the doorjamb, using it to ground him, while a cold sweat broke out beneath his jacket and chambray shirt.

"Mr. Wolfe?" a female voice called out. He recognized the tone as belonging to the nurse who took his temperature each morning, precisely at seven o'clock, rousing him from a perfectly good sleep. "Are you all right, Mr. Wolfe?"

"I'm fine," he lied.

"Are you sure you're okay?" She touched his arm. "You look pale."

He couldn't make out her face or her body, but he saw a halo of green settle around his elbow where her hand cupped him. He stiffened and stood up straight, releasing his hold on the woodwork.

"I'm fine, Miss Anderson. I'm checking out."

"Stay here and I'll get a wheelchair to take you downstairs."

"I don't need a wheelchair."

"Hospital regulations, Mr. Wolfe."

He watched her blob of color flow toward the nurses' station and then squeezed his eyelids shut. Damn hospital regulations. He wasn't about to be pushed around in a wheelchair. Maybe he would have to enlist his mother's help after all.

He turned. "Mom, where's the car?"

"Out front, Taylor, but you heard the nurse—"

"Never mind her." He stepped away from the door. "Come on." All he had to do was make it to the elevator and out to the main lobby exit. He trailed his fingertips along the wall and limped in the opposite direction from the nurses' station, knowing another set of elevators was just down the hall.

By the time he stumbled into the elevator he was bathed in sweat. He couldn't even see the numbers well enough to select the lobby. He had to ask his mother to do it for him. Scowling and frightened, he leaned against the back of the elevator, knowing he would never make it on his own if his vision didn't get any better. Maybe he *would* have to take it easy for a few weeks.

"Mom," he said, running a tongue over his dry upper lip. "Did anyone ever buy Aunt Julia's place?"

"Brierwood?" she replied. "Oh, here's the lobby, dear. Can you see well enough to walk?"

"Yeah," he lied. Carefully, he followed her lavender glow out of the elevator and onto the tile of the main floor. His cane clicked on the hard surface, startling him. He tried not to let it show, but he felt increasingly rattled with every step he took in the unfamiliar surroundings. People and potted plants loomed up unexpectedly. Voices came from nowhere. He was conscious that his breathing came in agitated spurts.

"Brierwood?" his mother repeated. "No, it's still empty, except for the caretakers, that is. Why?"

"I'm going there." He heard the whisk as the automatic doors slid open and felt the cool rush of air on his face. Thank God. A few more steps and they would be in the car.

"All the way to Seattle? Why don't you stay here, dear, where I can keep an eye on you? You aren't doing that well, you know. You look terrible."

"Thanks a lot, Mom." He raised his face up to the sun, basking in the natural heat after more than a month trapped in the controlled environment of the hospital. "But I'm going."

A remote place like Brierwood would keep him out of the public eye, at least until he got a handle on the mysterious blindness that plagued him. And Brierwood had nothing to do with the Wolfe estate. It had belonged to his mother's eccentric sister, Julia, who had been estranged from the family before she died. Taylor had often been told he favored crusty Aunt Julia both in coloring and temperament. He only wished he had known her. He imagined they might have gotten along very well, for they had more than looks and temperament in common. Neither of them had possessed one shred of respect for Richard Wolfe, his father.

Brierwood, two days later

Rose heard a thud down below and jerked to attention, listening intently. Ever since Donald Jacoby's death, she hadn't slept well, hadn't been able to turn out the lights in the house or shake the feeling that she was being watched. She felt like a scared child and chided herself for being silly and high-strung, but no matter how much she tried to rationalize her fears, she could not put them aside.

The noise downstairs had sounded like a door shutting. Had she forgotten to lock the front door? Had someone come in? She should answer the door before Bea woke up and went downstairs. Bea needed all the sleep she could get these days. The death of her husband seemed to have drained her of energy. The last thing Rose wanted was to put Bea's health in jeopardy.

Rose set aside her brush and capped her dye. Then, pulling off her rubber gloves, she walked around the end of the six-foot length of silk stretched over a long worktable.

After graduating early from college, she had started a business designing one-of-a-kind scarves for wealthy clients in the Seattle area. In a year her business had blossomed enough to show a small profit, and she considered herself lucky to be doing something she loved for a living. But since Donald's death, Rose felt as if her luck were fading like cheap pigments left too long in the sun. Something had changed at Brierwood. Something was different. The air seemed heavier, the shadows darker. She couldn't put her finger on the reason for the change, but she attributed it to the untimely and inexplicable death of Donald Jacoby.

Before Rose reached the doorway to the hall, she was startled by a flapping noise and turned around to see a huge raven alight on the window sill behind her.

"Edgar," she admonished. "Don't scare me like that!"

He cawed loudly and soared over to her, landing on her wrist, then turned a shiny eye to her, as if trying to tell her something.

"What is it, you rascal?"

He clacked and bobbed his head, agitated.

Another door thumped closed down below.

"Has Mr. Wolfe arrived?" Rose glanced at her watch as she walked out to the hallway. 8:55. Had she gotten the arrival time wrong? She distinctly remembered Bea telling her that he would be at Brierwood at half past ten. Perhaps Mr.

Wolfe had come earlier than planned. If that were the case, she should go down and welcome him and try to explain Mr. Jacoby's absence, for Bea hadn't informed the Wolfes about Donald Jacoby's death.

Edgar refused to accompany her to the lower level, which was odd, because he was usually interested in the comings and goings of people at Brierwood. Perhaps he lingered behind because it was early evening, the time when he generally went to roost. Putting his odd behavior out of her mind, Rose flowed down the stairs, wishing she had had time to change. Her painting clothes—an old summer smock and a bandanna spotted with dye—were not at all flattering, certainly not appropriate attire in which to greet Mr. Wolfe. But since he had arrived hours early, he couldn't expect her to be ready to greet him in her best dress.

Frowning, Rose pulled off the scarf and ran her fingers through her long red hair as she approached the study. She could hear Mr. Wolfe moving around in the room. The door stood ajar.

Rose rapped on the woodwork, wondering how she could explain the odd circumstances of Donald Jacoby's death and her own lengthy and secret presence at Brierwood.

"Come in," a dry voice commanded.

Rose passed into the study, lit by the eerie glow of a small desk lamp with a green glass shade. Mr. Wolfe had drawn the curtains, plunging the room into shadow. The hairs on the back of her neck stood up, but she attributed her reaction to her childish fear of darkness. In the dim light, she could barely make out Mr. Wolfe as he stood near the wall of shelves at the other end of the room, a book in his hand, his face and figure bathed in shadow. He was a tall man, and from the shape of his body, not the old man she had assumed he would be.

"Welcome to Brierwood," she said.

"Thank you."

"We didn't expect you so soon."

"Oh?"

His eyes glittered at her from the shadows, and his glance raked her up and down. She felt as if he were touching her with his hands. Rose resisted the urge to step backward, closer to the open door, and forced herself to utter the proper inanities.

"Did you have a pleasant journey?"

"As pleasant as can be expected." He shelved the book, turning slightly. "But not as pleasant as seeing you. You are more beautiful than I had hoped."

Rose paused. What an odd thing to say. As far as she knew, Mr. Wolfe wasn't even aware of her existence, let alone her appearance. Maybe he thought she was Bea.

"I'm not Mrs. Jacoby," she put in.

"Oh, I know that." He pulled out another book and looked down at the cover. "You're Roselyn Bastyr."

"I'm afraid you're mistaken. My name is Quennel."

"Perhaps you have been told you are a Quennel. But you are a Bastyr, my dear, through and through."

"What makes you say that?"

"I can tell just by looking at you. That peculiar shade of red hair is a family trademark in the Bastyr women."

Rose faltered. She had been told she was a foundling with no links to her past. Where the Quennel name had come from, she hadn't the faintest idea. To hear someone say she belonged to a family and bore a strong resemblance to someone—anyone—made her heart surge in her chest. More than anything, she wanted to belong to a family, a real family, with whom she shared bloodlines and her heritage. But most of her life she had lived with Donald and Bea Jacoby, who swore they knew nothing about her, or whether or not a Quennel family even existed.

"You know about me?" she asked.

"I know many things about you, Roselyn."

How much did he know? And what did he know of the current status of Brierwood? Did he know that Donald was dead? That she had kept secret the news of his death in hopes that Bea Jacoby wouldn't be fired? She was certain that no one would want to retain an old woman as housekeeper after her husband, who had served as grounds-keeper and handyman, had died. Worse yet, Rose herself had been living at Brierwood for fifteen years without the Wolfes' knowledge. Bea had been convinced it wouldn't matter, that no one ever came to Brierwood anyway or cared what happened there. Yet Taylor Wolfe, son of the owner of Brierwood, now stood before her in the study, claiming to know all about her.

He hadn't thrown her out, though. Not yet, anyway.

"You say you think I'm a Bastyr?"

"I know you are a Bastyr."

"Who are they?"

"All in good time, my dear." He chuckled as he shut the book. "We'll speak of that later."

She stepped closer. "Then it's all right with you that I'm here? I can stay?"

"For now, of course." He looked up at her. She wished she could see his face and his expression, but the darkness concealed everything, even the color of his hair. She clasped her hands together, feeling uneasy in his presence.

"Can I get you anything?"

"Thank you, no. I will talk with you later, Roselyn."

"All right."

She was grateful for the dismissal and hurried back upstairs to her work.

Seth Bastyr watched her go and smiled in the dark. Engaging little creature. She thought he was someone else. He had a mind not to set her straight, not just yet. If she thought he was someone else, she might accept his sudden appearance without putting up much of a fight. Then all of Deborah Bastyr's schemes and plans would be for naught. He wouldn't mind besting that bitch at last. He wouldn't mind it at all. And to vanquish Deborah by taking her daughter, Rose Quennel, would only make the victory that much sweeter. So far, the road to victory hadn't been difficult. Donald Jacoby was dead and buried. That left only Bea. And then Roselyn would be his. Seth thought of the ritual to come and closed his eyes to savor the sharp thrill of anticipation.

CHAPTER TWO

"Brierwood, sir," the taxi driver announced.

Taylor lifted his head from the back of the car seat as his taxi pulled through the entrance pillars. He had asked the driver to inform him of their arrival so that he could spend most of the journey resting; the flight from San Francisco to Seattle had exhausted him. He opened his eyes, hoping the colors would not appear and blot his sight and was relieved to find his vision normal. Wincing from the cramp in his neck, he looked out the car window at the grounds of the old family estate, illuminated by the headlights of the taxi.

So this was Brierwood.

He had never set foot in the place. His Aunt Julia had cut herself off from her sister upon her sister's marriage to Richard Wolfe. Taylor had always been told there was a mutual dislike between his father and his aunt, but he often wondered if a deeper reason existed for the animosity. After Aunt Julia died years later, the estate passed to Taylor's mother, with the stipulation that the caretakers remain employed until they reached retirement age. For over a decade the estate had remained untouched, for Ruth Wolfe had never concerned herself with the affairs of the place, mostly because it was more of an albatross than an asset.

On the three occasions when his mother had tried to sell the estate, not one buyer had come forward. Looking around, Taylor could see why. Even in the encroaching darkness, he could tell that Brierwood was overgrown and unkempt, a tangle of vines and trees and unfettered gardens. He had never seen such vegetation except in the steamy jungles of the tropics. He had heard that the rains of the Seattle area, coupled with mild winters, created a friendly environment for plants, but he was surprised by the lushness of his northwest surroundings. He made a note to himself to speak to the caretakers about the grounds. Obviously the couple were shirking their responsibilities.

The taxi swung around a curve in the drive, and Taylor looked ahead, glimpsing the facade of a Tudor mansion rising up from a sea of hedges, three stories of half-timbered nooks and crannies that rambled into the shadows of twilight. The entire face of the house was draped in ivy, with only the windows and casements showing, and all of them were dark, as if no one lived in the house.

Taylor glanced around, searching for a lighted window or door, but found none. It appeared that his arrival had been forgotten. He sank back, his fingers tightening around the handle of his cane. So much the better. If he should suffer a vision attack on arriving at Brierwood, he would rather suffer alone than in front of complete strangers. There was no telling when his world would burst into color, which kept him on edge around other people.

Rose woke at the sound of a door slamming again. She scrambled to her feet, shocked that she had fallen asleep so quickly. What time was it? She glanced at her watch. Ten-thirty! She had slept for nearly two hours, slumped in her chair, too exhausted to stay awake. She wondered if Mr. Wolfe had called her and she had slept right through his summons. At this point, it wouldn't be a good idea to make him angry. Mr. Wolfe seemed to be the kind of man who would get angry easily. She walked to the door and out to the railing, looking over the edge to the entryway two stories below. A dark-haired man stood in the foyer, two suitcases at his feet.

"Hello?" His deep baritone voice rang out, echoing up to her position on the third floor. Rose stiffened. He *was* looking for her, probably to take care of his luggage. "Is anybody here?"

"Just a moment!" Rose called out.

The man looked up, trying to locate her, and finally backed up to get a view of the third-story balcony. "You there!" he called.

"I'm coming!"

Edgar appeared out of nowhere and soared down to the foyer while Rose took the stairs, wondering why Edgar had suddenly decided to come to life, especially at this hour of the night.

Just as she gained the bottom of the two flights of stairs, she saw Edgar soar past Mr. Wolfe. Something metallic hit the floor and skidded toward her while Edgar disappeared into the shadows of the drawing room at the front of the house.

"Hey!" Mr. Wolfe exclaimed.

What had Edgar done this time? Rose stepped forward and saw a key glinting in the dim light. In an attempt to make off with the shiny object in Mr. Wolfe's possession, Edgar must have knocked the key out of his hand.

Rose reached down for it at the same time Mr. Wolfe did, and they nearly bumped heads. She straightened, holding out the key, smiling at the humor of the situation. But all amusement died when she looked into the face of the man before her. For a moment all she could do was stare at him.

He looked like a pirate—that was the only way she could describe him—with his shining black hair and sardonic slash of a mouth. But this pirate wasn't laughing. In fact, his dark brown eyes studied her with a guarded intensity that unnerved her. He had a prominent nose with a narrow bridge—a nose some might call aristocratic—and she had the distinct feeling that he was looking down that nose in disdain at her. A strand of black hair fell over a forehead crossed by a scar. Another scar paralleled the line that stretched from cheekbone to chin on his lean face. His jagged wounds branded his good looks with the mark of a brigand, compounded by the ebony fire that smoldered in his unusually dark brown eyes. But even more unsettling to Rose was a sudden flare of familiarity in his features, as if she had seen him before.

"And what are you staring at?" he demanded.

"Nothing!" Chagrined, Rose dropped the key in his outstretched hand. "And I apologize for my friend."

"Friend?" His long hand snapped around the key. "I can't believe a wild animal is loose in the house."

"Edgar isn't wild. He's quite tame. And once you get to know him—"

"I have no intention of getting to know him." He turned away and limped to the doorway of the drawing room. Had her reaction to his face upset him? Rose surveyed Mr. Wolfe as he walked. She hadn't noticed the cane when she had first met him in the study, but he hadn't been walking around then, either.

In the dim light of the house, she studied him, wondering at the queer feeling of déjà vu she had felt a moment ago. She noted how his hair glinted blue-black and was neither straight nor curly, but full of lights and body where it curved over the tops of his ears. His shoulders were wide and straight, which she assumed was the product of the expert tailoring of his leather jacket. He didn't look much older than his late twenties, but even with the limp, he moved with the confidence of a man who usually got his way, no questions asked. Who was he?

Puzzled and more than a bit annoyed by his gruff behavior, Rose stood at the foot of the stairs, her arms stiff at her sides. Mr. Wolfe glanced down the central hall, which led to the parlor, morning room and the kitchen, and then pivoted, his jacket creaking softly. "Where is Mrs. Jacoby?"

"She has retired for the night," Rose replied, wondering what had happened to his earlier mood when he had told her she was beautiful. Now he was looking at her as if she were an escaped criminal.

"And Mr. Jacoby?"

"He hasn't been here for quite some time."

"Obviously. The lawn is overgrown. And the outlying gardens look like a jungle."

"We have done the best we could, considering."

"We?" he quipped. "And who might you be?"

She knitted her brows in confusion. What kind of game was he playing?

"Well?"

"Have you forgotten? Rose."

"Rose what?"

"I told you before. Rose Quennel."

He paused for a moment and glanced away, as if running through a mental list. Then he looked back at her. "I don't recall your name on the list of people employed at Brier-wood."

"I'm not exactly employed here. The Jacobys are my guardians."

"Guardians?"

"Yes." She wondered why he was questioning her again after he had already told her that she could stay. Hadn't he mentioned the fact that he knew a lot about her? It certainly didn't seem like it now. She sighed in exasperated confusion.

"And how long have you been here?"

"Fifteen years."

"I see." He tilted his head and narrowed his eyes, inspecting her in a way that brought a flush to her cheeks. She half expected him to prod her with his cane as if she were an animal on an auction block. She drew herself up as straight as she could, but she was still more than a head shorter than Mr. Wolfe.

"And how do you earn your keep, Ms. Quennel?"

"I help in the garden, I cook—whatever Mrs. Jacoby requests of me."

He gave her splattered smock another scathing look. His eyes were cold and opaque, almost black, in perfect complement to his curt questions. Once again her gaze strayed to the scar that ran across his forehead, just above his left eyebrow, and the other angling down his cheek. Rose wondered what had happened to him, to leave him scarred and crippled. His scars added a primal ruthlessness to his expression, which caused her heart to patter more quickly in her chest. She stared at him while he inspected her. Then he switched his cool regard to her face, and she quickly glanced away so he wouldn't catch her staring.

"I called ahead to the Jacobys, instructing them to prepare for my arrival. They've run off, haven't they, knowing they have been remiss in their duties?"

"The Jacobys are quite old, you know—"

"They've been living at Brierwood all these years without lifting a finger to take care of the place! They couldn't face me, could they?"

"Mr. Wolfe, you've—"

"And like cowards, they left you here to make excuses for them."

"No—"

"What did they do—drink away my aunt's money?" He pivoted, leaning on his cane "Look at the place. It's in a complete—"

He broke off suddenly, and his hand flew to his face, his long fingers splaying over his eyes. He swore and stumbled backward, as if dizzy or ill.

"Mr. Wolfe!" Rose exclaimed. She rushed to him and, without thinking, clutched his arm, afraid that he would fall.

"I'm all right!" he growled, wrenching his arm away.

She stepped back, staring at him in alarm as he staggered to a settee near the foyer. Was he having a migraine attack? It served him right for losing his temper and subjecting her to an angry tirade without allowing her to speak in defense. He collapsed onto the settee and leaned back, closing his eyes. His cane clattered to the wood floor. Rose reached down and picked it up.

"Are you ill, Mr. Wolfe?"

"No." His heavy breathing belied his words. She could tell something had disturbed him.

"If you had let me explain, Mr. Wolfe, you might not have gotten so upset."

"Leave me alone."

"And just because you're a Wolfe doesn't give you the right to act like an ogre."

"Leave me *alone*, Ms. Quennel."

"And if you had taken the time to look around, you'd see that the inside of Brierwood has received excellent care."

"You've said your piece, Ms. Quennel, now go."

"Not without an apology."

He raised his head and squinted at her. "An apology?"

She nodded.

"All right. I'm sorry. Et cetera." He sighed and let his head ease back. "Now, will you just leave me alone?"

"You don't make it sound as if it came from the heart."

"So I'm a heartless bastard, Ms. Quennel. Ask anyone."

She measured him with her eyes. He sounded gruff, and his lips were stern and tight, but what he said didn't ring true. It was as if he were relaying someone's opinion of his character, an opinion that had offended him.

She lingered, curious to discover his real character, the one she suspected might lie beneath the gruffness.

"Can I get you something—a glass of water?"

He sighed again, as if realizing he was not to be rid of her. "Scotch, if there's any around."

Carefully she leaned his cane against the end of the settee and then walked to the drawing room, where Mr. Jacoby had kept a well-stocked liquor cabinet. Rose selected a bottle of Scotch and poured some into a glass. She wondered if she should add anything else, but since Mr. Wolfe hadn't requested it, she decided to take it to him straight. She shut the doors of the cabinet and hurried out of the drawing room.

Mr. Wolfe was still sprawled in the settee, his head resting on the back, his lips slightly apart.

"Here's the Scotch," she said softly, not wishing to startle him.

He put out his hand without opening his eyes, and she placed the tumbler in his fingers.

She was surprised to hear him mutter a gruff thank-you. Then he raised his head slightly and brought the glass to his lips.

She surveyed his face while he drank. At first glance she had considered him handsome, but upon closer inspection she decided he wasn't handsome in the classic sense of the word. Instead of working together as a harmonious whole, his features battled each other for dominance once his intense eyes were closed. His sharp nose and cheekbones contrasted with his wide sensual mouth and generous lower lip. Staring at him, she saw power and authority in the ridge of his pointed nose and strong jaw, which was offset by the sardonic upturn at the left corner of his mouth. His face seemed a contradiction in terms, and she wondered if such a face reflected the character of the man.

He pinched the skin between his dark brows, leaning back again.

"Is there something wrong with your eyes?" Rose asked as she stepped closer.

He ignored the inquiry. "I'll be all right in a moment."

She clasped her hands and waited for him to recover.

"Ms. Quennel," he said at last, "do you hear a buzzing sound?"

She looked around the entryway as if she could glimpse visual proof of the sound. "No—"

"I thought not." He scowled, pressing his lips together, then releasing them. Rose regarded his mouth, wondering what he was talking about, and wondering what it would be like to lean over and kiss those firm lips. It almost seemed as if a kiss would be a familiar gesture with Mr. Wolfe, when in fact she had never kissed a man in her life. She flushed, glad that his eyes were still closed and he couldn't see her blush.

Her reaction to his mouth confounded her, especially after he had been so arrogant and rude. She put it out of her mind, chiding herself for being as hot and cold as Mr. Wolfe. Then she lifted one of his bags and struggled with it to the foot of the stairs.

Though Mr. Wolfe was foul-tempered, he held her future in his hands. She shouldn't antagonize him any further, in case he might tell her to pack her bags and leave. She couldn't jeopardize her position at Brierwood, because it was imperative that she finish her fabric project before the end of the week, when her client was to pick it up. Then she would have enough money to rent a place of her own, where she and Bea could live.

Mr. Wolfe finished his Scotch and rose to his feet, his bad leg making him appear clumsy.

"I assume there must be a free bedroom somewhere."

"Yes." Rose had cleaned and polished every inch of the master bedroom, taking great care to see to Mr. Wolfe's comfort. She hoped that he might overlook the condition of the rest of the estate once he saw evidence of her hard work in his room. She hadn't anticipated the fact that he had difficulty walking. Had she known, she would have made arrangements for him on the ground floor. But it was too late for that now.

"The master suite is on the second floor, Mr. Wolfe. Do you think you can make it up the stairs?"

"Of course I can." He glanced up the curving walnut staircase. "I'm not a cripple, Ms. Quennel." He reached for his two bags, tucking one under his arm and grabbing the second with the same hand, leaving a hand free for his cane. Rose warily watched him out of the corner of her eye, expecting him to collapse at any minute. But he continued up the stairs without incident.

She waited until the sound of his uneven gait died out. Then Rose returned to her workroom by way of the servants' staircase at the back of the house.

Upstairs, Taylor quickly unpacked his clothes and took his shaving kit to the bathroom. As he walked around the master suite, he eyed the room appreciatively. Something about the dark greens and burgundy of the wallpaper and bedcovering made him feel at home. The pile of pillows on the bed looked soft and cozy, and the old-fashioned frame of the painting above the fireplace spoke of a grand and opulent era, a far cry from the minimalist decor of his mother's home in San Francisco. His gaze roamed over the plants near the window and caught the green of the Boston fern hanging in the bath. They were real plants, not silk imitations. For some reason the genuine article pleased him. He sighed and pulled his shirttails out of his jeans. Idly, he unbuttoned his cotton shirt as he looked around.

He had never felt comfortable sleeping in a house since taking up residence on his ship, the *Jamaican Lady*. A house didn't rock a person to sleep. A house wasn't full of the sounds Taylor loved so much—the cry of a gull, the *thwank twank* of rigging in the wind, the lapping of water against the hull. Yet this chamber in his aunt's house set his spirit at ease. Maybe it wouldn't be so bad here at Brierwood.

As he unfastened the last button on his shirt, Taylor heard a rap on his door. He limped across the floor to find Rose Quennel standing in the hallway holding a tray of cookies and a tea service. Two cups sat near the pot, as if she expected to sit and talk. He had no patience for chatty women or teacups, especially when he was so tired.

"I thought you might be hungry after your trip." She held up the tray and smiled at him. Taylor quickly looked away from her face, struck by the lack of guile in her expression. Most of the women he had met in his travels were college girls looking for adventure funded by daddy's bankcard, tavern veterans, dockside hookers or the stuffy little debutantes his mother lined up for him during his rare visits to San Francisco. But Ms. Quennel had an open face and a bright steady gaze intent with honesty, much like that of a child. She was a far cry from any of the women who had crossed his path.

"Mr. Wolfe?"

Taylor briefly inspected the tray, not in the least interested in the food. "I usually don't eat at this time of night, Ms. Quennel."

"They're homemade cookies. Bea and I made them this afternoon."

He glanced at her again. She looked like a Rembrandt painting—all red-browns and ivory—as she stood framed by the darkness of the hall, her deep red hair tumbling around her shoulders and her white skin glowing in the lamplight. He had the strongest urge to cup her cheek in his palm and see if she felt as smooth and soft as she looked. He hadn't been with a woman for months and felt the ache of repressed release, but he was well aware that he would have to get accustomed to the feeling. What woman would want to be touched by a scarred, half-crippled, half-blind man?

"Mr. Wolfe?"

He must have been staring at her like a besotted schoolboy. Angry at his lack of self-control, he motioned toward the sitting area near the fireplace. "Put the tray over there if you want. And no more Mr. Wolfe. Just call me Taylor."

"Okay." She smiled sheepishly and then swept into the room.

Formality had never been Taylor's strong suit. He thought of his parents and their impoverished beginnings and how they had become more stilted and formal with each million his father acquired. Formality was a sham that meant nothing to him, and he would not practice it.

"Is everything all right with the room?" Rose Quennel asked, walking to the coffee table in front of the sofa.

"Yes. It's fine." Taylor trailed behind her, unbuttoning the sleeves of his shirt while he surveyed her tall, lithe figure. She had changed into a gauzy summer dress in a tapestry design that swept past her knees and bared the tops of her arms. The dress was plain, but on her it looked like a ball gown.

She turned, and he realized why the dress seemed so attractive. Every movement she made was graceful, even the way she lifted her hands from the tea tray and stepped away from the table. She wore a square cut emerald on her right hand, a simple ring that complemented her slender fingers.

Taylor dragged his gaze from her hands and turned his attention to his sleeve, which he rolled up with exaggerated care, even though there was no reason to fuss with it, since he planned to undress as soon as she left.

He rolled up his other sleeve and saw her glance dart to the sinews of his forearm, which had caught the glow of the lamp on the nightstand. She quickly averted her gaze, however.

"Are your eyes still bothering you?"

"They're fine." His voice came out more gruffly then he had intended.

She paused, as if unsure whether to continue the conversation. Taylor hoped she would go. She was doing something to his senses. He felt as if his sight, smell, hearing and touch had been put on full alert and were aching to leap into action. His loins tightened in response, and he limped away from the tea table in an effort to distance himself from her tantalizing presence.

She ventured forward. "I know a bit about herbs and healing, Taylor. Perhaps I could—"

"All I need is some rest." He walked to the coffee table and hoped she wouldn't trail him. "And if you would excuse me, I'm very tired."

He glanced sidelong at her face and saw her friendly expression fade. Why did he feel like a jerk for dismissing her? She was only hired help, as far as he knew, a person with whom he wasn't required to sit and chat. Yet there was something about her that made him review his usual tendency to classify women according to their value to him and whether or not he wanted to take time out for them. Women were dangerous, as far as he was concerned. They could tie a man down and lay claim to his independence. He hadn't let many women get close to him, and never once had he allowed himself to become romantically involved with one. There was something to be said for having a woman in every port. It allowed a man his freedom and his pleasure at the same time. He wouldn't give up such a life-style without a fight.

Still, he felt like a jerk. As if to deny it, he reached down for a cookie, even though he wasn't hungry. "Thanks for the snack."

"Be sure to try the tea. It's my own special blend."

"Of what?"

"Herbs to help you sleep and make you heal more quickly."

Herbal concoctions? Homemade cookies? He was more accustomed to a good Scotch and water. Taylor grimaced and saw her expression darken. Had he offended her again?

"To heal yourself," she put in, her tone cool, "you must believe that you can be healed."

"If the best doctors in the country can't heal me, Rose, I doubt a cup of tea is going to do the trick."

"With an attitude like that, no." She walked to the door and turned. "Good night—Mr. Wolfe."

"Good night."

She closed the door behind her while Taylor stared after her. For household help, she had quite an attitude. Who did she think she was—his personal faith healer? Taylor bit into the cookie and chewed mechanically, ignoring the delicious flavor. He didn't need her help, and he didn't need to complicate his stay here with an entanglement. She was too young and innocent for him, anyway. And besides, he'd seen the way she glanced at his scars, trying not to be obvious about it. She was probably repulsed by the sight of him.

Taylor wasn't accustomed to women being repulsed by his looks. If anything, he had used his outward appearance to win whatever woman he desired at the time, well aware that ladies appreciated his dark looks and six-foot height. He'd never thought twice about using his physical attributes to get what he wanted. Now, however, he would have to depend on his personality. Taylor grimaced. People had called him a heartless bastard. Cold. Impossible. That didn't say much for his personality. And it didn't bode well for his love life, either.

Taylor grabbed two more cookies and ate one as he limped to the table where he had set up his wooden boat model. He would concentrate on finishing the three-masted schooner and stay away from that red-haired beauty. And after a week of peace and quiet here at Brierwood, perhaps he would be on the road to full recovery.

Later Rose tossed and turned in her bed, dreaming of Mr. Wolfe smashing her cookies with his cane, claiming that she had put rocks in them. She tried to protest, but the words wouldn't come out. Then she felt a warm hand on her shoulder and knew a slight sense of relief.

Someone was talking to her in a low, singsong voice. Was she still dreaming? The hand on her shoulder felt very real. Yet she couldn't quite open her eyes, couldn't quite gain consciousness. Had Mr. Wolfe come into her room? He had stared at her in a strange way when she had arrived with his snack. Was he the type of man who would try to take advantage of her? Somehow, she didn't think so. But if this wasn't Mr. Wolfe in her dream, who was it?

"Roselyn, Roselyn," a voice said near her ear. The voice was dry, seductive, and she eased onto her back, trying to see who stood near her bed, but she couldn't open her eyes.

"Roselyn, you hear me, don't you, my dear?"

She stirred, heard herself mumble an incoherent phrase.

"Roselyn, you must tell me where your mother has hidden her possessions."

My mother? I don't have a mother.

"You did. You just don't remember."

Maybe I don't want to remember. My mother gave me up, sent me away. Why should I want to remember a mother like that?

"It's true. Your mother was not a nice lady, Roselyn. But I believe she gave you something that belongs to me."

I have nothing of my parents'. Not even their name.

"Roselyn, my beauty." He kissed her bare shoulder, and Rose felt a warm, melting feeling spread through her. She sank farther into her bed. "Such bitterness. You have been hurt, haven't you? You suffer."

Yes, I suffer. But why should you care?

"Because I want to help you. I can give you back the family you lost so long ago."

She ached to know about her family, but she was afraid of the truth, of the guilt and shame associated with being a foundling. Surely if her mother and father had loved her, they would have kept her. So the truth was that they had not loved her and that they had rejected her. Rose didn't want to face that particular truth or learn the reasons for the rejection.

"Roselyn, I can show you the family you once knew."

No, I don't want to see. I don't care about them.

"Yes, you do, Roselyn. I know you're curious. You are looking back now. See, you can just make out a candle at the end of the corridor."

Yes, she could. Was she sleepwalking? She tried to turn her back on the candle, tried to close her eyes, but couldn't seem to command the movements of her own body.

"Go toward the light, Roselyn, and tell me what you see."

CHAPTER THREE

The light startled her. Rose scrambled to her feet as her mother bent over her crib and then hurriedly dressed her.

"Shh, baby," Deborah Bastyr whispered. "Mother's taking you for a walk."

Rose looked to the window, wondering why they would take a walk so early in the morning. They'd never done that before. She yawned and held out her arm so that her mother could slide on the sleeve of her red dress. She liked the dress, which was decorated with lots of bows and hearts, so different from the plain black-and-white dresses she usually wore. Her mother had bought the red dress for her, but for some reason she rarely got to wear it. She didn't know why that was. It was such a pretty dress, after all.

"There you are, pumpkin," her mother crooned, pulling a sweater on over the dress. "Good girl."

Rose put a knuckle to her mouth and sucked on it while her mother lifted her out of the crib. Her mother was wearing her black coat, the one with the fuzzy collar that felt so soft. She reached out and stroked it as her mother carried her across the room. Maybe when she was big, like Mother, she would get a coat just like it.

"We're going to play a game now, Rose," Deborah said, grabbing a cloth bag from the bed. "Let's pretend we have zippers on our mouths and we can't open our lips."

She made a zipping movement across her mouth. Rose smiled and copied the motion.

"Good. Now, once we zip our mouths, we can't speak. Not until I unzip yours, okay?"

Rose nodded, eager to play the game. Mother hadn't been playing many games with her lately, and she was glad to see that life was getting back to normal, although she wasn't too certain about walking around before breakfast. But if she was with her mother, it would be all right.

The house was dim as her mother carried her down the hall to the stairs. She wondered why her mother didn't turn on the lights. Perhaps when she was big, she wouldn't be afraid of the dark, either. She clung tightly to her mother's neck as they passed Uncle Enoch's room near the top of the stairs. His room was a spooky place she wasn't allowed to visit, and the dark wood of the sealed door seemed even scarier in the dark. Once she had caught a glimpse of him sitting naked in a chair in his room with drool hanging from his mouth.

Down the stairs they hurried. Her mother clutched her too tightly, and she squirmed, wanting to complain but remembering the zipper on her lips. Daisy, their big hound, lifted her head as they walked past the kitchen, but her mother made a motion for her to stay. That was odd, because Daisy always went with them on their walks. Rose looked over her mother's shoulder at the dog, her head bouncing, and hoped Daisy wouldn't feel too bad about being left out.

A light rain started to fall as they headed across the rear lawn. Why weren't they walking down the lane, as usual? Why was Mother headed to the woods in back of the house? Wasn't she afraid of the wild animals that lived there? Rose clutched her mother's neck even harder.

"It's all right, baby," Deborah murmured softly. But never once did she put her down to walk, even though she seemed out of breath.

It was still too dark to see much. All the pretty flowers were closed. And once they left the yard, there was nothing to see but trees and shrubs shrouded in morning fog. Rose's eyelids felt heavy, and pretty soon she put her cheek down on the fuzzy collar and shut her eyes, hoping her mother wouldn't get lost. Her mother's hair smelled nice.

The next thing she knew she was being handed to someone in a car while her mother crooned a reassurance that she would be all right. Then her mother slid in beside her and shut the door. All she said was "Let's go." With a lurch, the car sped away, and Rose snuggled against the curve of her mother's shoulder and fell back to sleep.

* * *

In her bed at Brierwood, Rose felt another kiss on her shoulder, but the physical contact barely registered. She had dreamed of her mother. She had seen the face of her mother for the first time, had felt her gentle touch and heard her soft voice. Overwhelmed by the sudden memory, Rose couldn't concentrate on the words of the man at her bedside.

"A man was in the car. Your mother's lover."

Leave me alone, Mr. Wolfe. I can't talk right now. Can't think.

"Your mother was an adulteress, a disgrace to the family."

Rose scowled, still not able to wake up. The dream she had just experienced disturbed her. She had never dreamed of her mother before. Why now? And was the dream based on actual childhood memories, or was it simply the result of her desire to create a past with which she could be satisfied? In the dream her mother had held her, crooned to her and reassured her. Was that the kind of mother who would reject her child? What sort of nonsense was Mr. Wolfe showing her? She tried to wake up, wanting to rid herself of the memories and the man at her bedside, but she couldn't open her eyes.

"Her lover wanted her to run away, to leave your father."

Father? I don't remember having a father at all.

"Oh, you had a father, Roselyn. You still do. He's looked for you for years. You are his only living heir."

That's not possible. I am an orphan. My father is dead.

"He isn't dead, Roselyn. And he's very anxious to get to know you after all these years. He's pleased that you have grown up to be such a beautiful young woman. Very pleased."

The man at her bedside touched her breast. Rose turned away, and she sensed that he had straightened but was still regarding her.

"You will be worth waiting for, Roselyn Bastyr. But the waiting will be hard indeed."

Rose shifted, disturbed by the intimate touch and his cryptic words. Her mother had loved her? Her father was alive? It couldn't be true. She had simply experienced an odd dream.

I don't believe you.

"The truth, Roselyn," said the voice near her ear, "is sometimes hard to accept. But in time you will realize how many lies you have been told. Now sleep."

Rose woke up late the next morning and jumped out of bed. It was nine o'clock, very late for her. She usually rose at six and was at work by seven, especially during the hot summer months, when the workroom got unbearably stuffy in the afternoons. As she dressed and arranged her hair into a loose braid, she had a fleeting glimpse of her dream during the night. How odd to recall a vision from so far back in her childhood. She usually had a hard time remembering any incidents before she was five, when she had arrived at Brierwood. Frowning, Rose glanced at her white face in the mirror and gazed at her bare shoulder. Another memory came back in a rush, and she drew her hand over the skin where two kisses had been pressed. Those kisses had been real. She was certain a real man had caressed her. And the only man at Brierwood was Taylor Wolfe. He might seem familiar to her, but that didn't permit him to take such liberties.

She would have to set him straight about what she would allow him to do. Coming into her bedroom at night was simply unacceptable behavior. She didn't know why she hadn't put up a protest last night. But she would make her objections plain first thing this morning. She would also lock her bedroom door from now on.

Anxious to confront Mr. Wolfe, Rose hurried down the hall, her anger mounting with every step. Perhaps he hadn't even gotten up yet. Too bad. She would interrupt his sleep just as he had interrupted hers.

Rose rapped on his door and waited impatiently as she heard the sound of his uneven gait approaching. He opened the door, his jaw covered with shaving cream and his neck and shoulders draped in a towel. He wore a pair of faded jeans belted loosely around his trim hips and no shoes or socks. Last night she had assumed his figure had been en-

hanced by the expert tailoring of his jacket, but she had been
wrong. Mr. Wolfe's bare, well-developed shoulders and
arms needed no enhancement whatsoever.

Flushing at the sight of his naked torso, she raised her eyes
and forced herself to attend to the reason she had come to
his room.

"Yes, Rose?"

"I want to talk to you about last night."

"Do you mind? I'm in the middle of shaving."

"What I want to say will only take a moment."

He looked at her expectantly, as if he wasn't the least bit
ashamed of his behavior. Rose felt her anger flare and
crossed her arms over her chest.

"Your family may own this house, Mr. Wolfe, but that
doesn't give you the right to behave in such a fashion."

"What fashion?" He grabbed both ends of the towel with
his hands. "What are you talking about?"

"You know perfectly well."

"Don't tell me you're still angry about the tea? Good
God, woman!" He turned and limped toward the bathroom. Rose followed close behind, fuming.

"Wait a minute!" she demanded. "I'm talking to you!"

"You're ranting, that's what you're doing." He picked up
his razor and leaned over the sink. His Adam's apple
bobbed in his throat as he swallowed.

Rose watched him scrape the blade down his lean face,
enraged that he wouldn't even stop to listen to her.

"I am not ranting. And I'm not talking about the tea, either."

"What, then?" He glanced at her in the mirror as he
rinsed the razor in the basin. "My lack of faith in your so-
called herbal remedies?"

"No. And I don't like to be toyed with, Mr. Wolfe."

"Neither do I. So quit talking in circles." He concentrated on his shaving while she took a deep breath to keep
from attacking him with both fists.

"Okay. You may be accustomed to slipping into the bed-
rooms of young women, but I am not accustomed to enter-
taining men in mine."

His shaving stopped in midstroke. "What?"

"Don't you ever, *ever,* come into my bedroom again, Mr. Wolfe. Is that clear?"

He half turned, his razor submerged in the sink, a look of surprise on his face. "Perfectly. But I—"

"I'm not the kind of woman you're probably used to. And if you take one step into my room again, I'll call the police."

"I have no intention of stepping into your room."

"Then what were you doing last night—sleepwalking?"

"I was working on my model." He indicated the table nearby, where his schooner stood partially built. "I didn't come to your bedroom. Hell, I don't even know where it is."

"How can you stand there and lie to me? You were there. You talked to me. You hypnotized me. You kissed my shoulder, touched my—" She broke off, too embarrassed to tell him all.

He tilted his head and gave her that narrow-eyed look.

"Don't try to deny it, Mr. Wolfe."

"Fine," he replied, dabbing his face with the towel, his movements sharp with anger. "You seem sure it was me, anyway."

"Why can't you just admit it?"

"This conversation is going nowhere. You aren't hearing a word I'm saying."

"And you're not hearing me!"

"The hell I'm not. I've met women like you, victims of their own hysterical imaginations."

"Hysterical imaginations!"

"Yeah." He slapped the towel over his shoulder and faced her. "And the women I've seen who are worried about men taking advantage of them are usually the type that I wouldn't look at twice."

"And what is that supposed to mean? That I'm hysterical *and* unattractive?"

"Lady—" he put his fists to his hips "—you can take it to mean anything you want."

She glared at him, so enraged that she couldn't speak. She was not the hysterical type. Besides that, he wouldn't even admit that he had come into her room. He had blamed it on her imagination. Her *imagination!* She turned on her heel and stormed out of the room, slamming the door behind her.

Rose fumed to the end of the hall and all the way down the stairs. Before she entered the kitchen, however, she took three deep breaths to calm herself and then smoothed back her hair and the skirt of her dress. She didn't want to disturb Bea needlessly or have to explain what Taylor Wolfe had done to her while she slept. But she was curious to find out about the Bastyr family and wondered if Bea knew anything about them.

Bea looked up from the cutting board, where she was mincing bacon and green onions for an omelet. "Good morning, dear," she greeted Rose with a smile.

Rose walked across the tile floor and gave her a hug. "How are you feeling, Bea?"

"Much better. But you should have awakened me when Mr. Wolfe arrived last night."

"I thought you could use the rest."

"That was thoughtful of you, Rose, but I was worried what Mr. Wolfe might think, seeing you."

"He was full of questions, but he didn't tell me to leave."

"That's a relief." Bea scooped up the bacon and dropped it in a sauté pan. "But I suppose he'll want to know all the details from me."

"Don't worry. The worst he can do is send us packing. I can handle that."

"But not until you sell your scarf, Rose." Bea turned to glance at her as she stirred the sizzling bacon. "We must convince him to let us stay that long."

"I'm almost done. Don't worry."

"You're a good girl, Rose." Bea gave her a warm but troubled smile. Rose shrugged it off, knowing in her heart that she wasn't *that* good. Good children didn't get banished from their families.

Rose stepped closer to the stove, though she stayed far enough away so the bacon grease wouldn't splatter her. "Bea, I have a question."

"Yes?"

"Have you ever heard of a family called the Bastyrs?"

Bea lost her grip on the fork, which slid into the hot pan and lay half-submerged in the bacon grease. "Oh, there, look what I've done!" she exclaimed, reaching for a sharp knife nearby with which to fish out the fork.

Rose noted Bea's fluttering movements, so unlike the calm, reserved woman Rose knew her to be, and realized the mere mention of the Bastyr name had sent Bea into a flurry of nervousness. Why?

"Ouch, that fork's hot!" Bea cried, dropping the utensil on the counter. "I'm just Miss Fumble Fingers this morning, aren't I?"

"Bea, you didn't answer my question."

"I'm sorry, dear." Bea walked to the sink to strain off the grease. "What was it again?"

"The Bastyrs. Have you ever heard of them?"

Bea pushed up her wire-framed glasses and turned from the sink, still holding the pan and spatula. "The Bastyrs?"

"Yes. Mr. Wolfe said I bear a marked resemblance to the Bastyr women."

Bea's grip tightened on the spatula. Rose could see the knuckles of her pudgy hand turning white. "Mr. Wolfe said that?"

"Yes. He said my red hair gave me away."

"Your red hair? Lots of people have red hair." Bea set the pan on the counter and quickly turned to the refrigerator. "I wouldn't take him seriously. He was probably just trying to break the ice with you." She rose up, holding a carton of eggs. "It's a typical male ploy when meeting a pretty girl to say she reminds him of someone."

"He said he knew all about me, though."

"How could he? He didn't know you were here until last night." Bea cracked the eggs into a bowl. Her hands shook.

"What aren't you telling me, Bea?" Rose demanded, gripping the edge of the counter. "You're hiding something from me. I can tell."

"Now, why would I hide anything from you, dear?" Bea retorted, whisking the eggs. The loose flesh on her forearms jiggled. She looked up at Rose and smiled, but Rose could see the tarnish of fear and insecurity dulling the sparkle in her eyes.

Bea picked up the bowl of eggs. "Perhaps you misunderstood him, Rose. I know you must be tired, driving yourself as you do. You haven't been getting enough sleep lately."

"I didn't misunderstand him." Rose frowned again, remembering how Mr. Wolfe had acted upon meeting her the second time, as if he had never talked to her before. He hadn't known her name and wasn't aware of her presence at Brierwood. What was going on? Was he deliberately trying to confuse her? And if so, why?

"I'm making an omelet for Mr. Wolfe, Rose," Bea put in. "Would you like one?"

She snapped out of her musings. "No, thanks. I've got to get to work. I've lost too much time as it is."

"You shouldn't skip breakfast, Rose. It isn't healthy."

"I'll be all right, Bea. I'll just take some coffee up to the studio."

She reached for a mug from the cup hook under the cupboard and poured it full of the fragrant, freshly brewed coffee. Taking a sip, she surveyed Bea as she poured the egg mixture into the omelet pan and hovered over the stove, carefully monitoring the cooking process. Was Bea lying to her? She had certainly seemed upset at the mention of the Bastyr family. But Bea wouldn't lie to her. She had known Bea for fifteen years, and in all those years she had never once distrusted anything the elderly woman had told her. No, if anyone was lying to her, it was that awful Mr. Wolfe.

"Well," Rose said, walking to the door, "see you later, Bea."

"Don't stay up there all day," Bea called over her shoulder. "And don't take that ring off when you're working."

Rose glanced down at the simple emerald ring she had worn since childhood. Bea insisted that she wear it always, and she did keep it on her hand most of the time, just to humor her. In fact, she'd even been wearing it at night since Donald's collapse in the herb garden. Rose pushed through the swinging door, worrying about Bea's nervous behavior and the strange unease that had settled over Brierwood.

* * *

Taylor sipped his coffee in the morning room just off the kitchen while Bea Jacoby shuffled to the table and slid a plate of steaming food before him. He breathed in the aroma of the omelet and homemade cinnamon roll, anxious to taste the offerings of the Brierwood kitchen. One thing he appreciated was good cooking, since he possessed only the basic culinary skills. He picked up his fork, waiting for Mrs. Jacoby to leave his side, but she just stood there staring at him.

She studied him, her brown eyes taking in every detail of his face and hair. Taylor, still unaccustomed to people staring at his scars, tried not to flush beneath her regard.

"Is there something you need, Mrs. Jacoby?" he asked, slicing through the omelet with the side of his fork.

"Yes. I want to know who you really are."

Taylor paused, a forkful of egg poised in midair. "Pardon me?"

"I want to know who you really are." Bea Jacoby clasped her hands in front of her ample belly, making it clear that she was not about to move until she got an answer.

"I'm Taylor Wolfe."

"I don't think so. None of your relatives have lived at Brierwood for twenty years. Then all of a sudden you show up. Why?"

"Personal reasons, Mrs. Jacoby, which are none of your business." He popped the egg in his mouth, hoping Mrs. Jacoby would see fit to remove herself.

"Personal reasons?" she persisted. "And might those include Rose Quennel?"

"I hardly think so. I don't even know her."

"You told her that you knew all about her."

Taylor nearly choked on his omelet. What nonsense had that hysterical Ms. Quennel been spreading? The next thing he knew, he would be accused of rape, perhaps taken to court and thrown in prison. He might very well have stepped into a plot designed to get a piece of the Wolfe fortune, something he had always guarded against but had never considered a possibility at Brierwood. Once a family had money, they were constantly besieged by people who were after that fortune in one way or another, whether through marriage or crime or a combination of both.

"I never said that I knew anything about her."

"Rose is unusually bright, Mr. Wolfe. When she tells me something, I have no reason to doubt her memory or her reason."

"Then maybe she's just confused." He took a sip of coffee, wishing he could enjoy his breakfast in peace and quiet. As it was, his meal lodged in his chest, bound up by the terse words between himself and the housekeeper, and by the idea that he might be in the process of being framed.

"Whatever you may think you have found in Rose, Mr. Wolfe, be assured that you are wrong about her. She has no family. Do you understand? None. Just because she has red hair doesn't mean she is connected to any family."

"I never said she was." Exasperated, Taylor sighed. "Look, Mrs. Jacoby, I have no interest in Rose Quennel. None whatsoever. How many ways do I have to say it?"

She studied him, staring at him from the corner of her eyes as if to judge the veracity of his words. He kept his gaze steady, willing her to believe him, until she turned and left the morning room. Taylor watched her, wondering what in the hell was going on.

One thing he was sure of, he wasn't about to become a victim of a frame job, no matter how beautiful the bait. The sooner he recovered his normal eyesight, the better. And that meant finding out all he could on the subject of the human eye and related diseases. He finished his breakfast and then limped up to the study on the second floor, where he spent the rest of the morning on the phone ordering books about the human eye, vision and anything else remotely related to his peculiar problem. He was determined to get his normal sight back, no matter what the doctors said. Doctors had misdiagnosed their patients before. They could be wrong in his case, too. Taylor hoped to God they were.

Rose stayed in the third floor workroom for most of the day. She didn't want to take the chance that she might run into Mr. Wolfe in the parlor or on the stairs, and she certainly wasn't in the mood for waiting on him. But by three o'clock she was suffering from hunger and heat. Her hair was damp, and her dress clung to the backs of her legs. She couldn't bear another minute of the heat. A dip in the pond just outside the grounds would revive her and give her the impetus to continue her work. She had made great strides in finishing the scarf and deserved a break.

She slipped out of the house and caught a glimpse of Mr. Wolfe walking down the lane. Rose took the opposite direction and headed for the back gardens, toward the pond at the rear of the property. As she got closer to the pond, her anger faded, replaced by the joy she always felt when walking through the canopy of fir trees. Stellar jays squawked as she strolled down the path, alerted by the presence of Edgar, who soared ahead.

Just as she was about to turn off the path to the pond, she heard a snuffling noise and a growl. Rose stopped at the Y in the path and listened again. The growl was closer this time, coming from the curved trail ahead of her. Though she knew it was impossible, she could swear she heard her name—*Roselyn, Roselyn, Roselyn*—as if some kind of creatures were chanting her name as they ran. The hair on the back of her neck rose, and she turned to flee just as four black-and-orange rottweilers burst around the bend in the path and thundered toward her, panting and snarling. They had huge blocky heads and powerful jaws frothed with white foam.

Rose knew enough about dogs not to run or show fear. If she did either, chances were that they would attack her. If she could stand her ground and intimidate them, she might buy enough time to find a way of escape.

"Back!" Rose shouted, glancing around for a stick with which to defend herself. The dogs trotted around her, sniffing the ground and growling. They had massive chests, as big a man's, and muscular legs and necks, and she was certain she would be no match for them. She backed toward the berry bushes where the two paths joined and looked down. A rock lay on the ground near her feet. Without taking her attention off the dogs, she crouched down and picked up the rock.

"Get back!" she shouted again, brandishing the rock. "Get!"

The dogs showed no fear. Where had they come from? The nearest neighbor was miles away, on the other side of the dense wood. She had never seen rottweilers in the vicinity. Were they a pack of wild dogs?

Roselyn, Roselyn, Roselyn, they growled, pacing in front of her. One padded closer and showed his teeth. The other three trotted up behind him, barking and snarling.

Desperate, Rose threw the rock at the leader. It hit the dog's chest and thudded to the ground. He didn't even take notice of the impact and lunged forward.

Rose screamed and scrambled backward, over the soft bank of the path. The earth gave way beneath her weight, and she toppled over, landing in the briers.

"Oh!" she cried, impaled by hundreds of little thorns tearing at her shoulders, arms and legs. Tears sprang up, but she blinked them back, too worried about the rottweilers to indulge in crying. The dogs paced at the top of the bank, glaring down at her, their jowls dripping froth on the blackberry leaves. Apparently they knew better than to jump down into the brambles. But how long would they stay there?

Grimacing in pain, Rose tried to look behind her for an escape route beyond the brambles, only to discover that her braid had come partially undone and her hair was caught in the briers. The more she twisted and turned, the more entangled she became, and she couldn't turn her head far enough to see how to free herself. Like a rabbit caught in a snare, she panicked and nearly pulled her hair out by the roots, until the pain in her scalp and in her arms and palms made her fall back, exhausted and frightened. What would she do? How long would the dogs stand guard over her? How would she ever get loose? Bea was slightly deaf and would never hear her cries for help. The only person who could help her was that awful Mr. Wolfe. And who knew if he was within earshot? And if he did hear her and came to her aid, what would the dogs do to him?

She glanced at the rottweilers and noticed they had turned their attention to something on the path. Their ears pricked forward as if they were listening.

"Ms. Quennel?" a familiar voice called.

The dogs turned and loped off in the opposite direction. But for the stickers in her back, Rose would have wilted in relief.

"Mr. Wolfe!" she shouted. "I'm over here!"

CHAPTER FOUR

Taylor leaned on his cane and wiped the sweat from his brow with the back of his hand. That was Rose calling him, and she sounded as if she were in trouble. Regardless, he had to pause for a moment and catch his breath. He hadn't realized how tired he would get after such a short walk, or how hot it was outside in the afternoon. Even though the garden and grounds looked cool and inviting from the house, they offered little relief from the close air. His leg throbbed and his breath came hard as he continued to hurry down the trail, following Rose's raven, who soared ahead of him.

"Help! Mr. Wolfe!"

"Coming!" He was certain now that the plaintive voice must belong to Rose Quennel. She didn't appear to be the type who would beg for anyone's help, yet who else would be here in this remote place? Taylor limped along the sun-dappled trail until he came to a clearing, where the path forked off toward a small pond.

"Mr. Wolfe!"

He caught sight of a white figure spread-eagled in a thicket of blackberries at the edge of the trail and limped closer.

"Rose?" he gasped in disbelief.

"Watch out for the dogs, Mr. Wolfe!"

"What dogs?" He glanced around. "I don't see any dogs."

"There were four rottweilers. They attacked me."

"I don't see them."

"You don't? Maybe you scared them off."

He nodded and looked down at her. "You look as if you've gotten yourself in quite a spot."

"My hair is caught. And I'm in a great deal of discomfort."

Taylor surveyed the situation, wincing when he noticed the bright red scratches on her fair skin. Dressed in denim cutoffs and a T-shirt, he didn't relish the idea of wading in after her, but he couldn't leave her and go back for an ax to chop her out. With his slow walk, he wouldn't make it back for half an hour, at least. He couldn't let her suffer that long.

Scowling, he stepped down the bank, using his cane to fend off the encroaching brambles. Even so, he received more scratches on his already scarred face and legs. A lusty brier brushed the gash on his leg and ripped off part of the bandage. Taylor could feel a warm trickle of blood on his skin, but he ignored it and blocked out the throb of pain as he hacked his way to Rose.

"How'd you manage to fall into these?" he grumbled, whacking at a stray vine.

"The dogs lunged at me. Please hurry."

Taylor bent over her and inspected the intricate maze of hair and briers. Gingerly he pulled a strand of red hair free, trying not to hurt her. He was accustomed to working with his hands on small difficult details, a talent honed by many hours spent building his models. The practice provided him with unusual patience and concentration, which he could apply with ease to his ships but found nearly impossible to grant to people.

He pulled on another strand, and she let out a gasp.

"Easy, Rose," he encouraged. "It's coming."

He put aside his cane and slipped a hand under her head, supporting its weight to take the strain off her neck. She sighed in relief, and he felt her relax somewhat. If this were a ploy to get them together, she had certainly placed herself in considerable pain for the cause. He wondered whose idea it was, Bea Jacoby's or Rose Quennel's, and whether she had become far more entangled than planned?

He worked quickly, freeing tangle after tangle, until the last vine was released from her hair. "There," he said, helping her to her feet, one hand on her wrist, the other on her hip, knowing he should step away from her as quickly as possible. She rose gracefully and stood before him, slightly dazed and pale, brushing her tangled hair out of her face. Her actions and expression seemed too genuine to be mere fabrication. Worried that she might collapse back into the thicket, Taylor slid both hands to the sides of her slender waist and surveyed her critically.

"Are you all right?" he asked.

"I—I think so," she murmured. "Thank you." In wonder, she looked up at him, as if seeing him for the first time. "You saved my life."

"I wouldn't say that."

"I might never have gotten away."

"You'd have managed." His eyes locked with hers, and he wasn't even sure what he was saying. All he knew was that he longed to bend down and kiss her lips, so red against her pale skin. She was lovely, even covered with scratches, and the paleness of her skin accentuated the blue of her eyes, the same periwinkle blue of the forget-me-nots growing at the edge of the briers. Beads of moisture hung in her lashes, adding to their lushness.

"I just can't understand where those dogs came from," she said. "I've never seen them around here before."

"And they attacked you?"

"Yes. And I don't know what I'd have done if you hadn't come along when you did."

Suddenly Edgar swooped down at them and landed on the grass nearby, cawing raucously. Rose glanced at the bird, breaking off the tender possibility that had hung between them.

"And where were *you*, Edgar?" she admonished. "You could have gone for help."

"He did. He guided me over this way."

"He did?" Surprised, Rose looked back at the bird.

Edgar bobbed his head.

Taylor came to his senses and realized that he had been considering succumbing to Rose just as they planned for him to do. This was no time to play the fool. Immediately, he released his light hold on her.

Rose backed away and lowered her lashes, while two patches of crimson blossomed on her cheeks. The shock had worn off, and it was obvious she was embarrassed. Flustered himself, he picked up his cane and gently took her wrist to lead her out of the briers, thankful to occupy his hands with something other than her soft curves. If he touched her again or gazed at her any longer, he would forget his vow to steer clear of her.

Once they reached the trail, he released her. "There you go, Brier Rose. Safe and sound."

He heard her suck in a sharp breath.

"Mr. Wolfe, your leg!"

He looked down. The slash on his right calf had broken open and painted his leg in blood.

Rose knelt beside him to inspect his wound and brushed at the trickle of blood with the hem of the slip beneath her dress.

"How did you hurt your leg, Mr. Wolfe?"

"In a car accident."

"On a piece of glass?"

"I don't know how it happened. I was unconscious."

She dabbed at his leg with the corner of her slip, her touch more gentle than that of any of the doctors or nurses who had attended him at the hospital. Taylor looked down at her, wondering why he was letting her fuss over him.

"It's quite a deep wound, as if you were cut with a knife."

"It's nothing."

"How long ago were you injured?"

"About two months."

"It should be healed by now." Rose straightened and deftly pulled the half slip down, stepping out of it with her inimitable gracefulness. The slip was a frothy concoction of lace trim and rosebud embroidery, and for a moment Taylor stared at it. He hadn't seen such a feminine piece of clothing for years. "Here," she said, kneeling down again. "Let me stop the bleeding, at least."

"Wait. You'll ruin your slip."

"I'd rather soil my slip than have you bleed to death, Mr. Wolfe."

Before he could back away, she was removing the old bandage in a way that didn't pull at the hairs on his leg. Then she tied torn strips of the slip firmly but comfortably about his leg. Taylor watched her, marveling that she would take such care of a virtual stranger—unless, of course, she was doing it only to ingratiate herself with him.

When Rose finished, she stood up. "I'd get that taken care of, Mr. Wolfe. It could get infected. It looks like it may be infected now."

"The doctors did all that could possibly be done."

"Have you tried plantain?"

"What?"

"Plantain. It's a plant, one of the best remedies for cuts and infections. I'm going to gather some for my scratches and yours."

"Forget it." There she went again with her herbal advice. Taylor had no use for quacks, even beautiful ones. He didn't like her staring at his scars, and he didn't want to be her patient. Most of all, however, he hated appearing as a wounded weakling in her eyes. "My leg needs time to heal, that's all."

He hobbled away from her. He didn't want her fussing over him and touching him. And he didn't want some novice healer messing around with his health. He also couldn't bear another moment looking at the vision she presented as she stood in a pool of sunlight—a luscious, flame-haired nymph with a crestfallen expression.

The farther he stayed away from Rose Quennel, the better. All he had to do was straighten out the question of the missing caretaker and then he intended to avoid Rose for the rest of his stay at Brierwood. Even now, he knew he had to get clear of her tantalizing presence before he made a fool of himself.

Taylor turned on the path to glance back at her. She hadn't moved.

"I want to talk to you later," he said. "In the study at four o'clock, if you can fit it into your busy schedule."

Her chin rose at his sarcasm.

"I'll be there," she replied.

He turned and limped away, suddenly realizing that he hadn't even thanked her.

* * *

Sitting on the edge of the desk in the study, Taylor looked at his watch. Ten after four. The woman was late. He should have expected as much. From all appearances, Rose was one of those flighty, artsy women who didn't quite fit into the modern world. He had never spent much time with women like Rose, preferring the type who played hard and loved on the run. Impatiently, he tapped the cane on the tip of his shoe and mentally counted the minutes, all the while listening for her step in the hall and wondering why he didn't do something more productive than sitting there waiting for her.

Out of the corner of his eye he saw the new bandage he had wrapped around his shin to stop the bleeding. Not only did the dressing look crooked and ineptly applied, it wasn't doing a very good job of staunching the flow.

He was about to get up and return to the bathroom for a towel when he heard a flutter of wings and Rose's voice in the hallway. Immediately he straightened his spine and faced the door, making sure to put on one of his sternest expressions. With the correct approach, it shouldn't take long to get to the bottom of Mr. Jacoby's unexplained absence.

Rose hadn't changed her dress, which was stained and torn by the berry bushes and spotted with her blood. One look at her drawn face and he felt his scowl slide away. Hadn't she taken care of her scratches? No wonder she could barely move. Didn't she know how to set priorities or manage her time? Such disorganization annoyed Taylor, especially when he suspected that she had been out foraging for plantain after he had specifically told her not to concern herself with his wound. Blinking back his anger, he watched her mince into the room and stand in front of him, her shoulders unusually stiff.

"You're late," he blurted.

"I was picking plantain for your leg."

"I told you to forget my leg."

She glanced at his bandage and then back to his face. He kept his expression impassive, even though he knew she disdained his clumsy handiwork. He could read the thoughts in her eyes as clearly as if she had spoken, and her silent criticism rankled him more than anything she might have said.

The interview was not going as he'd intended.

Before he could think of a way to get back on track, however, he was forced to duck as Edgar flew past his head and landed on a bust of Victor Hugo near the window. Taylor rose, a scowl on his face.

"I thought I told you to keep that bird out of the house."

"You said nothing of the kind."

"Didn't I?"

"No, you simply wondered why we would let him in the house."

"Wild animals belong in the wild."

"Edgar is not wild. And I assure you, Mr. Wolfe, he will not be a problem."

"Then you pick up after him?"

"Pick up?" she repeated vaguely.

"You know—clean up his droppings."

"Edgar doesn't disgrace himself in such a fashion."

"He's housebroken? Whoever heard of a bird being housebroken?"

"Apparently *you* haven't." Her level stare brought him down a peg.

Taylor stared right back, surprised that his stern countenance had no effect on her. Most people went on the defensive in the face of his censure, stumbling and stammering in their haste to please him. She didn't even seem to notice that he was upset.

This interview was not going well at all.

He stood, walked around the desk and motioned to a chair. "Sit down for a minute."

She looked at the chair, then back to his face. "I'd prefer to stand."

"Suit yourself." He sank into the burgundy leather chair and hooked his cane on the arm beside him. Then he faced Rose.

"So, what's going on around here?"

"What's going on?"

Did he see a hint of uneasiness cross her face? Good. "Yes. Something to explain why Brierwood is in such a state and why Mr. Jacoby is nowhere in sight."

She stared at him, her eyes widening.

"Well?"

"Didn't Mrs. Jacoby explain?"

"No, she didn't. So why don't you just sit down and enlighten me."

Rose clasped her hands together in front of her. "Mr. Jacoby is away."

"I know that." He leaned forward. "But where is he?"

"He's..." She licked her lips. "Well, honestly, Mr. Wolfe, I don't see why you should worry. I can fill in while he's gone."

"Can you?"

"I'm perfectly capable."

He studied her in a calculated sort of way that would have put most people on pins and needles. But Rose stood tall, never flinching, her eyes never blinking.

"That isn't the point."

"No?"

He shook his head at her feigned innocence. "You haven't told me where he is. If I were a suspicious kind of person, I might think you and Mrs. Jacoby were hiding something from me."

"Why would we hide anything from you?"

"Damned if I know. You two seemed to be hatching all kinds of trouble." He put his forearms on the blotter and leaned forward. "So where is Mr. Jacoby?"

Her blank stare didn't fool him in the least. She might be a great little actress with a commendable blank look, but her blue eyes glinted with an intelligent gleam that betrayed her mask of innocence.

"Damn it!" He lost patience and slapped the desk top with the flat of his hand. "Where is he?"

"I—"

"Where, Rose!"

"He's dead."

"Dead?" He sat back, shocked.

"Mr. Jacoby died over a month ago."

"Why didn't you tell anyone?"

"I thought no one would care if we kept silent for a while."

"You did, did you?"

She nodded, her eyes even wider.

"Why keep it secret?"

"I was afraid Bea and I would be sent away." She stepped closer. "It's not that I'm trying to trick you or anything, Mr. Wolfe, it's just that I need to stay here, at least for this last week, because—"

He held up his hand to silence her outburst. "That's not the point, Rose. The Wolfe family has been paying good money for wages that have not been earned."

"I'm sure the Jacobys didn't cheat your family. They've just been getting on in years and—"

"Letting the place go to seed. So that's what's been going on here." He grabbed his cane and pushed away his chair with the backs of his legs. "And how do you figure in all this? Why are you at Brierwood?"

"I was left on the doorstep as a child. The Jacobys took me in—"

"At my mother's expense. That was big of them."

"Show some mercy, Mr. Wolfe. Your family doesn't seem to be hurting for money."

"Really? And how did you come to that conclusion?"

"Well, they own Brierwood, after all, and I'm sure much more than—"

"Looking to get a piece of it, are you?"

She stared at him, her face blanching. She had such amazing control over her expressions that he had to admire her acting abilities. Taylor walked around the desk, his cane tapping on the parquet floor.

"Just remember one thing, Rose Quennel. I may share the Wolfe name, but that doesn't mean I share their wealth."

A shadow of confusion passed through her blue eyes, as if she didn't know what he was getting at.

"I may not be as wealthy as you assume. Think about *that* the next time you jump into a brier patch."

She stepped back, her hand splayed across her breast. "You're not implying that I—"

"Don't bother with theatrics, either. If I want to watch melodrama, I'll take in a play downtown." He motioned toward the door. "Now go on and get yourself cleaned up."

For a long moment she said nothing, but he could tell from her expression that she was furious. Then, without breaking eye contact with Taylor, she held out her forearm "Come, Edgar."

The words and the tone of her voice could have formed icicles on the Taj Mahal.

Taylor felt the tips of his ears burning as he stared at her. Her rage gave her a majestic bearing he had never witnessed before, as if she had turned into a marble statue— chilling, regal and unforgivingly rigid. For an instant he wondered if he was wrong about her, if he had misjudged her actions. Then again, she could still be acting. Before he could decide, he saw the raven glide across the room and perch lightly on Rose's wrist.

She turned and walked stiffly out of the study. Taylor watched her go and didn't move until she had disappeared from view, as if her coldness had frozen him in place. What if he had misjudged her? What if Mrs. Jacoby had jumped to conclusions about him that had nothing to do with Rose? He hadn't even given her a chance to explain herself. Taylor straightened his leg and winced. It didn't really matter, anyway. He didn't care what Rose thought of him. And he didn't have to concern himself with her feelings. In fact, having her angry at him would create an emotional distance between them that would make it easier for him to avoid her. He might find some peace and quiet here at Brierwood after all.

Yet he hadn't the faintest idea what he would do if he *did* manage to acquire peace and quiet. Being locked away in a huge dark house on an overgrown estate was a far cry from the peace he found in the open air of the sea. On board the *Jamaican Lady,* there was always something to fix, polish or adjust. He hoped his books would be delivered early tomorrow, so that he would have something constructive to do. The pace at Brierwood was so damned slow that he might regain his vision but go mad in the process.

* * *

Rose hurried to her room to take off her dress and try to pull some of the briers out of her back. The tiny brown spines were hard to see in the light of her bathroom, and the job was made doubly hard because she had to operate by looking in a mirror, which meant each movement had to be made in reverse. The mirror frustrated her by making her feel clumsy and uncoordinated, and the heat in the upstairs bathroom only added to her foul humor. The entire time she was plucking briers, her mind centered on her maddening conversation with Mr. Wolfe. He had all but accused her of lying. He hadn't listened to a single word she'd said and had told her she was melodramatic. *Melodramatic!* Fury and frustration bubbled within her until the tweezers shook in her hand.

With a frustrated sigh, Rose gave up plucking the briers and realized she had succeeded in removing only a fraction of them. Since Bea's vision wasn't good enough for such a close-up job, Rose would probably have to see a doctor to get them removed. But she hated going to doctors and knew she would put off the inevitable for as long as possible.

Steeling herself to endure the irritation of her scratches meeting water, she took a quick shower and gingerly dressed in a light cotton shift she had hand-dyed with stamps made from Edgar's feathers. Then she twisted her hair into a simple knot at the base of her neck and slipped her feet into a pair of sandals. She probably wouldn't meet Mr. Wolfe's expectations of the way household help should dress, but she couldn't bear to wear anything else on her injured skin.

Stiff and sore, Rose went down to help with dinner.

Bea's nervousness of the morning had increased to the point where she was dropping mixing bowls on the floor and forgetting to check the chicken breasts under the broiler. While Rose made a romaine salad, she watched Bea drop and break a water glass, a measuring cup and a plate.

Rose put aside the long green romaine leaf she had been tearing. "Bea, what's gotten into you today?"

Bea shot an agitated glance her way and then opened the oven door to get the singed chicken, burning the top of her hand on the oven rack in the process.

"Oh, heavens!" she cried, running to the sink. Rose rushed to her side, took the rack of chicken and turned on the cold water so Bea could hold her hand under the cool flow. "Oh, thank you, Rose! Oh, that smarts!"

"Bea, I know there's something wrong. You're a nervous wreck."

Bea blinked, looked at Rose as if searching for an answer in her face, then focused her attention on her injured hand.

"Is it Mr. Wolfe?" Rose asked, leaning closer to see the changes in Bea's expression. "Are you worried that he'll fire you?"

"No, it isn't Mr. Wolfe. It's just that—" She broke off and looked down.

"What, Bea? Tell me!"

"We have to leave here, Rose. We have to pack our things tonight and leave."

"What?" Rose stepped backward, stunned. "Why?"

"I can't tell you why. But we must get out of here."

"But what about my scarf? My client?"

Bea turned off the water. "Some things are more important than money, Rose."

"What's going on?" Rose put her hands on her hips, as if to trap Bea at the sink until she revealed all. "Tell me, Bea. I know you're hiding something from me."

"Don't you understand, my dear?" Bea laid her hand on Rose's arm. "I can't tell you. You simply must trust me."

"Trust you?" Rose jerked her arm away. "Why can't you tell me what's happening? I am a grown woman, Bea. I'm not a little girl anymore. If there *is* something going on here at Brierwood, I deserve to know about it. You're getting on in years, Bea. You may think you can protect me forever, but you can't. And you can't keep me in the dark like this."

Bea pinched her lips together and shook her head. "It's just that I promised someone." She hugged herself. "I promised! But I never thought—" She shuffled to the pantry door. "We didn't think they would find—" She turned back to face Rose. "It's almost your twenty-first birthday and if—" Bea cut off the jumbled confession and stared at her, a plea in her eyes. "Please, Rose. Just this once don't ask me to explain. Just do as I say and pack your things."

"No!" For the first time in her life, Rose defied Bea Jacoby. She'd had enough coddling. She wanted answers now. Bea's distress had something to do with the Bastyr family, of that she was certain. Were the Bastyrs connected to the Quennel family? Did Bea know of the connection? And what did her twenty-first birthday have to do with anything? Rose stared at the old woman and felt her chest constrict with heartache and betrayal. Had Bea lied to her all these years, claiming that she knew nothing about the Quennel family? Had she kept the past a secret from Rose, the very person to whom that past belonged?

A hot snake of outrage uncoiled in Rose. How could the people she had trusted and loved as her own parents have lied to her for fifteen years? Was anything they had told her the truth? Reeling with shock and betrayal, she stumbled out of the kitchen and fled up the stairs.

Rose skipped dinner, too disturbed to eat, too shattered to look at Bea. Instead, she spent the early hours applying more silver swirls to the scarf, working carefully, even though her mind was a million miles from the silk beneath her brush. The night was warm, the air unmoving, yet taut with an unnatural calm, as if a huge storm were coming over the horizon. Edgar sat on a perch by the window, quiet but watchful, and Rose was thankful for his steady friendship. At least Edgar had never told her a lie.

To blot out her thoughts and nagging unease, she put in a cassette and turned on Mozart, filling the old ballroom with the lively strings and brass of the overture from *The Magic Flute*. She worked on, but the music raised her spirits only slightly.

At eight, someone knocked on her door.

Though Rose didn't want to talk to either Bea or Taylor Wolfe, she bade the visitor to come in.

Bea slipped into the workroom, carrying a small chest made of wood and carved in an intricate pattern of circles and stars. Rose's glance darted from the box to Bea's face, which was lined with worry and fear. For all Rose's anger at her, she couldn't help but feel pity for the old woman.

Bea shuffled past the desk and stood near the end of the long table, as if waiting to be asked to stay. Her lower lip trembled, but her eyes remained steady and intense. For the first time Rose saw Bea for what she was: an elderly, plump, gray-haired woman who had aged ten years in the last few hours. She seemed tired, frazzled, but undeniably focused. Rose knew that beneath Bea's soft and nurturing exterior beat a heart of iron, which had been displayed over the years whenever Bea thought Rose was in danger. Now the iron was back, but Rose wasn't certain how long Bea would be capable of defending her. Bea was old and had been shattered by the death of her husband.

Rose wondered if the roles were reversing and she would soon be the one rising to the defense of Bea. She sighed and capped her paint.

"Oh, Bea!" Rose walked over to her and slipped her arm around Bea's rounded shoulders. "I didn't mean to yell at you in the kitchen like that."

"It's all right, dear. I understand."

"I don't deserve to be lied to, Bea, that's all."

Bea nodded. "I know. It was for your own good, though, Rose. You must believe we did it for your own good." She threw a furtive glance over her shoulder. "Come, child, I must show you something. But we mustn't be seen or overheard."

"By whom? Mr. Wolfe?"

Bea nodded again, her mouth drawing down at the corners.

Rose glanced around the old ballroom, wondering where they could find the best privacy. She decided on a salon across the room, once a place for playing cards, now used as a storage area for yard goods. The sound of their voices would be muffled by the bolts of fabric and the hanging panels of cloth. There were no windows or doors to the salon, other than the one opening onto the ballroom. If someone wanted to eavesdrop, they would have to resort to mechanical means.

She turned up the music as an added precaution and then led Bea across the parquet floor to the salon. A spiderweb stretched across the doorway. Rose batted it away and opened the creaking door. She flipped on the light, a small brass fixture that hung from the ceiling and barely afforded any light. In the old days, most of the light would have been furnished by decorative wall sconces, but the bulbs had long since been removed. Dust wafted up as she urged Bea to sit on an old straight-backed chair with cabriole legs, which had lined the ballroom to seat wallflowers who had no dancing partners. Bea held the box securely on her knees and looked up.

"All right, Bea," Rose said, closing the door and pulling up another chair. "Suppose you tell me what the big secret is all about."

CHAPTER FIVE

"I thought you were safe, Rose," Bea began, shaking her head. "I thought there would be no reason to tell you everything. For fifteen years you lived here with us, and not once did anything occur to make me suspect that they had found out where you were."

"Who's they?"

"Your family."

"The Quennels?"

"No." Bea sighed and looked up at her, reaching for her hands. "The Bastyrs."

"Wait a minute!" Rose pulled her hands out of Bea's grasp. "I don't understand. Why wouldn't you want them to find me? They're my relatives!" She felt rage welling up again. "What did you and Donald do—kidnap me when I was a child and then tell me I was an orphan?"

"No, nothing like that, Rose. Please, don't judge us so harshly."

"How do you think it feels to know you've been tricked for fifteen years?" She jumped to her feet. "Lied to! Kept apart from your real family! And you wouldn't ever have told me, would you, if Mr. Wolfe hadn't shown up!"

"Rose, listen!" Bea pleaded. "I *am* your family. I'm your paternal grandmother."

"My what?"

"Your grandmother. Donald was your grandfather."

Rose stared at her, feeling as if her heart would break in two. All these years she had thought of herself as an abandoned waif, with no one in the world to call her own. And now she was expected to believe something entirely different—that she had a family? That she had a grandmother? The idea was so foreign to her that she couldn't even accept it.

"You're my grandmother?" she countered. "Why didn't you tell me?"

"I couldn't. Believe me, dearest Rose, I *couldn't!* Telling you might have meant your death!"

"Why? Were my parents criminals? Were they members of the underworld or something?"

"Your father was my son and a very good man." Bea blinked. "But your mother was from a strange family."

"Why would my own family want me killed?"

"They don't." Bea opened the box. "The Bastyrs want something far worse for you, Rose." She drew out a folded paper, sealed with a circle of red wax. "But I think this letter will tell you everything you need to know."

Shattered by shock and disbelief, Rose took the clutch of yellowed papers and turned it over. Her first name was written in flowery script on one side. For a moment she hesitated and glanced at Bea.

"Who wrote this?"

"Your mother."

"My—my—mother?"

Bea nodded solemnly and pointed to the red seal on the other side.

"Where is she? Is she still alive?"

"No." Bea shook her head. "She wrote the letter before her death fifteen years ago."

"And my father?" The words *father* and *mother* felt awkward on her tongue, almost as if she had no business saying them.

"He is no longer living, either, Rose."

"What happened to them?" she asked. "Did they die in an accident or something?"

"No. Read the letter first. Then we'll talk."

Rose sank into the chair. With a trembling hand she broke the seal and unfolded the paper within. She didn't know what to expect. Was it a litany of the wrongs she had done as a child that had caused her family to give her up? Had another, younger child caused her to drop from favor? Had she been implicated in the death of a family member—perhaps of her own mother? A million reasons for rejection—all the reasons she had come up with during her lonely childhood—flitted through her mind as she stared down at the distinctively small handwriting of her mother. She dreaded the truth. She didn't want to find out just what kind of problem she had caused or face the grim reality of her true nature. Heart pounding and teeth clenched, she refolded the paper and gave it back to a shocked Bea Jacoby.

"You arcn't going to read it?"

Rose shook her head, holding back tears, then scrambled to her feet.

"But, Rose, you must!"

"I can't." She opened the door. "I—I don't know what to think right now, Bea. I have to be alone!"

"But, Rose . . . !"

Rose could hear Bea close the box and push back the chair as she hurried after her. "You must come away from Brierwood this very night, Rose!"

"I can't! I've got to sort this through!"

"No, Rose, I beg you!"

Rose blocked out the sound of Bea's pleas and plunged across the floor, her footsteps echoing off the walls and ceiling of the huge chamber, creating the illusion that a flurry of maidens ran with her. Edgar swooped down to her, flying alongside as Rose ran out of the ballroom and out to the hall. She had to be alone. She had to get out of the house. Frantic and desperate, she ran down the stairs, careened through the hall to the rear of the mansion, flung open the back door and stopped in her tracks. The garden was draped in shadow. The only object she could make out clearly was the gnomon of the sundial gleaming in the moonlight. Her childhood fear of the dark loomed up in an even blacker shadow, forcing her back, making her return to the gloomy rooms of Brierwood.

With a sob, Rose shut the door and leaned on it, so upset that she felt as if she would jump out of her skin. Where could she go so no one could find her? If one more person told her she was someone other than Rose Quennel, made her question everything she had ever been told or accused her of doing things of which she was totally innocent, she would absolutely burst.

"Oh, Edgar!" she cried, overwrought.

He cocked his head and cawed, then took off from the hall table. Lacking a better direction, Rose followed him. He flapped upward, through a wing of the house that the Jacobys had closed years ago. Rose hurried through the quiet house, ignoring the dust and cobwebs and the sheet-covered furniture. Edgar glided to stop at the door of a room Rose had never been in before and cocked his head again, giving her a meaningful stare.

Rose opened the door and passed into a huge bedchamber, which she surmised had been a master bedroom at one time. The bed was hung with emerald-colored velvet and huge golden cords with tassels. The rest of the furniture was draped in sheets. Edgar hopped over the thick green carpet until he reached French doors that led to a balcony. Rose followed, gazing at a silver brush-and-comb set lying on the dressing table, monogrammed in a filigreed JC. This room had been inhabited by Julia Curtis, the long-dead mistress of Brierwood.

Quietly Rose opened the French doors to allow Edgar to go outside. He sailed to the banister of the balcony. Rose ventured out a few steps and looked at the ebony landscape below. The bedroom was located at the front of the house, with a view of the drive, the front entry gate and a dense wood that ran all the way to the shores of Lake Washington. The moon sprinkled glitter over the lake far away, and the stillness of the scene afforded a calm that was full of serenity, completely different from the dense hush of Brierwood.

Rose leaned against the banister and breathed deeply, feeling the serenity settle into her.

"Thank you, Edgar," she whispered.

She stayed on the balcony, and when she felt more calm, she found an old wicker chair and sank into it, while she thought through all that Bea had told her. But her restless sleep of the previous night, coupled with the heat of the summer evening, made her drowsy. Before she knew it, she was leaning on the palm of her hand. Soon afterward she drifted off to sleep, sinking onto the crook of her arm.

Much later, she felt a light touch on her shoulder.

"Roselyn, Roselyn," a voice crooned in her ear. "Beautiful Roselyn."

Go away. I'm tired.

Smooth, warm hands caressed her bare shoulders, spreading a strange heat through her chest, and warm breath fanned the side of her face. She tried to pull away but seemed paralyzed with lassitude.

"I have a question or two for you, my dear."

Don't touch me, Mr. Wolfe.

"Just a few questions and then you can rest."

I'm too tired. Go away.

"Roselyn, see the candle at the end of the corridor? I want you to go toward the light."

I don't want to go back there again.

"You don't want to learn the truth?" Warm hands slid around her torso and brushed the undersides of both breasts. Rose felt herself rise up slowly in the chair, her breasts tingling and aching. She shouldn't allow herself to feel pleasure at the hands of a stranger.

No, I—

"Once you learn the truth, we can be together. Then I will show you the glory of being touched by a man. Really touched, Roselyn."

Mr. Wol—

"Don't fight me, Roselyn. I'm here to help you. But you have to see these truths for what they are."

I don't want to go back, I don't want you to touch—

Now the hands were caressing her, kneading her in a way she had never known before. She could hardly breathe, could barely form a coherent thought. She should resist, push him away, flee.

No—

"You see the light, Roselyn. I know you do. Walk toward it, my beauty. Keep walking, keep walking. Only this time, don't go back as far as you did the last time."

No—

The light from the Bastyr house faded as five-year-old Rose closed the door behind her and crept down the back steps, hurrying over the dew-laden lawn with a heavy satchel in her right hand. She had no idea where she would go or what she would do, but she could no longer stay in the house, not when everyone yelled all the time and Uncle Enoch kept trying to get in her room at night. The thought of him breaking into her room again to stand there drooling and touching himself made her heart race with fear. Even now her heart banged in her chest. But she wasn't sure if it was the memory of her uncle that struck fear in her or the shifting shadows of the trees bordering the high rock wall that ran along the edge of the Bastyr property.

Beyond the gate in the wall she could see the narrow lane that led to the main road. The lane sure looked spooky at night. Rose shuddered. She hated being in the dark by herself, especially outside, but if she was going to run away, she had to be brave. Gathering her courage, she opened the heavy iron gate and slipped past it to the lane.

Once outside the Bastyr grounds, Rose set the suitcase down, rolled her shoulders and picked up the bag with her other hand. She couldn't believe how heavy the suitcase seemed to have gotten. Maybe she shouldn't have packed so many books. Sighing resolutely, she pressed on.

Where would she go? She hadn't traveled very far from home and wasn't sure where a real town was. In fact, the only times she ever went anywhere were to church and on Mother's special trips. She never paid much attention to which direction they took on their trips, because mother always had a fascinating activity for her to work at—puzzles, needlework or learning to read. She wished her mother was with her now, but for the last two months Deborah Quennel had spent her days in her room, and no one was allowed to see her until she felt better.

Mother had told her that Rose would soon be going to school and then she wouldn't be stuck at home all the time, but a year was too long for her to wait. Besides, she didn't want to go to school. She already knew how to read and could recite her multiplication tables all the way up to the twelves. Surely a five-year-old could get a job somewhere as long as she could read and figure. She wouldn't want to be a printer, though. Everyone blamed ink fumes at the printing shop for making Uncle Enoch go crazy. Mother always grew silent when the subject was brought up, as if she didn't believe the others, but Rose was pretty sure they were right.

Rose walked until the lane curved and the trees blocked the faint glow of the house lights. She paused, her heart still hammering. The night was black—as pitch-black as described in some of her books. She didn't know what pitch was, exactly, but it couldn't be much darker than the gloominess ahead.

Rose held a knuckle to her mouth and blinked. Her mother had told her there were no such things as monsters, but she had never believed it. Adults didn't know everything. And what if they were wrong? What if they just hadn't *seen* a monster before? One could jump out of the bushes on the other side of the road and gobble her up before she could scream. Even if she did scream, no one would have time to run out and save her.

Suddenly Rose found she couldn't move. She was too frightened to take another step. If she took her eyes off the far side of the road for just one second, she would give a monster enough time to leap out and get her.

She stood in the road, staring at the blackness until her eyeballs ached, until her hair felt wet with sweat and fear.

Then the screech of a cat fight ripped through the silence. Rose shrieked, jumped into the air and dashed for the house, pumping her short limbs as hard as she could. She ran and ran, afraid to look back, afraid she would see a hideous monster nipping at her heels. Panting raggedly, she careened toward the gate, thankful that she had left it ajar. Just as she gained the gate, however, she heard it slam shut and saw a tall dark shape materialize on the other side.

"Roselyn!" a stern voice called from the shadows.

She ground to a stop, recognizing the deep, dreaded tone.

"No-o-o!" Rose screamed on the balcony, flailing her arms. She had to wake up, had to stop the dream. "No-o-o!"

"Rose! Rose!" Taylor's voice rang out.

Hands reached for her. She fought them off and scrambled to her feet, jerking back to consciousness. Her eyes fluttered open, and she saw movement out of the corner of her eye as a black figure slid out of her range of vision. She whirled around to follow the vision but saw nothing other than the edge of the balcony and the fingers of ivy crawling up the side of the house. No one could have possibly disappeared so quickly without jumping over the balcony, and to jump from such a height would mean certain death.

She whirled back around, convinced that Taylor was the one who had been touching her. His hands had caressed her shoulders and stroked her breasts, and she had enjoyed the sensation. A deep sense of shame washed over her at her base reaction to him. What kind of woman would let a stranger do that to her? Outraged at Taylor and herself, she raised her hand and soundly slapped him on the face.

For an instant they stared at each other—Rose with her hand still raised and Taylor with his palm to his cheek—and for an instant she thought she had just made a terrible mistake in striking him. Then Rose tried to dash away, but he caught her elbow. He wrenched her back to face him, holding her arm so high that he nearly pulled her off her feet. In the darkness, his eyes blazed at her.

"What in the hell was that for?" he demanded.

"Let me go!"

"What's the matter with you!"

"You monster! Let me go!" she tried to yank her arm free, but he held her tightly. She raised her other arm to pummel him into releasing her, but he caught her forearm in midair and pinned both arms to his chest, trapping her between his body and the railing of the balcony.

She froze, highly aware of the great drop behind her, while he stepped closer until each hard plane of his lower body pressed into her soft curves. Up close, he seemed even more magnificently built than he had appeared that morning with the towel draped around his shoulders. And the intimate posture of his hips against hers sent a flush creeping up her neck.

"Bad dream, Brier Rose?" he growled, tightening her grip on her wrists.

"It was no dream!" she retorted, glancing up at him in fright. His face was much too near, his mouth far too close for comfort. She struggled, but he only stepped closer, impressing his male flesh against her. To her alarm, she noticed he was becoming aroused. Frantic, she arched backward in an attempt to distance herself from the powerful plane of his torso, but she only managed to present her breasts to him. He looked down at her, and she flushed anew with shame and helplessness. "Let me go!"

"Not until you tell me what's going on. Why did you hit me?"

"Because," she retorted, "you crept up on me when I was sleeping and touched me."

"I didn't touch you."

"You did so. In places you had no business touching."

"The hell I did." His grip eased, but he didn't let her go. "Why are you up here anyway?"

"Why are *you?*"

"I heard something and came up to investigate."

"A likely story, Mr. Wolfe."

"You were ranting and raving out here. You were having a nightmare."

"Nightmare, ha!"

"Probably from a bad batch of that herbal tea of yours."

Rose glared at him. Was he trying to be funny? She was in no mood for humor. Not in the least. But he obviously wasn't going to release her until she quieted. She tried but failed to break eye contact—disturbed by the way his eyes had changed from impersonal black to an intimate brown full of warmth and dancing lights. Even his posture had changed. He still pressed against her, but the pressure had gone from rigid strength to a languid weight that created an unfamiliar tightening between her legs. The sensation soon blossomed to an intense throb. She felt as if she would melt from the inside out if she allowed Taylor to go on touching her.

She knew she should pull away, but the sensation drugged her. She seemed to have no self-control when it came to this man. How could she react this way to him? She hardly knew him. He had insulted her, had dismissed her with a wave of his hand, had taken such liberties with her that she should be slapping his face again, not succumbing to the touch of his body. She had to get away from him, had to sort through

the flood of emotions he unleashed inside her. Rose forced
herself to relax, knowing the only way to free herself would
be to trick him into thinking she was calm. She closed her
eyes, willing her breathing to slow, even though she was
highly conscious of Taylor's own uneven breathing.

While she stood there with her eyes closed, she felt him
bend down to her lips. He touched them lightly as if to taste
her, his fingers snaking more tightly around her wrists. Rose
choked back a cry of protest as he crushed her forearms
against his chest and slanted his mouth over hers for a
deeper, more lingering kiss. The tip of his nose brushed hers
in a surprisingly suggestive way. For an instant Rose tilted
her head back, surrendering to his probing mouth. His lips
were warm and soft, much softer than they appeared. And
the taste of him was surprisingly wonderful. He had mentioned showing her how glorious it could be to be touched
by a man—really touched. Was this what he had meant?

As he kissed her, she forgot about her disturbing dreams
of the past, about Bea's shattering revelations, and about
her frantic attempt to escape her own thoughts. And for one
wonderful moment she felt nothing but the glorious blank-
ness of rapture as worry gave way to pure physical delight.

Then she remembered the way he had treated her and the
things he had said to her, and she pulled away from his
mouth.

"Don't you ever do that again!" she exclaimed breath-
lessly.

"You liked it."

"You're mistaken, Mr. Wolfe. Now let me go!"

"All right," he replied huskily, but he still didn't let go of
her wrists. "If you promise not to slap me again."

"Only if you promise not to touch me again."

"I don't know if I want to agree to that." Smiling crook-
edly, Taylor released her wrists, only to slide his hands
around her shoulders. She flinched at his touch, her flesh
even more tender now that the briers had had time to ag-
gravate the surrounding tissue.

"What's the matter?" he asked.

"I've got stickers in my back."

"Sorry." He immediately lifted his hands. "I forgot."

As if he cared. She grimaced, mostly to hide an acute attack of nerves, and was surprised when he stepped back, pulling the heat and pressure of his body away from hers. The sudden freedom confused Rose. She stumbled sideways along the rail to put some space between them should he consider capturing her again.

"I'll bet those briers caused your nightmare," he ventured.

"I don't think so."

"You move as if you're in pain."

"I am, Mr. Wolfe."

"Is there something I can do to help?"

"I don't want your help."

She saw him blink twice and step toward the wall as she passed by. If she could make it to her room and lock herself inside, she just might escape him for the night. Then in the morning she would decide what to do—stay at Brierwood or give in to Bea's odd fears and flee.

Before she had gone more than a few steps, however, she heard the clatter of Taylor's cane and looked over her shoulder to see the cane slip through the uprights of the banister and sail down to the ground below, where it bounced end over end and skidded across the grass near the entryway.

Rose whipped around to see what had happened to Taylor. He had stumbled through the French doors and was holding his hands to his ears as if trying to block out a loud noise. He staggered forward, bumping the dressing table and knocking off bottles and the brush and comb. She could sense his fear as he propped himself against the bedpost to keep from banging into something else and falling.

Against her better judgment, Rose ventured back to him but kept at arm's length, in case he was trying to trick her.

"Taylor?" she queried, peering at his face. His skin was pale, his mouth parted as he gasped for breath, and his eyes were tightly shut, causing sunbursts of creases to bloom at the outer corners. The scar on his cheek pulled awkwardly to the left, dragging up that side of his mouth into a pained sneer.

"Taylor?" she repeated. "What's happening?"

"The noise . . . it's so loud—"

"I don't hear any noise."

"I do. And it's about to break my eardrums." He reached out for her, feeling the empty air. "Rose, get me away from here."

She stared at his outstretched hand, wondering if he would grab her again and not release her. But if that were the case, why would he have let her go in the first place?

Rose stepped closer and slipped her hands around his upper arm. The feel of his firm flesh sent a bolt of desire through her. She had to keep herself from gliding her hand along his well-defined biceps, so hard beneath his shirt-sleeve. Whatever Taylor had done before his car accident, he had kept himself in excellent shape.

"Get me out of here," he gasped.

"Where?"

"Anywhere! Downstairs."

She pulled him toward the stairs, urging him in a loud voice to watch for the first step. Slowly she guided him to the landing and then all the way down to the foyer.

"Any better yet?" she asked, wishing he would open his eyes.

"A bit." He unclamped his left hand from his ear. "Take me outside, Rose."

"It might help if you opened your eyes."

"It won't do any good. I can't see a damn thing."

Rose glanced at the front door. What if the rottweilers tried to attack her again? She wasn't crazy about being out-side at night. In fact, she hadn't gone outside in the dark since she was five and had tried to run away—the same in-cident she had just relived in her dream. Blocking out the frightening memory, Rose reached for the doorknob. If she refused to go outside, she would have to tell Taylor her rea-sons for doing so, and she wasn't about to discuss her childhood with him, not under hypnosis and certainly not when she was awake and completely lucid.

She opened the door and guided him out to the walk, carefully checking to see that the front door was unlocked behind them. Then she turned to Taylor.

"Any better?" she asked.

He nodded and brushed his fingertips over his eyelids.

"It's cooler out here."

"Yes." He breathed heavily, as if he had been relieved of a great weight.

"Is the noise gone?"

"Fainter, anyway." He opened his eyes and looked around.

"What does it sound like?"

"Ever hear a pipe organ?" Taylor asked, running a hand through his hair.

"Yes, in church."

"Well, the noise sounds like someone playing all the keys full blast."

"Funny, but I didn't hear anything at all."

At least not this time. But she distinctly recalled the sound she had heard the night of Donald's death. A pipe organ played at full blast. Taylor had described perfectly the sound she had heard. Was there some connection? Why hadn't she heard it this time, though? Did it mean that she was in danger? Could Taylor have something to do with the sound and Donald's death? Yet he hadn't even been at Brierwood at the time and had acted genuinely surprised when informed of the death of her supposed grandfather. Rose didn't know what to think or what to say, or whether or not to trust Taylor, especially since Bea didn't trust him.

Instead of confiding in him, she walked across the grass and retrieved his cane. She returned to his side.

"Here's your cane, Mr. Wolfe," she said, holding it up to his hand.

"Thanks." His fingers curled around the wooden handle.

Rose looked at him in the darkness. His face was full of sharp shadows in the dim light, and his expensive watch twinkled as he moved. He was taller than her by about a head and looked to be in top condition, with the exception of his leg. Either his clothes were hand-tailored to fit him or his figure had the proportions ideally suited to the conservative cotton shirt and jeans he was wearing. Rose guessed that his wide shoulders and slender hips would look good in anything he chose to wear, be it twills or tuxedo, and that he would feel at home in both.

At his sigh she looked up at his face, hoping he was recovering and would want to go in soon. This talk of strange noises and being out in the night air turned her skin to gooseflesh and made her teeth chatter, even though the evening was balmy. She clenched her jaw and hugged her chest with her arms, keeping a close watch for any sign of the dogs in the shrubbery.

Taylor pinched the bridge of his thin nose, as if he had a headache, and Rose realized he wasn't ready to return to the house.

"Have you seen a doctor about your eyes?"

"Yeah. Lots of them."

"And?"

"If they knew what was wrong, do you think I'd be here at Brierwood falling over my own shoelaces?"

He turned and walked away from her. She trailed after him.

"How long have you had these spells?"

"For a month or so, ever since the accident."

Rose looked down. "The same accident when you hurt your leg?"

"Yeah. The accident that ruined my life."

"Ruined? What do you mean?"

He laughed bitterly and looked up, his body outlined by the moon. "I can't see, Rose. I've been physically disabled and disfigured. My life will never be the same."

"And what *was* your life like?"

"It was my own. But it won't be again if I don't lick this vision problem."

"Why?"

"Because I'm as good as blind. Can't you understand?" He hobbled away from her, down the walk into the deepening shadows.

She clasped her hands in front of her, reluctant to follow, but afraid of being left behind. "What is your life really like?"

"What do you mean?"

"I mean, is it happy? Sad? Do you have a wife, children, lots of friends? Do you do anything creative?"

"What does doing creative things have to do with life?"

"Life *is* a creation, Mr. Wolfe. I think that if we aren't creating something new here and there, then we aren't really living. We're simply marking time."

Taylor paused and looked back at her. "Where'd you hear that?"

"Nowhere. It's just how I feel."

He gave a derisive snort. "Why all the questions?"

"I was simply wondering."

"Well, I don't appreciate nosy people." He turned toward the house, walking as quickly as he could with his injured leg. Rose followed, wondering if his brusqueness was a front to disguise his feelings of hopelessness.

He yanked open the door, and she looked up at him.

"What's wrong?" she asked.

"Nothing. My eyes are fine now. And so is my life."

"I was simply trying to—"

"From now on, keep your questions to yourself, all right? I am not your concern. Is that clear?"

"Perfectly." She squared her tender shoulders and swept past him into the house.

She heard the door latch behind her and the thump of Taylor's gait as he moved toward the stairs.

"By the way, that kiss upstairs meant nothing, either. I was merely trying to snap you back to your senses."

She glared at his back. "I quite understand, Mr. Wolfe."

At her acerbic reply he turned on the stair. "I don't want you to get the wrong idea. Some women read more into kisses than they should."

"Really?" She raised her chin, not about to admit that the kiss upstairs had been her very first. "Actually, I had forgotten all about it. We hysterical melodramatic types must have bad memories, too."

For a moment he coolly regarded her. She felt a frisson of unease shimmer down her spine. Had she overstepped her bounds again? Was this man a threat to her, as Bea suspected? And why did he bring out the worst in her? Rose's heart thumped in her chest as he continued to survey her.

Suddenly the grandfather clock near the foot of the stairs struck midnight, shattering the tense moment between them. Taylor waited until the last chime faded away. Then, without a word, he turned and hobbled up the stairs, leaving a heavy silence in his wake.

Outside, a huge crack of lightning split the stillness, echoed by a rumble of thunder that rattled the windowpanes. The storm had arrived.

CHAPTER SIX

Later, Taylor lay in bed, his fingers laced together behind his head as his thoughts raced. What was it about him that Rose distrusted? He had never done anything to hurt her or frighten her. In fact, he had been far more reserved than he was with most women. And why had he been so cruel, telling her that the kiss meant nothing, when he damned well knew he had wanted to brand her as his own with that kiss?

He sighed, thinking of the way her soft mouth had opened beneath his, and a rush of heat passed over him. What would it be like to embrace her and really kiss her, to feel her graceful arms around his neck, her hands in his hair? His loins tightened with desire at the slightest thought of her. Yet such musings only served to torment him. As long as she didn't trust him, he would have to keep his distance.

What could he do to earn her trust? Words wouldn't be enough. Somehow he would have to prove that he was all he said he was. Yet how? Taylor sighed in frustration and flopped on his side, trying to drown out the voice that droned in his ear, telling him that he was a crippled wreck incapable of helping anyone.

He slept fitfully and much later had a strange dream, the same dream he had experienced during his car wreck, when he had sat pinned by a tangle of metal and the twisted steering column, his leg crushed and his senses swimming. In the dream, he had risen out of his cloud of pain and hovered above the foggy highway, surveying the line of smashed cars with an odd sense of detachment, as if he weren't even involved. He saw his body in the demolished Jeep, his face a bloody mess, and barely recognized himself or the car. In fact, he felt immensely relieved that he wasn't bound in that body any longer.

Then he heard his name and felt himself float upward. He looked up and saw a bright light above him. At first the light seemed to glow just above his head. Then he realized the glow extended as far as he could see into the heavens and was tremendously bright at the far end. He felt wonderful and unafraid, and more than happy to travel to a new dimension. Heaven knows, his life on earth hadn't been all that fulfilling. He headed for the glowing light and knew he was grinning like a fool.

"Taylor," called a woman's voice he didn't recognize.

He looked to the side, his grin slipping, wondering who was keeping him from his path toward the beckoning light. A figure stood in silhouette against the light, a figure of a tall, slender woman with long hair. She raised a hand to reach for him.

"Taylor," she called.

He slowed his progress and stared at her, but the light blurred his vision, and he was unable to see her features or the color of her hair. All he could make out was the graceful curve of her body and the sweep of a long gown.

"You must go back."

"Go back?" Taylor replied in surprise. "But why?"

"You have been chosen."

"Chosen for what?"

"A task. Just like the other times."

"What other times?" He glanced at the light beyond, impatient to continue, wondering who the woman thought she was, trying to detain him like this. "I don't remember being chosen."

"You were chosen, Taylor, but failed. Maybe this time you will complete your task and end the cycle."

"I would rather just go to the light."

"If you go to the light, you will be damning someone else."

"Who?"

The woman answered, but Taylor couldn't hear over the sudden whine of a siren as a highway patrol car sped to the scene of the pileup.

"Who?" Taylor demanded, while the vision of the woman flickered before his eyes. Was she going to fade to nothingness?

"Go back, Taylor. I beg you. You are my only hope."

As the image of the woman flickered, the light that poured around her touched off a scarlet-and-gold nimbus that blinded him. Taylor staggered backward, holding his forearms up to ward off the glare.

"I give you a special gift, Taylor Wolfe. Use it and save yourself this time."

The siren grew louder as the patrol car pulled to a stop on the highway. Taylor looked down but saw only blobs of color dancing before his eyes. He blinked rapidly, trying to focus, and his vision gradually returned. Below him he could see the flashing blue light and hear the distant whine of another siren. Then, as if he had lost his focus on the wonderful light above, he felt himself being pulled back to the Jeep, to the pain, to the rusty taste of blood in his mouth.

"No!" he wailed.

"Taylor!"

He moaned and tried to shake his head. He didn't want to go back. He didn't want to feel the agony in his leg and head. If he could just concentrate on the light above instead of the sounds of the highway patrol cars...

"Mr. Wolfe!"

"Mr. Wolfe, are you awake?" Rose knocked on Taylor's bedroom door, hoping he wouldn't be too long in answering. She had made his breakfast, as Bea had gone back to bed with one of her debilitating migraines. On the tray were a wedge of blueberry whole-wheat coffee cake, fluffy eggs, sliced melon, freshly squeezed grapefruit juice and steaming coffee. The food sat under silver domes, but the coffee was open to the air, sending a feather of fragrant steam into the chilly morning air. Luckily Taylor was up, and he opened his door shortly after she knocked. He was dressed in a pair of jeans and a wrinkled blue-and-white-striped shirt with the sleeves rolled to his elbows. The shirt was unbuttoned and revealed a narrow glimpse of his well-developed chest as he held open the door. Rose wondered if he had slept in his clothes.

"Well!" he exclaimed. "Where's Mrs. Jacoby this morning?"

"She isn't feeling well." At his cue, she swept into the room and deposited the tray on the table in front of the sofa. The movement pulled her dress over her shoulders, and she couldn't suppress a small cry of pain.

"What's the matter?" Taylor asked, coming up behind her.

"It's the briers. They're sore."

"Why don't you take them out?"

"I would," she turned and faced him, "but I'd have to be a contortionist to reach most of them."

He tilted his head slightly and studied her, and she could see the realization dawn on his face that he might be able to help her. She backed away. The last thing she wanted to do was to show the location of the offending briers to Taylor. Some were on skin she hadn't revealed to another human being since she was a child.

"Eat your breakfast, Mr. Wolfe. Your coffee's getting cold, and the coffee cake is best eaten piping hot."

"They can wait. Right now I think I should have a look at your back."

"No," she protested, backing up even farther. "I'll be all right."

"You don't want the briers to get infected, do you? Of all people, you should know that."

"I know, but I—"

Taylor ignored her protests and turned on his heel, limping into the bathroom without the use of his cane. He came back with a pair of tweezers.

"Lie down on the bed," he instructed, motioning toward the rumpled burgundy comforter.

She stared at it, her feet rooted to the floor. Lie on his bed? It seemed like such an alien place now that he had branded it with the shape of his body and the scent of his skin and hair. The thought of reclining in his nest mortified her.

"Rose, lie down, or I won't be able to help you."

She glanced at his face and then back toward the bed. What he said was true. She needed help, and he was the only person around who could relieve her suffering. Rose took a nervous step toward the bed and then paused.

"The briers are all over my back, Mr. Wolfe." She felt herself blush fiercely. "And . . . well . . . lower."

"You mean on your . . . derriere?" he asked, a slow grin lifting the left corner of his mouth.

"Yes." She stared at the far wall, trying to maintain some decorum during this most humiliating experience. "On my bottom."

"I'll tell you what, Rose. We'll unbutton your dress at the back there and do the top part, and then work on your, er . . . bottom. That way you won't be completely naked at any one time."

She was relieved at his thoughtfulness.

"That sounds like a good plan," she replied stiffly, putting a knee on his mattress.

"Go ahead and lie down," he urged, his voice less harsh than usual. "I don't bite, you know."

But he did fondle. She remembered the way he had touched her breasts in the study and made them ache and tingle. She remembered the way his kiss had melted her from the inside out. Rose lay on the bed and vowed she would keep this session as businesslike as possible. Being in his bedroom and lying on his bed was a dangerous situation for someone who had no experience with men.

As the side of her face sank into the down comforter, she was enveloped in his scent, a tangy fragrance with a hint of sweetness, as if he had been out in the wind and had captured it in his hair. Rose closed her eyes and scrunched the comforter with her fists, blotting out the image of Taylor's eyes and the way they had melted to a deep brown when he had held her in his arms the night before. She felt his fingers unbuttoning her dress. He didn't fumble once with the tiny buttons. Under ordinary circumstances, when in full command of his body, Taylor probably never fumbled or stumbled with anything. She was seeing him at his worst in his wounded, semiblinded state and wondered what he had been like before his accident.

Cool air swept over her burning back as he gently pulled away each side of her bodice. Rose breathed in and held herself stiff as he unfastened her bra and laid aside the straps.

Taylor winced when he saw her back. Her shoulders were scratched and dotted with tiny brown briers, as were her shoulder blades and the muscles along her spine. Even the backs of her arms were sprinkled with stickers. Removing the briers might take quite a while. Fortunately he was accustomed to working for hours on his models, which required immense concentration and a steady hand.

He looked down at her back, imagining how it must appear without the briers. Her skin was like flawless porcelain edged in rose—the kind of skin possessed by a mere handful of women, the kind of skin that cried out to be caressed and protected from harsh elements. He paused, his hand inches from her shoulder, as he realized that he was a harsh element, a broken-down man with years of experience and bitterness behind him. To touch such perfection would be like cutting chiffon cake with a rusty rasp. He had no business stroking such fair, lush skin.

Gingerly, he moved aside the long strands of her dark red hair, marveling at its silkiness. Most women he knew treated their hair with permanent waves, or sprays and gels that stiffened it and made it feel crispy. And then there were women who wore their hair nearly as short as his, a style that robbed a woman of her femininity, as far as he was concerned. The texture of Rose's hair was unlike any he had ever felt. It seemed virginal, if the word could be applied to hair.

Taylor closed his eyes. He could smell the soft scent of lavender wafting up from her. He swallowed back a strong physical urge to run his fingers through the ripples of her shining tresses and let the strands titillate the sensitive flesh between his fingers. He could almost imagine the way her hair would hang around him in a fragrant russet cloud should she ever lean over him in bed, her graceful white hands planted on his chest. Much to his annoyance, he felt himself swell with desire for her, only this time the desire was sharp and insistent, because she was in his bed already. All he would have to do was straddle her, trap her delicate wrists beneath his palms and take her from behind. That way he wouldn't even hurt her scratched skin. He could have her right now if he wanted to take her by force.

Taylor breathed in sharply and turned away from the bed, wondering what had come over him. He had never taken a woman against her will, had never forced himself on anyone. Yet he wanted Rose so acutely that he felt dangerously desperate, heightened by the fact that he hadn't had a woman for months and knew his desire must go unslaked. The odds that Rose might someday hunger for his touch were minimal, if not downright nonexistent.

He snatched the tweezers from the nightstand and sat down beside her, willing himself to inspect her back as a doctor might inspect a broken toe, making himself view her back as a separate entity and not part of a glorious whole. God help him in the second phase of this operation, when he had to look at her lushly rounded bottom. If he could control himself then, he would be a candidate for sainthood.

"Mr. Wolfe?" Rose asked, her words muffled by the comforter.

Her voice startled him, and he realized he must have been gawking at her longer than he should have.

"Okay, I'm ready," he replied, his voice gruff. "Are you?"

"Yes."

He raised the tweezers while he searched for a good place to start. He decided to work from top down, doing the backs of her arms first. Gently he pressed her flesh with his left thumb and forefinger, forcing the brier to pop to the surface. Then, one by one, he pulled out each tiny brown dagger.

Rose never made a sound, even though he was certain he caused her pain when he squeezed out the more deeply embedded stickers. After a while he felt her relax on the bed, which made her muscles slacken so that his job was a bit easier. She never said a word the entire time he worked on her back, for which he was grateful. He wasn't the type who could concentrate and talk at the same time. Pointless chatter annoyed him, as well.

After a quarter of an hour he sat back and brushed the hair off his forehead with the back of his wrist. "So far so good, Brier Rose," he said.

"Are you done?" she asked, twisting on the comforter.

He nearly caught a glimpse of her naked breast. Knowing he would be torturing himself if he saw any more of her torso, he averted his gaze.

"Yes—on the top, that is. Just as a precaution, though, I think I should apply some kind of antibiotic."

"My comfrey salve would do well in this case."

"What in the heck is that?"

"Comfrey is a plant that fights infection. I mix powdered comfrey with cocoa butter and beeswax to make the salve."

"I suppose it would be better than nothing. Do you have some?"

"Yes." She rose on one elbow, holding her loose garments to her breasts this time. "In the bathroom that's in my bedroom."

"Stay right there. I'll get it." He traded his tweezers for the cane, which was propped against the nightstand, and hobbled to the door. Then he turned. "Where is your room, anyway?"

She gave him a funny look, as if she didn't believe him, and then pointed to the left. "Down at the end of the hall, near the back stair."

"And what does this salve look like?"

"It's in a green glass jar marked Comfrey. It should be in the cabinet above the sink."

"I'll be right back. Just stay where you are."

He walked down the hallway, wondering why he was so eager to help her. If he were honest about it, he would have to admit that he liked the idea of Rose Quennel lying in his bed and wanted to keep her there as long as possible.

Taylor opened the last door on the left in the hall and peered in. This room had to belong to Rose. The feminine decor of white lace curtains and wine-colored floral-print fabric fit Rose's personality, as did the jumble of books on her dresser and writing table, and the bouquet of bird feathers she had arranged in a small crystal vase. A collection of impressionist prints graced her walls, most of them by Mary Cassatt, whose subjects were women and children. His gaze lingered on a painting of a woman bathing a child, and he felt a twisting jab in his chest.

Somewhere there was a woman who had borne a child in shame. He could have done something about it. But as a sixteen-year-old, he had allowed his father to override his sense of honor. Taylor had been forbidden to step forward with the truth, for the truth involved speaking out about the no-good son of a prominent businessman with whom Taylor's father was arranging a construction deal. The deal went through, establishing Wolfe Construction as the premier firm in San Francisco. The young woman's accusation of rape, on the other hand, was squelched, but not before her reputation and life were ruined. Taylor felt like hell for years afterward and never forgave his father for demanding such a costly silence from him. After graduating from high school, he left home and never saw or spoke to his father again. He never accepted a penny of the Wolfe fortune for college or anything else, even though his father constantly wrote checks and bought him cars, as if trying to make up for the past. The checks were returned uncashed, the vehicles never accepted. And only when his father had died four years ago had Taylor returned home to visit his mother.

He still burned with anger and shame, even now, after all these years. He turned sharply away from the painting.

Taylor walked past Rose's four-poster bed, which looked plump and fresh, the lacy shams frothy white. He could imagine that her bed would smell pleasantly of lavender and that the linen would be spotlessly clean—a virginal bed.

Taylor smiled sadly at his private joke and hobbled into the bathroom. As far as he was concerned, her bed should remain virginal and his celibate.

He found the comfrey salve and—thinking of Rose's modesty—a large white towel with which to drape her, and then returned to his bedroom.

When Taylor walked through the doorway, he saw Rose flop back down on her stomach to shield her body from sight.

"Found it," he remarked, walking forward. "Shall I put some on you?"

"Please. And gently."

"Have I been hurting you?" he asked, hoping he hadn't caused her too much discomfort.

"No. Actually, you have a light touch, Mr. Wolfe."

Her words pleased him. He sank down beside her and removed the lid from the jar, setting it on the nightstand.

With feather-light strokes he applied the salve to her back and arms, trying not to imagine what it would be like to caress her for reasons of pleasure, not pain. Even so, the touch of his hands must have had a soothing effect on her, for at one point she sighed. The sound shot right to his loins. He shifted.

"Do you want me to fasten your bra and dress?" he asked, his voice hoarse. "I brought a towel in case you don't want to get the salve on your clothes."

"The towel would be fine. Thanks."

He lightly draped the terry cloth over her back and then started to unbutton her dress all the way to the hem. With each button, his breathing grew more uneven and his arousal more intense. Ah, but this was exquisite torture. She wore no slip beneath the dress, only pure-white panties.

"Your panties," he began, clearing his throat. "I'll have to take them down just a bit."

She was as stiff as a board.

"Do what you have to, Mr. Wolfe," came her muffled reply.

He groaned silently. If she only knew what his body was screaming for him to do, she wouldn't grant him carte blanche. Taylor reached for her underwear and slid it off her slender hips. The round flesh of her small, white, incredibly virginal bottom popped into view. Taylor sucked in a breath and held it. How would he live through this torture without going crazy?

She stirred. "There are quite a few briers, aren't there?" she asked.

"Yes."

"I couldn't bear to sit down this morning."

Taylor clenched his teeth. He could hardly sit down now. His jeans were uncomfortably tight beneath his zipper. He reached for the tweezers, figuring the best thing he could do to keep his mind off visions of making love to Rose was to start plucking briers and try to make small talk, as much as he hated it.

"I noticed the clothes you had on yesterday," he ventured. "Have you been painting the house?"

"No." She propped her chin on her balled fists. "I've been working on a piece of fabric for a client."

"A client?" He pulled out a brier, trying to fill his mind with their idle conversation instead of the sight of the dimple in her right buttock. Her rump was so slender and delicate, he had an overwhelming urge to nip it with his teeth. He forced himself to look only at the very tip of the tweezers. "Do you run some kind of business here at Brierwood?"

"Yes. I'm a fabric designer."

"What exactly is a fabric designer?"

"Well, in my case, I paint designs on cloth. Some designers use computers to create patterns, which are produced by machines, much like a printing press. But my work is all done directly on the fabric, freehand."

Freehand? He could imagine his hands freely cupping the pale moons before him and crushing her against his aching body. What a feeling that would be! And how good it would feel to release himself in her tight depths.

Taylor moistened his lips. "Where... um... do you work?"

"I have a studio on the third floor. Would you like to see it sometime?"

"Yeah." He would like to see anything, anywhere, if he could just survive this brief moment in time. Carefully he pulled more briers, squeezing her skin as gently as possible. "Do you... do you have many clients?"

"Enough to keep me busy. Right now I'm trying to finish something by the end of the week. Then I'm going to take a small vacation."

"That sounds good. Where?"

"I don't know. Someday, when I have enough money, I'd like to go to Great Britain to research textiles in the museums there."

"Ah." Four more little hummers and he would be done. Taylor caught his lower lip between his teeth and bent to his task, knowing a greater test lay beyond—that of rubbing comfrey salve on the expanses he longed to caress with more than just the tips of his fingers.

He leaned forward, dropped the tweezers on the nightstand and picked up the salve.

"Almost done, Rose," he said in encouragement, more to himself than to her.

"It feels much better already, Mr. Wolfe."

"You should have asked me to help you yesterday." He dipped his fingers in the creamy yellow salve.

"I was too embarrassed."

"Has it been that bad?"

"No." She turned her head enough to look over her shoulder at him. Her blue eyes were smoky with an emotion he didn't recognize. All he knew was that he'd never seen anyone look so alluring and so innocent at the same time. "But I didn't expect you to be such a gentleman."

"Gentleman?" He forced a chuckle and spread the salve on her rump, stroking her with just one hand, which made it less of a temptation to run his palms all the way up the sides of her body and make her his prisoner.

The truth was, he hadn't expected her to be such a lady, either. Her behavior baffled him. If she had wanted to engage him in a compromising situation, this would have been the time to do it, and yet she had made no move to seduce him. He had to admit that he was somewhat disappointed.

"You wouldn't say I was a gentleman if you knew what I was thinking."

"And what are you thinking, Mr. Wolfe?"

For an instant he thought of revealing his attraction to her, of leaning down and kissing her, but an instant later he thought better of it. He pulled back his hand. "Things better left to the imagination." He rose and turned his back so

she couldn't see the physical evidence of his reaction to her.
"All done, Brier Rose."

"Thank you."

He hobbled over to his cold breakfast. Rose followed a
moment later, wrapping the towel around her. He dared not
turn around and look at her.

"Let me make you another breakfast, Mr. Wolfe. It's the
least I can do in return for your kindness."

"That's all right." He lifted one of the covers and sniffed.
He had choked down many a cold meal of crackers and beer
aboard the *Jamaican Lady*. Lukewarm eggs and coffee cake
seemed like heavenly fare to him. "There's nothing wrong
with the food."

He heard her walk toward the door and glanced at her
over his shoulder. Her grace and bearing made her look like
a queen even when she wore a plain terry-cloth towel. Why
had he ever accused her of being hysterical? Melodramatic? The more he got to know her, the more he realized
that "proud" and "noble" were far better descriptions of
Rose Quennel. He was just about to ask her to share his
breakfast when someone pounded on the door.

"Rose?" Bea called from the other side. "Are you in
there?"

Taylor saw the color drain from Rose's face.

CHAPTER SEVEN

"Oh, no!" Rose cried, clutching the towel at her breasts. "It's Bea!"

"So?"

"She'll see me like this!"

"Don't worry." He limped to the door and opened it. "What's up, Mrs. Jacoby?"

Rose looked around his shoulder and saw Bea standing in the hall, her gray hair wild around her face and her dress wrinkled, as she held up a huge green gem in one hand and a pistol in the other. Rose was surprised not only by her disorderly appearance but by the very fact that she was standing there at all. When Bea had a migraine she usually got so sick she couldn't function. To be on her feet and talking must have taken all the willpower she possessed.

Bea took one glance at Rose's disheveled hair and towel and then pointed the gun at Taylor's chest.

"All right, Mr. Wolfe!" Bea declared. "I've had enough!"

"You're going to shoot me, Mrs. Jacoby?" he drawled.

"Don't think I won't, young man!" Bea waved the gun and leaned forward, trying to clutch Rose's hand, even though she still held the emerald. "Come out of there this instant, Rose."

Rose hung back, abashed. "It's not how it appears."

"And how is it?" Bea retorted. "You tell me you'll take in his breakfast. Fine. My head is pounding so hard I can barely stand up. Then I notice the time and wonder why you've taken half an hour to hand Mr. Wolfe his tray!"

"Mrs. Jacoby, I can explain—" Taylor interjected.

"Oh, I'm sure you could, Mr. Wolfe. You probably have a million slick explanations. But I don't want to hear a single one. Come along, Rose!" She grabbed Rose's wrist.

"Bea, please!" Rose yanked free, mortified.

"I've done nothing but pull out her briers."

"Pull out her *what?*"

"Her briers." Taylor motioned toward Rose's shoulder. "A pack of wild dogs forced her into some brambles yesterday. She couldn't reach the stickers in her back, so I talked her into letting me help her remove a few."

"Wild dogs? Here at Brierwood? A likely story."

"It's true, Bea! There were four of them. Rottweilers!"

Bea stared at Rose's shoulder and then returned her glare to Taylor. "Be that as it may, I don't want you touching my Rose. Do you hear? I don't want you near her!"

"Bea!" Rose exclaimed, shocked by the vehemence in Bea's voice. "He was only trying to help me."

"Help you, my foot!" She clutched Rose by the arm. "You're going to get some clothes on, girl, right now!"

Rose let Bea pull her down the hall toward the room only because she was too embarrassed to remain in Mr. Wolfe's presence.

At her bedroom door, she broke free of Bea's grip and stormed to the closet, her embarrassment flooding to anger. Bea followed her.

"Thanks so much, Bea, for treating me like a child!" Rose exclaimed, throwing the towel in the laundry hamper. "I've never been so humiliated!"

"I was only trying to protect you."

"With a gun and that emerald?"

"I had the gun in case he was who he said he was—a Wolfe. I had the emerald in case he was who he pretended not to be—a Bastyr."

"Oh, Bea, not that again!" Rose grabbed the sides of her unfastened bra. "I'm a grown woman, Bea. And I'm perfectly able to protect myself and make my own decisions."

"You think undressing in the bedroom of a strange man is a wise decision?"

"Yes! Mr. Wolfe is a gentleman."

"You have no idea what Mr. Wolfe is." Bea stepped closer "Listen to me, Rose. We must leave this place, at least until your birthday on Saturday."

"Why? What is it about my twenty-first birthday that makes you so nervous?"

"On your twenty-first birthday," Bea replied, lowering her voice, "should the Bastyr family find you—and I believe they have—they will do anything in their power to make you a ritual bride."

"A what?" Rose cried, pausing with a dress in her hands.

"A ritual bride. Please, Rose, you must let me explain about the box, about the letter."

For a moment all Rose could do was stare at Bea, wondering if the old woman had lost her mind. Who had ever heard of such a thing as a ritual bride? A fantastic image of white robes and goat entrails popped into her mind. Yet Bea seemed dead serious. In fact, she seemed truly frightened. Rose lowered her arms, allowing the hem of the dress to puddle on the floor at her feet. She decided she would have to hear what Bea had to say about Mr. Wolfe, her mother and the Bastyr family before she did anything else, just to assuage Bea's fears. The poor woman had probably suffered the migraine because of it.

"All right, Bea," she sighed. "I'll read the letter."

Relieved, Bea put her hands to her mouth and nodded.

Rose pulled on the dress. "Meet me up in the ballroom in about five minutes, okay?"

Bea nodded again and hurried out of the bedroom.

In the salon off the ballroom, Bea leaned forward. "First read the letter. Then we'll talk about our options."

Hoping she wasn't doing the wrong thing, Rose took the papers and broke the seal. She had a terrible feeling in the pit of her stomach, as if she were launching into territory best left unexplored. But Bea's distraught behavior forced her to continue.

Rose took a deep breath and plunged ahead, carefully deciphering the small handwriting of her mother.

My dearest Roselyn,
When you read this letter, you will be nearing your twenty-first birthday. How I wish I could have seen you grow into a woman. I'm sure you must be an accom-

plished lady by now, and a lovely young woman, as well, knowing what a precocious little beauty you were at the age of five. It may come as a shock to you to learn about your father and mother, since I have sworn to secrecy any and all people who had a hand in abducting you from the Bastyrs. They were instructed to raise you as an orphan, so that you would have no ties to the past, and so the Bastyrs would have difficulty in discovering your whereabouts.

Do you remember your mother, my dear Roselyn? I hope you remember me with fondness and love, for I had only loving motives in mind when I sent you away from me. It was a terrible decision to make, but I made it hoping to break the chain that has imprisoned Bastyr women for centuries. I did not want that prison for you, Roselyn. I would rather have killed you myself than subject you to the life of a Bastyr bride.

By getting you away from the Bastyr family, I had hoped to keep you from the life that I endured and from the knowledge that tainted my heart. They are a dangerous group of people whom you must avoid at all costs. Their practices and appetites have brought my disease upon me and driven to madness many other members of the family. I could not let you be doomed to such a future, and that is why I gambled everything to get you away from them when you were a child.

On your twenty-first birthday you are destined to become a ritual bride, just as I became one when I was twenty-one. The Bastyrs rarely produce female offspring. But when they do, these females are bound to the patriarch of the family—Seth Bastyr. Therefore, my father became my husband when I was twenty-one. This does not seem heinous to the Bastyrs. It has been a family practice for countless centuries, and it is designed to keep the bloodline pure. As a result, the Bastyr family is riddled with geniuses and idiots, supermen and monsters. The monsters and idiots are not suffered. They are put to death. Such was the fate of the two children who came before you.

Once a Bastyr woman becomes a bride, she is supposed to forget her former self. She is charmed into forgetting what has happened to her, to overlook the heinous practice of intermingling with one's own kin. At first I did forget, but as time passed and I lost one child and then another, I remembered bits and pieces of my life before I became a bride. I realized that my marriage was unconscionable, but by then it was too late. I was in the first stages of my illness. I wasn't strong enough to get away. All I could manage was to smuggle you out when you were five, before the same thing could happen to you, before the Bastyr curse could damn you as it has damned me.

The Bastyrs have strange powers of which you must be wary, Roselyn. I am not certain they will be able to find you, but in the event that they do, I have prepared certain devices to protect you. One is an emerald, imbued with special powers, a discovery I found hidden in the Bastyr library. The other is a list of instructions that you must follow on Midsummer's Eve when you will turn twenty-one—the day you are destined to become a Bastyr bride. Bea Jacoby alone knows the location of these items, and she has promised to look after them until you need them.

Roselyn, you do not belong to the Bastyrs. Your father was not Seth Bastyr. Your father was a man I met after I became a bride. I loved your father very much, but he lost his life in an effort to save you. Bea Jacoby is your father's mother—your grandmother. Donald is your grandfather. They have changed their names to protect you all these years. And I trust that since you are reading this, they are both still alive.

When you were a newborn, you were branded with a mark to prove your identity to the Bastyrs. They didn't know at the time that you were not a true daughter. Perhaps they still do not know. I looked everywhere for the brand, hoping to obliterate it and save you. But I was unable to find it. I am afraid that the mark is there nevertheless, and that they will come for you and know who you are.

I did not want to ruin your childhood with fear, Roselyn. That is why I left instructions to keep all this knowledge from you unless the Bastyrs found you. I wanted you to remain forever separated from that heinous family. But since you are reading this, you must be in danger from them. Have heart, however, Roselyn. We Bastyr women are not as weak as they think we are. With the emerald and my instructions, I trust that you will be free of the fate I had to endure. Like the Bastyr males, I had my own powers during my life on earth, and I hope that my legacy to you, my dear child, was to pass some of that power on to you.

Keep in mind that it is imperative for you to remain a virgin until you are twenty-one. I am sure that Bea has told you this already. Do not take a lover before that time. In fact, do not fall in love with a man until you are past your birthday. Seth will use your love. He will feed on it and kill your lover. Should you lose your virginity before you are twenty-one, he will assuredly kill you.

I know this will seem odd to you, perhaps even frightening. But I have done everything in my power to safeguard you and break the chain. I pray that you will escape with your life and your soul.

Just remember that I love you, Roselyn, with all my heart. You have meant the world to me. And should it be in my power after death, I will be looking down on you from above and sending my love and protection to you in every way that I can.

Be strong, my dear child. Be brave. And know that we will see each other again, I am sure.

Your loving mother,
Deborah

Rose refolded the letter and looked down at her hands, which didn't seem to be part of her own body. She felt disassociated from reality, split down the middle by the truths she had just learned—that her mother had loved her beyond her wildest dreams, that her father had given his life for her, and that she came from a family with a history of incest and madness. Her vision blurred, and her throat felt as if a huge lump were lodged there. She heard Bea say something to her, but she couldn't focus on the words. She clung to the thought that her mother had loved her after all. She had sent her away to save her life. Her name was Deborah—just like in the dream—and she had loved her. She had loved her so much that she had given her up, never to see her child again. Rose felt Bea's arms come around her. And for the longest time she wept, encircled in the warm embrace of her grandmother, while she held the yellowed papers, the only link to the mother she had never really known.

"How did she die?" Rose finally murmured.

"She was a troubled woman, Rose. A troubled woman."

"How did she die?" Rose looked up, her eyes hot. "Tell me!"

"She killed herself. When she heard about your father's accident, she lost the will to live."

Rose swallowed. She could feel the blood surging in her temples and in her neck. "My father was in an accident?"

"Ostensibly. One night near the Bastyr place, it seems he fell and broke his leg. He bled to death out there."

"But you don't think it was an accident."

"No." Bea shook her head. Her gray eyes were like chips of flint. "Seth Bastyr killed him. I know he did."

"Oh, Bea!" Rose felt new tears pooling in her eyes.

Bea gently patted her back. "That's why we've worn emerald rings all these years, given to us by your mother to protect us from the Bastyrs. That's why I've always insisted that you wear yours."

"I'm sorry, Bea," Rose declared, wiping her eyes. "I'm sorry I doubted you. I—"

"There's no need to apologize, Rose dear. No need." Bea gave her a smile of encouragement and understanding, seeming much closer to her old self again, and then she stood up. "But you do realize that we must leave as soon as possible. We can't let the Bastyrs get you."

"And you think Taylor is connected to the Bastyrs."

"He told you about them, didn't he?"

"Well, yes." Rose pressed her lips together in doubt and wiped the tears from her cheeks.

"How could he know about the Bastyrs and you unless he is somehow connected to them himself?"

"He just doesn't seem . . ." Her voice trailed off. Deep in her heart she didn't feel a threat from Taylor, even though he had been arrogant and rude to her. She had suspected him of being the one to hypnotize her at night, but even that suspicion was faltering in the face of his kindness earlier that morning. He hadn't once tried to touch her, even though she had lain half-naked on his bed. The man who came to her at night surely would have taken advantage of her in a similar situation.

If by some chance Taylor was not connected to the Bastyrs, and if she could have just one or two more days, she could finish her scarf and all would be well. But if she didn't finish, she would miss her deadline and lose a most influential client, not to mention a tidy sum of money.

Her professional reputation was on the line. She didn't know whether to stay or leave.

"My mother mentioned a list of instructions and an emerald," Rose ventured.

"The same emerald I had a few moments ago." Bea turned to retrieve the box from the floor. She raised the lid. "Your mother gave this box to me to keep for you. I've kept it under my bed for fifteen years."

Rose peered into the velvet-lined box and saw a piece of parchment about the size of a paperback novel and a small ruby-colored pouch. Carefully Rose picked up the pouch and placed it in her palm. The drawstrings draped over her hand as she loosened the top of the sack. She could almost feel a glow from inside the pouch, as if something of enormous energy lay within.

Her fingers felt a hard, cool object about the size of an apricot. Rose drew it out.

"The emerald," she gasped, holding it up to the light. It glinted a rich green in the lamplight and was full of shifting depths that captivated her.

"Yes," Bea said softly, her voice full of awe. "Just look at it."

"My mother says it has some sort of power." Rose looked up at Bea. "That sounds like hocus-pocus to me."

"When it comes to the Bastyrs, Rose, you have to suspend your belief system. They don't follow the norm, from what your father told me. They have strange powers, strange ways. It's Seth Bastyr, the leader of the family, who has the most powers. But your mother seemed to have had many herself. She must have inherited them from the Bastyr genes. She could speak to animals with her mind. I saw it happen."

"Speak to animals?"

"Yes. She could call animals to her. They would bring things to her, do things for her, as she was always doing for them. She was a very gentle woman, your mother." She held the box closer, so that Rose could put back the emerald. "Haven't you noticed you have the same gift, Rose? With Edgar?"

Rose paused a moment. "Edgar and I are friends. But I've never consciously tried to communicate with him. I've never asked him to do anything in particular. He warns me, sometimes, that people are coming. Things like that."

"He is usually with you, though. He sits on your wrist, goes with you everywhere, and yet you've never trained him."

"I never thought twice about it. I thought he was smart."

"No, Rose. You taught him, simply by thinking about what you wanted of him. How do you suppose he came to Brierwood?"

"I don't know. Hasn't he always been here, Bea?"

"No. He came when you were six. He was hurt. You found him on the lawn, don't you remember? You said you had heard him crying and crying all night."

Rose smiled faintly as the memory resurfaced. "Yes, I remember now."

"But I hadn't heard a thing. And neither had Donald, and he had been trimming shrubbery in the area. Only you heard Edgar's cries."

"I'd forgotten about that."

"So you see, Rose, you do have certain gifts. Even though you aren't a full-blooded Bastyr, you still have powers of your own."

Rose nodded and drew out the piece of parchment. She looked up at Bea. "But what else is in my bloodline, Bea? My mother mentioned the Bastyr practice of incest. Doesn't that cause birth defects? Abnormalities?"

"Sometimes." Bea gave her shoulder a reassuring squeeze. "But you seem to have escaped such problems, Rose. You aren't a full Bastyr, after all."

"And my real father—what was he like?"

Bea's eyes softened. "You'll learn all about Will when we get away from here, Rose. I have so much to tell you!"

Rose smiled. A whole new life lay before and behind her, a life full of people with whom she was connected. She felt a glow inside and out, and wondered if holding the emerald had contributed to the warm feelings that were blossoming inside her.

"Look over the instructions, Rose," Bea urged.

Rose picked up the parchment and scanned the writing. The instructions included sitting at the foot of a fir tree and concentrating on the inner self.

"On your birthday, you must follow the instructions to the letter. Your mother made that very clear."

"I've never seen anything like this," Rose said, shaking her head. "It seems pretty weird."

"I'd take it seriously, if I were you, Rose. Seth Bastyr killed your father. He would kill again to get to you."

"This Seth—" Rose replaced the parchment in the box "—what does he look like?"

"Unfortunately, I don't know. I never saw him. I've been told he spent the daylight hours sleeping and the night hours keeping pretty much to himself."

Rose felt a chill race down her back. She remembered her dream of the previous night, when she had faced Seth on the other side of the iron gate. She hadn't seen his face, either. But she remembered him as being tall, lean and dark-haired. Was Taylor really Seth in disguise? Then she remembered the narrow shoulders and dry voice of Seth Bastyr. Taylor had a well-developed physique and a voice full of rich baritones. Could they be the same man? Or were they two completely different people? And if Seth went abroad only during the night, he would have had to change habits in order to appear as Taylor, who was quite visible during the day. To make matters more complicated, Seth Bastyr could have sent a courier in his place.

Rose frowned, uncertain of her own logic. Her intuition—her heart, if she truly admitted it to herself—told her that Taylor was not a Bastyr. But could she listen to her heart? She had no experience in such matters.

Yet could she trust the fantastic story of the Bastyrs? The man who came to her at night told her that everyone had fed her lies. Could Bea still be lying to her? The letter could be false. The emerald could be glass, for all she knew. Who was telling the truth? Whom could she trust?

"What's the matter, dear?" Bea questioned. "You're as white as a sheet."

"I—I— This is all too strange!" She stood up and brushed a stray strand of hair off her forehead. The glow she had felt only moments before had suddenly shriveled to a cold flicker of distrust and doubt.

"I know it must be hard to take all this in at once, but you must."

Rose turned at the doorway. "I must finish the scarf. That's what I must do."

"But, Rose, you can't!"

"My birthday is Saturday. That gives me two more days. If I work all day today I can probably finish. Then we can leave."

"No, Rose!"

"You said yourself that nothing will happen to me until my twenty-first birthday." She put her hand on the doorknob. "Besides, we have my mother's emerald and her instructions. If what you've told me is true, we are safe."

"Not necessarily. They've never been put to the test—"

"One more day, Bea. That's all I'm asking." She opened the door and looked back at her grandmother. Bea's face was full of doubt and worry, which deepened the lines around her mouth.

"One more day, Bea."

Bea sighed heavily and clutched the box tightly to her chest. "All right. But I don't like it."

CHAPTER EIGHT

By the time dinner was over, Taylor was in the mood for companionship. His books had arrived that morning. He had spent the entire day reading about the human eye and had discovered some odd information in one volume. He was eager to share his news with anyone but Bea Jacoby, who made an art form of avoiding him and cutting off all conversation with a hard stare. He really wanted to tell Rose what he had found out about his eyes, but she had been busy all day, and he hadn't had a chance to talk to her. Maybe she was avoiding him because of the morning fiasco, when Bea Jacoby had found her in his room. She might be too embarrassed to face him. Yet he couldn't imagine Rose hiding from anyone, not with her spirited streak. He smiled slowly as he finished his coffee. He liked that streak in her. In fact, there wasn't much about Rose Quennel that he didn't like.

Taylor rose and pushed back his chair. He was going to find Rose and talk to her, no matter what objections Bea Jacoby raised.

He hobbled up the stairs and knocked lightly on Rose's bedroom door but got no response. Next he checked in the study, wondering if she might be in there. But the room was empty. He glanced out a window that overlooked the back gardens but saw no evidence of her there, either. Just as he had decided to give up and go downstairs for another cup of coffee, he saw Edgar soar up to the third story and through an open doorway.

"Ah," Taylor mused to himself. "The workroom."

He limped up the stairs and passed over the threshold of the workroom. The place was huge. It must have been the ballroom in the old days when his aunt had entertained. A fairy-tale quality still pervaded the room due to the festoons of hand-painted cloth that Rose had hung from the ceiling and over the tops of the tall windows. Part of the room was taken up by four tables, each at least twenty feet long. Wooden racks took up another corner. Shelving filled with plastic gallon containers and a jumble of glassware sat in the shadows of early evening. Rolls of fabric, more tables, stacks of laundry baskets, a hot plate and a rack of plastic utensils lined the far end of the room. An old rolltop desk littered with papers and books guarded the doorway nearby.

Taylor walked farther into the room and looked around the desk. He found Rose standing at the end of another long table, her fingers curled loosely around the shaft of a paintbrush. She wore a spattered bandanna to keep the hair out of her face, but the rest of her russet tresses tumbled down her shoulders and back in a river of fire.

For a moment his eyes went out of focus and he heard a faint whirring sound at the same time that a rainbow-colored shimmer appeared around Rose's head. Startled, Taylor blinked, hoping his vision wasn't going to give out on him again, and in an instant the shimmer disappeared.

"Mr. Wolfe?" she asked.

"Hi," he replied, relieved that the vision incident had been so brief. He limped to the end of the table.

She looked at him expectantly and twirled the paintbrush between her thumb and forefinger. An awkward silence stretched between them. To break the tense moment, Taylor directed his attention to the fabric stretched over the table by a series of staples. "This must be the scarf you mentioned."

"Yes."

He moved down the side of the table in order to see the design from a better position. The jumble of colors and lines suddenly took the shape of an unusual mosaic in indigo and peach, a depiction of a man and woman embracing, their robes falling together as one, much in the manner of a Gustav Klimt painting. Tiny swirls of silver that reminded him of galaxies scattered over the night sky decorated the robe of the man. Squares of salmon, peach and the barest hint of lavender made up the robe of the woman. The indigos and silvers shimmered in a fantasy motif that seemed utterly magical. Taylor lost himself looking at it, captivated by the detail of the design and the graceful nuances of color, amazed that a woman as young as Rose could create such a masterful work.

He knew how many years it had taken him to learn the patience required to build a model ship. To control dye in such intricate lines on a piece of fabric must require a steady hand and a concentration that would put his accomplishments to shame.

Gradually Taylor became aware of Rose's gaze. He looked up to find her watching him. She blushed again, which turned her blue eyes to luminous pools of cerulean.

"Do you like it?" she ventured.

"It's incredible."

She rubbed the small of her back as she came forward. "It's to be a gift for someone. That's why I have to get it done by the end of the week."

"Ah."

She strolled up to stand beside him, apparently forgetting her distrust of him. "I only hope my client will share your enthusiasm. He's getting anxious to see it."

"He'll love it."

"Do you really think so?" She looked up and raised her fine eyebrows.

"I have no doubt. Where did you learn to draw like that?"

She shrugged. "I grew up here at Brierwood and spent a lot of time alone. I filled my hours with drawing."

"Time well spent." He reached out to trace a silver swirl with his finger. "Where did you get the silver paint? I've never seen anything like it before."

"My client sent it to me, insisting that I use it. When I asked him what it was, he couldn't tell me."

"It shimmers." Taylor wiped his fingers on his jeans, trying to rub off the silver residue on his skin. His fingertips tingled from the contact with the paint. "You sure it isn't toxic?" he asked.

"It could be." She picked up a jar from her desk and inspected it. Taylor glanced at the jar, which looked old and asymmetrical, as if it had been made by hand.

"It's the strangest stuff," Rose continued. "Rather gooey and insoluble. I had to experiment for a while, trying to come up with the proper amount of washing soda and water in order to get it to spread. I finally managed to get it to work, but it took up a lot of my time." She put the jar back down on the table.

"It reminds me of the trails left by slugs and snails."

She stared at him, then glanced down at the scarf and back again, incredulous.

"I realize the comparison isn't very flattering—"

"No, you're right," she replied, her eyes shadowed with disbelief. "You are absolutely right, Mr. Wolfe. I should have recognized the similarity long ago." She walked around the table, lightly touching the silver patches. "Strange, isn't it?"

"It's still quite beautiful." He limped behind her, hoping he hadn't offended her. "Are you nearly finished?"

"Yes, except for setting the dye and hemming the cloth. I'll meet my Friday deadline, though. That's when my client is coming for the piece."

Taylor looked down at the scarf. He knew women who would kill to possess such a work of art. Rose Quennel should be living in New York, not in Brierwood. She could be making hundreds of thousands of dollars with her scarves, given the proper exposure. All she needed was some encouragement and protection, both of which he could give her. His mother had hundreds of contacts in New York, not only in fashion, but in real estate. And Taylor had met quite a few artists over the years. He could find her an apartment, a studio, and introduce her to the right people.

Suddenly Taylor caught himself in midthought. What did he think he was doing? He had never considered taking a woman under his wing before, especially when the process would include cooperating with his mother. That he could even consider the concept made him weak in the knees.

Flustered, Taylor leaned his hip on the edge of the table. "How's your back?" he ventured.

"Fine." She averted her gaze. "Thanks to you."

"That Mrs. Jacoby has you on a tight leash, doesn't she?"

"She tries to protect me."

Taylor crossed his arms over his chest. "Do you think you need protection from me?"

Rose glanced at him, from his hair to his belt buckle. Amused, he noticed that her gaze didn't stray any lower. Then she looked back at his face.

"Should I?" she asked, reaching for a screwdriver.

"You tell me."

She blinked twice, regarding him from the corner of her eyes as she began to remove staples from the long edge of the table. "I'm not sure."

"Does Mrs. Jacoby hound you like this with every man, or is it just me?"

Rose paused at the question and then resumed her task. "Actually, there hasn't been anyone else."

"No boyfriend?" He straightened and ambled up behind her. "No senior prom date? No college beau?"

"No."

"I find that hard to believe."

She rose up and turned to face him. "I've led a rather secluded life, Mr. Wolfe."

Taylor could tell that she was surprised to find him standing so near to her. Her eyes grew wider as he stepped even closer, trapping her between the edge of the table and his body. He reached out and titled her chin up with his forefinger. "When are you going to drop the Mr. Wolfe business?" he asked lowly, staring at her full red lips. "I told you, I'm not one to stand on formalities."

"It's just that I don't know you very well."

He felt something brush his shirt and looked down, releasing her chin. She was holding the screwdriver between them. For her, the screwdriver probably represented a weapon. For him, it was a blatant sexual image that spoke of a bridge between them connecting their bodies, and of a vision of her holding him in her graceful white hand. Taylor's body responded immediately with a sharp twist of desire. He shifted uncomfortably, chiding himself for his lack of control in the presence of this woman. He longed to press her against the table and kiss her into surrender. But by all appearances she intended to run him through if he so much as laid a finger on her.

"I take it you don't trust me," he said at last. "Do you?"

"No, Mr. Wolfe, I don't."

"Why?"

"Bea thinks you are connected to my past."

"Why would she think that?"

"Because you knew about my family, the Bastyrs."

"Who?"

"The Bastyrs. Don't you remember? When you first arrived, you stood in the study and told me I was the spitting image of the Bastyr women."

"I didn't talk to you in the study that night."

"Yes, you did." She frowned, and her nose wrinkled pertly. "You arrived early. I heard you shut the door, and I came down to the study. That's when you told me I could stay at Brierwood. And that's why I thought it was so peculiar when you acted as if you didn't know who I was later that night."

"Wait a minute." Taylor backed up, knowing his chance to kiss her had vanished. "I didn't get here early."

"You got here at about nine o'clock, as I recall."

"No, I didn't." Taylor paced to the desk. "It was more like half past ten."

He turned and frowned at her. She returned the puzzled frown with one of her own.

"You're lying," she declared.

"I'm not, Rose." He never lied—only that once so long ago when he had let his father make his decisions for him. Ever since then he had told the truth with a vengeance, as if to compensate for the pain he had caused.

For a long moment she studied his face, her eyes dark with questions and distrust. He withstood her scrutiny, hoping she would see that he really was telling the truth.

"Then who did I talk to?"

"I don't know."

She brushed a stray hair off her forehead and glanced around the workroom, distracted, as if she thought she might find the answer to the mystery written in the wallpaper or scratched on the glass of the high windows.

"Could there be someone else here at Brierwood?" she asked, her voice quavering. "Someone who is hiding from everyone but me?"

That night Rose lay awake, worried that a stranger walked the halls of Brierwood. She had confided her fears to Bea and promised to leave first thing in the morning. But she would not, under any circumstances, venture out in the night, especially when the dogs might still be around. She also hadn't mentioned the nocturnal visitor to anyone, too ashamed to admit that she had let the man touch her.

Soon Rose fell into an exhausted sleep, only to be awakened by a dry silken voice calling her name and a hand caressing her hair. Try as she might, however, she could not open her eyes.

"Roselyn, my beauty. It is time again."

Time? Time for what?

"To look back and tell me what you see."

No. Leave me alone.

"You must. And this time, dear Roselyn, you mustn't scream. You must face the visions and face the truth, so that you will quit living a lie."

I'm not living a lie.

"Roselyn, you know so little of the truth that you wouldn't recognize it without my help. Your mother told you nothing but lies."

That's not true. My mother never lied to me!

"Has she told you of your family? Of the father who has tried to find you all these years?"

She said I didn't belong to them.

"A lie, Roselyn. Deborah told you that so you wouldn't try to find your kin. She didn't want to take the chance that you might discover what kind of woman she really was. Or what kind of man your father was. It wasn't right of her to rob you of your heritage."

Rose felt him lift her hand and kiss the palm with lips that were moist and hot. She murmured in protest, but the effect of the kiss trickled all the way up her arm like hot summer rain on a windowpane.

"Roselyn, let me help you see what you have missed—the closeness, the love, the devotion of your father."

She *had* missed that. What would it be like to have a mother? A father?

"Let me help you fill the void that has always darkened your heart, Roselyn."

It was true. She had always felt empty inside, never having known her family and her father.

"But you did know him at one time."

No, never.

"Yes, you did. Before you were kidnapped by your mother." He held her hand palm upward and slowly circled her flesh with his fingertip, until she could barely keep her mind on her own thoughts. The movement created a sensual whirlpool that drew her farther and farther from her room at Brierwood to a place of darkness and fear.

Please, no—

"You must remember, Roselyn. You must relive it and see your father. Allow him to speak with you. Allow the truth to come out and make you whole again. Then we can go on."

Round and round went his fingertip on her palm. Deeper and deeper she spun, until complete darkness enclosed her and the musky smell of nightshade and damp earth overwhelmed her senses.

Rose found herself standing at the wrought-iron gate outside the Bastyr house.

"Roselyn!"

"Let me in!" Rose glanced over her shoulder in fear that some night creature would pounce on her from the bushes. If she could just get through the gate to the safety of the yard, she would feel safer. "Please let me in. I'm scared."

"As well you should be, running away."

"Open the gate, please!"

"You are a bad girl, Roselyn. You have violated the rules."

"But I couldn't help it." She grabbed the cold metal bars. "Please don't make me stand out here."

"You were supposed to stay in your room."

Sweat broke out beneath her knee-length coat. "I couldn't stay there anymore! Uncle Enoch kept—"

"Your excuses are useless. I know what kind of girl you are. A bad girl, just like your mother."

"She isn't bad!"

"Yes, she is. She lies and cheats. And no daughter of mine will lie and cheat, so help me God."

"You're not my father—"

"That's a lie!" The tall figure rattled the gate so hard that Roselyn fell backward onto the ground. "And don't you ever repeat it!"

Stunned, she stared up at him, unable to see his face in the darkness. Her view of him was always the same, never quite in focus, never in the light, so she couldn't quite discern the features of the man who doled out punishment in the name of fatherly concern. He always stood in the shadows of a room, his back to the light of the doorway, always came down from his room after the evening meal and slept during the day. Never once had he shown his face to her, kissed her or held her on his knee. Rose wouldn't have wanted such attentions, anyway. She lived in terror of him and feared the sound of his measured step on the stair or in the hall.

She shuddered. He couldn't be her father. He just couldn't! How could her kind, soft-spoken mother be married to such a man?

Rose could see him seething, his narrow shoulders heaving as he glared at her. Rose knew his rages well, his sudden bursts of cruelty that could flare up unexpectedly. Once he had kicked a dog so viciously that he had killed it. Rose sat on the ground, too frightened to move, while the damp earth soaked through her dress and her underwear.

Finally he seemed to gain control of himself. His voice, more evenly modulated now, sliced through the night air.

"I'm only trying to save you from yourself, Roselyn, by teaching you what it means to be honest. You will thank me one day for being harsh, for only through harshness will the mind of a child remember."

His voice rumbled on as Roselyn hugged her knees, her panic overriding the words he was saying. His lectures were always the same and always followed by a punishment.

What would he do this time? Make her drink and drink and drink until she vomited, to cleanse her of evil? Make her pace for hours in the freezing cold in only her panties to rid her of the sin of vanity? Make her stand for an entire night with a book on her head because she had been caught reading past her bedtime?

"You can make it easy on yourself, Roselyn. You know why you were sent to your room. Tell me why, Roselyn."

"For lying." She scrambled to her feet. "But I wasn't—"

"Not telling the whole truth is just the same as lying, my girl."

"But I don't even know—"

"Do you take me for a fool?" he thundered, rattling the gate again.

Roselyn faltered backward, her knuckle to her hips.

"Speak up, child!"

"N-n-no."

"No one takes me for a fool. Not even your mother. She thinks she is getting away with her little affair, but I am wise to her. She's being very bad, Roselyn, and we must stop her before she brings ruin to the family."

He crouched, sliding his hands down the bars so that he was at eye level with her. "You can help me, Roselyn. You can help save our family. Just tell me the name of the man your mother has been seeing. That's all you have to do. I don't know why you're being so stubborn."

"What will you do to him if I tell?"

"Why, nothing, child. I'll ask him to stay away, that's all. And then we'll talk to your mother and tell her to try to be better in the future, to quit telling lies to us."

Rose studied him, distrustful of his sudden personable tone. He would punish her mother. He would probably make her stand out in the cold in her underwear, too. He might even hurt her mother. If he got really angry, he might kick her mother just as he had kicked poor old Buster.

The vision of her pretty mother curled up in pain on the floor gave her fresh resolve. She stuck out her bottom lip.

"If you tell me his name, Roselyn, I will let you in and have Mrs. Foster make you a nice cup of cocoa. I'll bet you're cold. You're very cold, aren't you?"

"Yes."

"Well? What is his name?"

"I—I—" She looked at the house behind him, with its lighted windows and promise of warmth, and then back at the figure crouched before her in the darkness. She swallowed. "I—I—"

"Come, Roselyn, it's easy. Just tell me his name."

She pinched her lips together. She couldn't betray her mother, not for a cup of cocoa. "I told you, I don't know!"

"Don't know?" he repeated, slowly rising to his awe-inspiring height. "Don't know?"

"No."

"Liar!" he bellowed. "Liar! You know his name, and by God, you'll tell me!"

"I don't know! I swear!"

"Perhaps you don't know the value of cooperation, Roselyn. Perhaps you don't know the value of a good home."

Rose's heart sank. Whenever he spoke of her lack of values, he always devised a punishment to fit the crime. She shivered, terrified of what he might invent.

"Perhaps a night away from home will teach you to count your blessings, Roselyn Bastyr." He released his hold on the gate and turned away.

He meant to leave her in the lane. He meant to leave her all alone in the dark.

Horrified, Rose ran forward and grasped the gate. "Please!" she cried. "Don't make me stay out here!"

He stopped and turned his head to glare at her over his shoulder. His eyes glinted in the darkness. "Ungrateful child. Let this be a lesson to you."

"But I'm scared! I want to come home! Please, open the gate. Please!"

"You brought this on yourself, Roselyn."

In disbelief, she watched him walk away and disappear into a ground fog that swirled out of the shrubs.

"Please, don't leave me alone!" Her plaintive request broke off in a sob as she sagged into a crumpled heap at the foot of the gate. Her clothes were damp, her knees and shins bare to the elements.

"Mother!" she cried, but she knew her mother couldn't hear her. She had probably taken her medicine so she could sleep during the night and had no idea that Rose was outside all by herself. Rose put a knuckle to her lips. She couldn't stay out here, not in the dark, alone with the unknown.

She had to tell.

"His name is Will!" she cried, shuddering.

The dark shape of her father appeared from the fog. "Will what?"

"I don't know!" She wept, heartsick and distraught.

"What is his last name, Roselyn?"

"I don't know! He lives by the zoo. He has a green car!"

"What's his last name, Roselyn. Think!"

"There's a big *A* on his screen door."

"*A* for Andrews? Will Andrews?"

"No. Anderson. His name is Will Anderson!"

Her father opened the gate. "Good girl, Roselyn. You have done well."

But Rose knew she hadn't done well. Out of fear of the dark, she had just betrayed her mother.

Rose was still sobbing when she felt a warm hand on her shoulder. Somehow she knew without opening her eyes that she had returned from her memory and was back at Brierwood.

"Your father was only trying to help you," the dry voice purred near her ear.

He was cruel.

"Seen through the eyes of a child, perhaps he seemed cruel. But he only wanted you to be the best that you could be, Roselyn—honest, brave and strong, like the rest of the Bastyrs."

And twisted.

"Oh no, Roselyn. Is that what your mother told you, that the Bastyrs are twisted?"

Yes. And I believe her.

"Why? Did your father ever strike you? Ever lay a hand on you?"

No, but—

"There, you see? He wasn't really cruel."

Rose stirred uncomfortably, trying to marshal her thoughts while he reached out and traced the opening between her lips. She turned away from his hand, but he only drew it across her cheek and down her neck, slipping his fingers into the top of her nightgown. He fanned his hand just over her left breast, and Rose sighed, knowing she should pull away, but longing to be touched all the same.

"He wanted to touch you, Roselyn, to show you his love. But he couldn't, because your mother had poisoned your mind and turned you against him. She kept you from him."

I was afraid of him.

"Because you wouldn't give yourself to him—your trust, your devotion, your obedience. If you had, he would have showered you with all the love in the world."

It didn't seem like it at the time.

"Perhaps." He drew the sheet away and eased down the elastic top of her nightgown to reveal her breasts. Rose felt cool air bathe her flesh before he leaned over her. His lips paused above her right nipple, expectation pulling it into a tingling peak. The anticipation of his mouth upon her sensitive skin made her gasp and arch her back.

Strong hands grasped her breasts while her eyelids twitched. She had to open her eyes, had to look into his eyes, to see if this was Taylor, to see if he desired her as much as she desired him at that moment.

"It's not too late, Roselyn," he murmured. She felt his weight upon the bed as he sat beside her.

"Promise to tell the truth and you will be loved beyond your wildest dreams."

Her breasts ached; her body was aflame for him. She opened her mouth but couldn't speak.

"Promise to obey, Roselyn, my beauty, and you will never be afraid again."

She tried to lift her arms, but they were like lead weights. She tried to speak but couldn't form a coherent word. Then she felt him ease his body onto hers, and she thought she would die from the glorious pressure of his chest against her breasts, the weight of his abdomen against her belly and the hard length of his thigh as he wedged his leg between hers. He moved his knee, and she gasped.

"Take the ring off, Roselyn. Give me the ring."

No. Bea told me to keep it on.

"Bea is making you a prisoner of her own delusions and fears, Roselyn. But you aren't afraid, are you?"

No.

"What she's been telling you is rather farfetched, isn't it?"

Yes.

"The ring makes you a prisoner. Take off the ring and you will be released from all her foolishness."

Somehow she found the wherewithal to slide off the emerald ring and hold it out to him. His breath swept over her cheek as he bent to her lips.

"You tempt me," he whispered. "Oh, you tempt me."

He kissed her at the same time as his hips ground against her thigh, surprising her with the carnal violence of both his body and his lips. His tongue thrust into her mouth, and even though she was a virgin, she knew enough of what went on between men and women to recognize his intent. His tongue wasn't there to pleasure her but to violate her. The violence shocked her, even in her groggy state. She struggled backward, pressing herself into the pillow, but his mouth only followed, his tongue in relentless pursuit, while he imprisoned her with his hands and the leg he had forced between hers.

What had begun as a light caress had suddenly become an invasion. He hissed her name and clawed the backs of her arms, raking over the scratches made by the briers. The pain shocked Rose to reality. This man wasn't showing her love, he was all but raping her, lost in satisfying his own desires without any regard for her.

No! The word screamed inside her head but never made it to her lips. She had to get away from him. Had to escape. But he was heavy. Rose struggled against her hypnotic state, trying in vain to push him away, surrounded by the smell of his heat and lust. She sucked in a breath, trying to get away, and caught the scent of nightshade. She froze.

Taylor had never smelled of nightshade. His hair had smelled of wind and sea. When he had kissed her, he hadn't been rough or violent. She had known a melting feeling in his arms, not this pummeling sensation of physical assault. Something was wrong here. Something wasn't as it should be. And if this wasn't Taylor on top of her, who was it?

She had to wake up.

Rose shut down the physical sensations—the smell of him, the taste of him, the feeling of his hands on her skin, the sound of his labored breathing. No matter what spell had been cast upon her, she had to wake up. She had to call upon the strength of her own mind to free her from the incubus who had come to her bed. Rose willed herself to think of nothing but waking from the lethargy of her body, concentrating on her goal as if it were a glowing dot that could grow larger from the force of her heart and soul. The dot increased and flickered to life, but not enough to blot out the curtain of blackness brought down by the man on top of her.

Rose knew she would be lost if she didn't get help. The man in her bed would have her, ruin her, and take her soul as surely as he took her virginity. Fighting the urge to cry, Rose prayed to her mother to help her. Wherever Deborah was in the great beyond, Rose needed her now more than ever.

Mother!

Immediately a sensation of warmth poured down, as if a golden light flowed over her, surrounding her. Rose concentrated, using the warmth to protect her like a shield, and willed herself to rise above the groggy sensation that drugged her mind. She must not falter, must not think for an instant about the man moving on top of her. She must think only of the light. Slowly the lassitude lifted and her dot of light flared into a swirling starburst. Rose focused with all her might on the vision of the starburst burning away the shadows of the dark curtain.

Then, in a twinkling, the darkness was gone.

Rose jerked upright and glanced to the side just in time to catch sight of a filmy dark figure moving toward her bathroom. Terrified, she lunged out of bed and bolted in the opposite direction. She flung open her door and burst into the hall, only to run into Taylor Wolfe.

CHAPTER NINE

"Taylor!" She launched herself into his embrace, threw her arms around his neck and clung to him. His chest was bare, and he wore only the bottoms of a pair of cotton pajamas, but she didn't care. His body was warm and solid and afforded a sense of security she needed more than anything else at the moment. She was so frightened that she couldn't form another word and resisted all his attempts to look at her face. Finally he gave up and simply held her, one hand at the back of her head and the other around her waist, until she had collected her wits enough to answer his questions.

"Rose?" he asked. "What's happened?"

"A man was—" She broke off, at a loss for how to explain herself without mentioning the shameful details of her nocturnal visitations.

"A man was in your room, Rose?" He clutched her shoulders. "Is that right?"

"Yes!"

"Who?" His fingers squeezed the tops of her arms.

"I don't know!"

Taylor leaned down to peer at her face. "Are you hurt?"

"No, just shaken up."

"What happened? Where'd he go?"

"I don't know. He might still be in there!"

"Bastard!" Taylor let go of her and grabbed his cane from the floor. He pushed the door open.

"I don't know how he got in. My door was locked."

Taylor made no response. She stumbled after him, afraid to be left alone in the dark house. He strode around the room, checking the window, the closed door and under her bed, and inspected her bathroom. In spite of his limp and scars, he cut a powerful figure, and she suddenly realized that he might not be as crippled as he appeared.

"You said your door was locked?"

"Yes. I can't figure out how he could have gotten in."

"And the window was locked?"

She nodded.

Taylor paused at the foot of her bed, perplexed.

"Did you see anything in the bathroom?" she asked.

"No. Nothing."

"That's where I saw him heading."

"He's not there now. I think he's long gone."

She ventured closer to pick up her robe off the foot of the bed, knowing that the cotton nightgown she wore would do little to conceal her nakedness, should she stand in brighter light.

"You okay, Rose?" he asked as she drew on the robe. "I mean, *really* all right?"

His solicitude warmed her. "Yes. He didn't—he didn't hurt me."

"What did he look like?"

"I don't know, really. He was wearing black. That's all I could tell."

"Do you have any idea who he could be?"

She paused, knowing very well who the intruder might be. Seth Bastyr. But to admit that to Taylor would involve telling him of her family. She wasn't ready to think about them, much less discuss them with Taylor.

"No, I haven't the faintest idea."

"Want me to call the police?"

"That isn't necessary. I don't think anything was taken."

For a long moment he studied her with his head slightly tilted and his brows drawn together. What must he be thinking? Then he reached out for her hand, and the sudden contact of his warm skin heated her all the way to her bare feet.

"Come on. You need a brandy."

"I don't drink."

"A nip will do you good." He pulled her down the hall to his room. "You should see your face, Rose. You're as white as a ghost."

He shut the door behind them and motioned to the bed, which was bathed in a pool of light from a lamp on the nightstand and covered with an assortment of books. "You're as cold as ice, too. Warm up there while I get the brandy."

He issued orders as if certain she would obey his every command. Yet Rose didn't want to argue. She was cold. She was afraid. And Taylor's rumpled bed, aglow in the darkness, looked like a haven of warmth and security.

"Just pile the books on the floor," he said over his shoulder while he unstoppered a decanter at a small cabinet in the sitting area.

Rose set the books on the floor and slipped under the covers, snuggling against the pillow as his scent wafted around her, warming her even further.

He walked to the bed, carrying two snifters, and offered her one. She murmured her thanks.

"Are you sure you're going to be all right?" he asked.

She nodded and watched him walk around to the other side, wondering if he intended to get in bed with her. She had never been in bed with a man, and the possibility that he would slide in beside her made her nervous.

Taylor sank onto the bed, his weight shaking the mattress as he eased against the pile of pillows at the headboard. Grateful that he hadn't slipped beneath the sheets, Rose took a gulp of her brandy.

The liquor burned like fire in her throat, and she choked.

"Easy!" Taylor chuckled, holding her drink steady as she hunched over in a coughing fit. "You're supposed to sip brandy, not swig it!"

"I didn't know!" she wheezed. She wiped away the tears that had sprung to her eyes. "I've never had any before!"

He gave the glass back to her. "Some things in life need to be taken slowly. Brandy's one."

His glinting eyes told her there were others, and she could guess what one of them might be. Lovemaking. Flustered, Rose took a careful sip this time, trying to avoid making eye contact with him.

"What are all the books about?" she asked, searching for a safer topic of conversation.

"The books? Research."

"About your eyes? Have you found anything?"

"Yeah, but I don't know whether I buy it."

She glanced at him in surprise. "Why?"

"The authors try to pass their work off as scientific theory, but it seems like farfetched bunk to me."

"For instance?"

"Here, I'll show you." He reached down and retrieved an old-looking hardback in dark green with gold lettering on the front. He touched the dog-eared corners and the slightly cracked spine.

"It's funny. I don't remember ordering this particular title," he said, "but of all the books that were delivered yesterday, it has the most information."

"What does it say about your vision?"

"Crazy stuff. That what I'm seeing is normal for some people."

"Normal?" Rose sipped her brandy, feeling much more at ease.

"From what it says here, the colored halos I've been seeing are called auras. They're emissions of energy that most animate and inanimate objects give off. Some people view auras as a key to personality traits. Different colors mean different things."

"Like what?"

"Take yours, for instance. You have what is called a crystal coloration."

"You've seen my aura?"

"Yeah. Yours is like a rainbow. It's the sign of a healer." He opened the book to a marked paged. "Crystals become the medium, or the conduit, through which healing passes." He ran his finger down to another paragraph. "Crystals can have the physical feeling of being fractured and are jealous of their private space."

He looked at her and grimaced. "The healer part I can accept. But the rest of it doesn't sound like you, does it?"

"Kind of." She thought of the way her life had splintered in the last few days as she learned of her past and her parents. Yet she had always felt somewhat fractured, as if she were not a whole being, with the big question of her parentage hanging over her like a cloud. "How about you, Taylor? What's your aura like?"

"I've never seen my own aura."

"How about Mrs. Jacoby's? Have you seen hers?"

"Once in passing. So what?"

"What color was it?"

"Mostly yellow."

"What does yellow mean?" Rose leaned closer, highly conscious of his bare shoulder inches from her nose.

Taylor flipped through the book. He found the section on yellow and tilted the book in her direction.

She read the passage out loud. "'Yellows are like puppies—warm, lovable, eager to please and loyal.'"

Taylor looked down at Rose and cocked an eyebrow at her. "That doesn't sound like the Mrs. Jacoby I know."

"You haven't seen her at her best. Bea is usually a dear."

"See what I mean? You can twist these things just like you can twist a horoscope to conform to the events of the day." He was about to pull the book away when a section caught his attention. "Wait a minute—"

"What is it?" Rose tipped her snifter to her lips. Taylor's company and the brandy were doing a good job of smoothing the rough edges of her fright and warming her toes. She felt unusually companionable and had the strongest urge to snuggle up against his arm.

"It talks about spots in the aura. I've noticed a black spot in yours. It floats above your right shoulder."

"A black spot? What does that mean?"

"It says here that we can carry images in our auras of people who have been significant in our lives or figures we have been thinking strongly about. It could be a family member or a character in a book you've just read."

"Does my spot have a face?" Certainly an image of a family member couldn't reside in her aura. Other than Bea and Donald, she hadn't known any of her family well enough for them to have been significant. And no amount of brandy could take the edge off the pain of that realization. Rose felt a wave of sadness pass over her and glanced up to find Taylor studying her.

"I don't know. I'll have to look at you more closely in the morning and see if I can get a clearer image." He paused, and she looked away, hoping to hide her melancholy thoughts from him. "Are you all right?" he asked, reaching backward to set his snifter and the book on the nightstand.

"Yes." She played with her nearly empty glass, hoping he wouldn't ask any personal questions. "I'm fine. The brandy is doing the trick."

He sat back and for a moment was silent. She was aware that he was gazing at her from the side. Rose tried to relax, but his presence unnerved her, for she had no idea what he was thinking or what he was going to do next. And she knew in her heart that his bed was a dangerous place for her to be.

Flustered, she thought of another subject. "What were you doing standing outside my bedroom door, anyway?"

"I heard that sound again."

"The pipe-organ sound?"

"Yes." He turned toward her. "Do you have any idea why a man would break into the house?"

Rose looked down. "Yes, but you wouldn't believe me."

"Try me." His voice was low and full of warmth. She looked up at him from under her lashes and found that he was still gazing at her, the sardonic slant of his mouth replaced by a grim, straight line. All the expression in his face was centered in his black eyes, which were on fire with an emotion she couldn't name. She knew only that her gaze suddenly felt just as hot and raw as his, and that she couldn't look away.

"Try me, Rose," he repeated, reaching for the side of her face. His hand slipped between her cheek and her hair to frame her jaw and ear. His head lowered to hers. "Trust me," he breathed. And then he kissed her.

The kiss deepened as his tongue swept into her and his fingers eased into her hair. The kiss made her dizzy, disoriented. She remembered her mother's warning not to succumb to a man and reached up to put a restraining palm on his chest. But the touch of his smooth, warm skin sent her over the edge of restraint and made her forget the letter and all its mysterious restrictions. Instead of pushing Taylor away, she ran her palm across the flat plane of his chest and over the tight muscle of his shoulder, marveling that his masculine flesh felt so different from hers—hard and uncompromising where hers was soft and yielding. What would the rest of him feel like?

Then, as if someone had dashed cold water over her, Rose realized that she would never find out what the rest of Taylor felt like, for she should not be here in his bed, kissing him and touching him. He had told her that his kisses meant nothing, which implied that his lovemaking would mean nothing, as well. Besides that, love with a man was forbidden to her. Shocked that she could let down her guard so easily, she pulled away just as Taylor broke from her lips.

"Hand me your glass," he murmured.

She gave the brandy snifter to him, and he set it aside.

Then he turned back and looked down at her, his eyes smoldering with desire. "I won't hurt you, Rose," he said softly. "You should trust me, you know."

"Why should I," she replied, "when you kiss me like that and then say it means nothing?"

She tried to duck out of the bed, but he grabbed her wrist to keep her beside him. Rose watched as if hypnotized as his hand slid up her arm and came to rest at the column of her neck.

"Maybe it does mean something," he admitted.

"Such as?"

"I'm not sure."

"Oh?" She pulled away from his hand. "And I'm supposed to let you take advantage of me when you don't even know your own intentions?"

"There's nothing wrong with exploring each other's bodies."

"Maybe for you. But not for me."

He smiled slowly, the left side of his mouth rising ever so slightly. Rose tried to ignore him, but she felt her body respond with a melting sensation. She saw his gaze drop to the front of her robe, which had come unfastened, allowing him a view of her breasts beneath the filmy nightgown.

"I may be inexperienced, Taylor, but I know where such explorations can lead."

His gaze flickered up to her face. "And where is that, Rose?"

"To—to bed."

"We're already in bed." He reached out and gently drew down her robe to display the tops of her ivory shoulders.

Rose fought to keep herself from melting into a spineless mass. "You know what I mean, Taylor. If I let you, you'd take off all my clothes."

"You're right." He circled her breast with his fingertip and then cupped it. "I'd love to see what you really look like, Brier Rose."

Rose sighed and closed her eyes. "But I can't allow you to do that, because you—"

"Shh," he replied, his voice gravelly, before he cut off her protests with a kiss. Rose tasted the brandy on his tongue and felt the press of his thumb beneath her cheekbone while the release of doubt burst inside her. Yes. She would trust him. She longed to trust somebody. And somehow she knew she should have trusted Taylor all along. The violence she had felt with the other man faded to nothingness under Taylor's firm but gentle hand as he urged her back onto the pillows, his mouth still angled over hers.

Then he lowered his head and took the tip of her breast in his mouth. She could feel the damp heat of him through the thin cotton fabric. Slowly he drew away, tightening his lips around the hard peak and using his teeth at the last moment. Rose gasped and arched toward him, hoping he would do it again, even though she knew she was courting danger with every moment she lingered in his bed. He took the other breast in his mouth. She reached up for him, running her hands along his straining neck and shoulders, reveling in the pure masculine power she felt beneath her fingers.

His hands slipped the robe off. A ragged sigh flowed from her as she let her arms slide from him and lay back to allow him to disrobe her, at least to the waist. He eased down the elastic neckline of her nightgown, baring both breasts.

"Look at you," he declared. Rose looked down and saw his hands pass over the rounded curves of her upraised breasts while his thumbs stroked her nipples. His skin was much darker than hers, and his long, blunt fingers be-

longed to the hands of a man, a sight she had never seen
before on her breasts. He caressed her, sighing heavily. She
sighed, too, and thought she would die of pleasure. He
kissed her breasts, her throat, her chin, her mouth.

Then he lowered his bare chest to hers and she realized
that the pleasure had only just begun. His skin was aflame,
and the pressure of his weight on her made her ache with a
sharp desire deep inside. Together they sank into the pillows, locked in an embrace of searching hands and searing
lips, of tumbling hair and writhing limbs. Taylor ripped
away the barrier of the sheet and blanket that separated
them, then came back down upon her, nudging aside one of
her legs with his knee and angling himself along the length
of her thigh. Rose felt the hard maleness of him and blossomed with heat and dew in the part of her that longed to
know him as a woman knows a man. She trembled, well
aware that she should stop him, but even so she held him,
one of her hands splayed across the expanse of his wide
back, the other buried in his shiny black hair. She knew this
moment was as inevitable as the rise of the sun, the circle of
the moon. This man was meant to lie with her, on her, inside her, and she was meant to take him in.

She felt the muscles of his back tense as he reached for her
nightgown and pushed it upward, his warm palm trailing up
her thigh. The thrill of the movement brought her back to
her senses.

"Taylor!"

"Don't worry, Rose." His voice was thick and breath-
less.

"We can't," she whispered. And yet she knew she should
open herself to him, give herself over to his desire and take
what he had to offer. She should open her heart to Taylor
and form a bond that would never break, the kind of bond
she had instinctively felt the first time she had seen him.

"Just relax," he said, his mouth near her ear, and the
rush of his warm breath made her skin tingle with a thou-
sand pricks of delight. "I won't hurt you."

Rose felt his hand near her belly and knew he was unty-
ing the drawstring of his pajamas. Could she allow herself
to see him that way? Touch him and know him that way?

She closed her eyes while every sense screamed at her to break down and accept him.

"Taylor, I can't," she whispered in anguish, pushing against his chest.

Taylor rose up on his elbows. "What do you mean, you can't?"

"I—I just can't. Don't ask me."

"You afraid of what Mrs. Jacoby will say?"

"No, I just can't—"

He pulled away. "It's my scars, isn't it? I don't turn you on, do I?" he asked bitterly.

"No, it's not that."

He sat up, taking his weight and warmth with him. "Don't lie, Rose. Just level with me."

"It's not you, Taylor. It's me!" She sat up and put her legs over the side of the bed. "I should go."

"No." Taylor rose from the bed and crossed his arms. "I don't want you going anywhere, Rose. If that intruder comes back—"

"I'll be fine." She got to her feet and adjusted her nightgown and drew on her robe.

"No. Stay here tonight. I won't touch you."

She paused. The last place on earth she wanted to be tonight was in her own bedroom.

"I'll sleep on the couch." Taylor motioned to the settee in front of the fireplace. "I just don't want you sleeping alone, Rose. Okay?"

She gazed at him, amazed that he could still take her welfare into consideration after she had refused his advances.

"I insist," he added.

"All right." Slowly she sank back down to the mattress. "Thank you, Taylor," she said, relieved. He hobbled to the cedar chest at the foot of the bed and took out a spare blanket, which he carried to the small sofa. Rose doubted he would be comfortable on the damask-covered cushions, but she had no recourse other than sharing the bed with him, and that was far too dangerous to consider.

She watched him shake out the blanket and then lower himself to the settee. "Good night," he declared with a sigh.

She watched his head disappear from view. "Good night."

With more sighs and a great deal of rustling, he settled himself down for the night. Rose removed her robe and climbed into his bed. She turned off the light and listened to his breathing. With every intake of Taylor's breath, she could feel her heart burgeoning. She slid her hands under her cheek and listened as he fell asleep, and knew at that moment that she was falling in love with him.

A tear slid from the corner of her eye and ran over the edge of her hand. If what her mother had said was true—that the Bastyrs would feed on her love for a man—she must never reveal her feelings to Taylor. In fact, if she really loved him, she should do everything in her power to push him away.

Rose fell into a fitful sleep and dreamed of running through a dense forest of oaks, her progress hampered by the long dress she wore. Surprised, she glanced down and saw she was attired in a strange long skirt made of dull coarsely-woven cloth. A green shawl flapped around her shoulders and she carried a satchel in her left hand.

Up ahead in a clearing, she caught a glimpse of a large table-like object, which materialized into a huge sundial made of granite, much like the sundial in the back garden of Brierwood.

But somehow she knew this landscape of her dream did not represent Brierwood, and her clothes did not reflect modern fashion. In fact, her homespun dress looked as if it belonged to the Puritan era of New England.

Just as she gained the sundial at the center of the raised clearing and dropped the satchel at her feet, she heard someone call her name.

"Constance!"

She turned to see Taylor running up the path to her. He was dressed in breeches, a long vest, and a white shirt with billowing sleeves. Her heart skipped a beat as she watched him sprint across the grass, both legs straight and strong. He was sleek and handsome and full of life, and she wanted more than anything to take him in her arms and kiss him, well aware that she had never felt his touch. Either she had forgotten what it was like to kiss him, or she had never really tasted his lips before.

But a sudden fear pressed upon her, blocking out her joy at the sight of him. What if Seth Bastyr should find them, here in the darkness?

"Hurry!" she urged. "We haven't much time!"

"They didn't see you go?" he asked.

"I don't think so. But they'll soon miss me and come looking. We've only a few minutes, Nathaniel."

Why had she called him that name? As a matter of fact, why had he called her Constance? Before she could ask, he pulled her into his arms and kissed her, backing her against the sundial. She returned the embrace and pressed into his body, forgetting everything but the feeling of his mouth on hers and her breasts thrust against his chest. She loved him. Ah, how she loved him. In a moment she would tell him, say the words, make him understand what he had come to mean to her.

"Seducer!" a strange voice rang out.

With a start, Rose jerked awake. She looked around warily, sure that Seth Bastyr had come to haunt her again. Perspiration beaded on her forehead and her heart thumped with terror as she visually checked each shadowed corner of the room. No one was there. Slowly she sank back onto the pillow and calmed herself by listening to the steady rhythm of Taylor's breathing at the sofa nearby.

The dream had been so real, just like the visions of her past which Seth conjured by hypnotizing her. But where had the dream of the sundial come from? Why had Taylor called her by another name? What did it all mean? Shaken and disoriented, she tried to close her eyes and relax, but sleep didn't come for many hours.

Just before dawn, Taylor heard the pipe-organ noise again. He jerked awake and sat up, blinking in the dim light that filtered through the windows of his bedroom. For a moment he forgot where he was and thought he was back again on the *Jamaican Lady*. But then he remembered that he was sleeping on a cold, hard settee in his bedroom at Brierwood, and that Rose Quennel was snuggled in his bed.

He threw off the blanket and looked at the bed where Rose slept.

For a moment he thought he was dreaming, because he imagined he saw a dark figure standing at the side of the bed, looking down at Rose. He blinked, sure that he was imagining things. But the figure was still there.

"Hey!" Taylor shouted, jumping to his feet.

The figure turned. In the dark, Taylor couldn't make out the features of the man's face or the details of his clothing, but he was acutely aware of a feeling of malevolence. Taylor paused, unsure of what to do. As a last resort he let his eyes go out of focus as he had done in the workroom with Rose. He saw the figure bounded by an aura of undulating black. As if in a trance, he watched as the aura of the figure pulsed and surged in an enormous murky cloud, reaching all the way to the ceiling. Taylor was sure that the intruder had returned. But what kind of person had a black aura? For the first time in his life, Taylor felt utter and complete terror. The tattered green book might have truths to tell him, after all. He knew without consulting the strange book that the aura of the man before him represented evil— pure, quintessential evil.

Taylor froze, unable to utter another word. He knew he should do something to protect Rose or at the very least warn her of the intruder's presence. But he was so frightened he couldn't move. The wound on his leg seemed to throb in time with the undulating aura, shooting spikes of pain up his shin and thigh. All he could do was watch in horror and agony as the figure dissolved into muddy-colored smoke. Then the murky cloud funneled into a swirling mass that poured into the pure colors of Rose's rainbow aura, condensing to conform to the confines of the black spot above her right shoulder.

"My God!" Taylor gasped.

CHAPTER TEN

Shaken, Taylor limped to the bed, his leg throbbing with each step. He reached Rose and was startled when she turned and mumbled in her sleep. For a moment he thought she would wake up and see him staring at her. He hung back, thinking twice about the impulse to wake her and tell her what had just happened, because he would have to explain his own inability to act at the same time. That impotence would not endear him to her. More than anything, he wanted Rose to see him as a capable man, perhaps even heroic, and not the hesitant, injured man he had become.

Since the time he was a teenager, he had climbed mountains and sailed the oceans, braving hardship and personal injury. He had spent his entire life facing danger and the possibility of death, as if he had been in training. Training for what, though? For Brierwood? How could he hope to help Rose when he could barely walk?

Full of anguish, Taylor turned away and limped to the balcony. He pulled aside the curtain and looked out the window as the first rays of light glowed behind the trees. The pain in his calf gradually subsided as he watched the sun come up. He scowled, trying to figure out what was happening at Brierwood and what was happening to him. At any other time he would have found it easy to walk away from a woman and her problems. He would board the *Jamaican Lady,* set out to sea and soon forget any and all entanglements. But his boat was moored hundreds of miles away in San Francisco, and he was here at Brierwood, caught in an ever-increasing web of questions. He couldn't leave, not physically, and certainly not emotionally, when Rose was in danger with only old Bea Jacoby to protect her.

He glanced over his shoulder at the beauty in his bed, her red hair fanned across his pillow and her white hands curled on her chest. Her bare fingers, bereft of her ever-present emerald ring, looked as delicate and soft as a child's. No, he could never leave Rose alone, especially after witnessing the black cloud entering her aura. Who or what had the figure been? Did it have something to do with the Bastyr family, with the stranger she claimed to have seen in the house?

Taylor walked back to the bed and sat down in an upholstered chair near the nightstand. Whatever he had seen, he planned to stand guard against it until Rose awakened. This time he would not let anyone talk him out of helping a woman, not even himself.

A few hours later Rose rolled onto her side and opened her eyes, surprised to find Taylor sitting beside her, his head propped on his fist, his dark eyes trained on her face. The sight of him sitting there watching her made a warm sensation spread through her languid limbs. How long had he been gazing at her?

Seeing her awaken, he raised his head. His lean cheeks were shadowed by a dark growth of beard, cut through by the jagged pale scar, and an unruly strand of black hair hung over his forehead. She remembered the taste of him and the weight of him and tried to dash it from her thoughts. She must never succumb to him again.

"Good morning, Rose."

"Good morning." She sat up. "What are you doing there?"

"Watching you."

She bunched the covers to her breast, suddenly wary. "Why?"

"I'm worried."

"Worried?" Had she talked in her sleep? Had she relived another painful shard of her past and revealed it to Taylor? She prayed she hadn't. She didn't want to admit that she came from a twisted family, not even to herself. "What are you worried about?"

"That intruder—who was he?"

"I don't know."

"Last night you said you might have an idea."

Rose got out of bed and slipped on her robe, wishing he had presented her with a cup of coffee instead of twenty questions.

"Well?" He stood up as if to prevent her from leaving the room.

"Taylor, I just got up. Can we talk about this later?" She stepped around him, but he grabbed her arm.

"No, damn it!"

Rose glared at him, and he instantly let go of her.

"Sorry," he growled. Frustrated, he ran a hand through his hair, as if to calm himself. "What I mean is, I don't think we should take the break-in lightly. And the more I know about you and Brierwood, the better."

"I don't see what I have to do with the intruder."

"What about the person who came to Brierwood before me? You talked to him. Who was he? And you said someone had come to your bedroom and touched you. What was that all about?"

"They must have been bad dreams, just as you said."

"Cut the crap, Rose."

Suddenly Rose felt very much awake, alarmed that he was pressing her so hard for the truth. She wasn't ready to confide in him, not when she didn't know what to believe herself. She straightened her shoulders. "Are you calling me a liar, Mr. Wolfe?"

"You know more than you're telling me."

"Perhaps it's personal."

"Maybe I want to hear the personal stuff."

He stared at her, his eyes glittering. She had never seen such opaque eyes, as if they were fashioned from obsidian. She had to get away from his eyes before she buckled and told him everything, dragging him all the way into her troubled life.

"Well, maybe I don't want to tell you."

"After last night, I thought—"

"Last night never should have happened, Taylor. I was frightened and vulnerable. And I had too much brandy."

"Don't blame it on the brandy, Rose. You wanted to be there."

"You think so?" She threw frost into her voice, hoping to come across as cruel and uncaring, so she could push him away. "Do you think I would go for you, with your scars and your lame leg? I can do much better for myself. Much better."

He blinked at her in shock, too startled to hide the flash of hurt that flared in his eyes. She tore her gaze from his face and stared at his model ship across the room while she hugged her robe around her, as if to hold the pieces of her breaking heart together.

"I was just using you, Mr. Wolfe. Don't you get it?"

She hurried past him to the door before he could reply.

After a shower, Taylor went down for breakfast and plowed through his eggs and fruit, trying to sort through the words Rose had flung at him. Those words had echoed his own thoughts, that he wasn't man enough to be attractive to her. Yet she was in danger, and no matter what she thought of him, he couldn't walk away.

He thought of the women he'd had—laughing, sultry, gorgeous females who had practically pulled off their clothes for him—and how easy it had been to bring them into his sphere. The method had been simple—a date, a tour of the *Jamaican Lady,* a bottle of champagne on the deck in the moonlight, and the lady was his for the night. Taylor paused with the coffee cup at his lips as a flush crawled over his cheekbones. Looking back, he could see the callousness of the operation. He couldn't imagine trying the old routine with Rose. In fact, he couldn't imagine asking her for a date. It seemed juvenile, somehow, as if they were far beyond dating. Yet apparently he was the only one who thought that way. From what Rose had told him, she didn't even want to get to know him. *I can do better than you.* Her words rang in his ears, forcing him to put down his mug before he shattered it beneath the pressure of his palms.

No matter how Rose felt about him, he had to look at the black spot in her aura and try to make out a face or feature to identify the figure he had seen last night. Picking up his dirty dishes, Taylor put a shoulder to the swinging door and pushed through to the kitchen, surprising Bea, who was working at the sink.

"Mr. Wolfe!" She turned around, and he noticed her glance down at a butcher knife on the sink board beside her. Taylor flushed anew, unaccustomed to being distrusted.

Wondering if she would actually arm herself, Taylor sauntered to the sink to deposit his dishes and watched as she sidled away. "If you'd feel safer, Mrs. Jacoby, go ahead and pick up the knife."

She glanced at the blade and then back at him. "I don't think you're funny, Mr. Wolfe."

"I'm not trying to be." Smiling grimly, Taylor looked down at her. "Where's Rose this morning?"

"Why do you want to know?"

"I have to speak to her for a minute."

"She's too busy. She has to finish hemming the scarf before her client comes today."

"Her client is coming here?"

"Yes. He was anxious to pick it up, so he's coming in person."

"When?"

"This evening."

Taylor crossed his arms and leaned against the edge of the counter. "So she's upstairs in the workroom?"

"I didn't say that." Mrs. Jacoby wiped her hands on her apron. He could see her fingers trembling and wished there was something he could say to allay her needless fear of him.

"Listen, Mrs. Jacoby." He sighed, wondering how to approach the subject of the Bastyrs. "I'm worried about Rose. I know you don't trust me, but I need your help."

She studied him from the corners of her eyes. "My help?"

"Yes. Something is going on at Brierwood. I think Rose knows about it, but she won't tell me."

"Why should she?"

Taylor stuffed his left hand in the front pocket of his jeans. He knew whatever he said must convince Bea to help him, and that meant he had to be absolutely frank. His gut feeling about Rose was very different from what he wanted to admit to anyone, especially since he had known her only a short while. But deep in his heart he knew Rose was special, unlike any woman he had ever known. He wanted her—in his arms, in his bed and in his life—and that thought scared the heck out of him. He could hardly look at the truth, much less say it out loud.

Taylor glared at the floor, fighting the urge to bolt out of the kitchen and Brierwood. But there was no turning back. He had to win over Mrs. Jacoby, and he could only do it with the truth. He sighed again and looked up at Bea.

"Because I care what happens to her, Mrs. Jacoby. I care a hell of a lot."

Bea's gray eyes pored over his face. "I don't believe you."

"I don't care if you believe me or not. I want to help her."

Bea wiped her hands again, bunching the hem of her apron between her palms. Taylor could tell that his words had shocked her into silence, and that she was trying to make sense of them.

"I need to know about this family you've talked about—the Bastyrs."

"Don't toy with me, Mr. Wolfe."

"I'm not!" He straightened and ran a hand through his hair. "Don't you understand, Mrs. Jacoby? I'm not a threat. I'm not part of that family. I want to help Rose. But I can't, not when I don't know what's going on."

"Ask Rose, then."

"I have, but she claims not to know anything. She says that she's just been having bad dreams. But I know for a fact that someone or something is here at Brierwood, coming to Rose at night."

"How do you know?"

"I've seen him."

"You saw someone?"

"Yes. And I don't know how to explain it, but I sensed he was evil."

Bea dabbed her forehead and temples with the corner of her apron and shuffled away, turning her back to him. For the first time since he had met her, he felt as if he had reached her. Could she be starting to believe him?

He stepped closer. "That's why I need to know, Mrs. Jacoby. I don't want anything to happen to Rose."

She lowered her head, as if in prayer, and then slowly turned to face him.

"Perhaps I've been wrong about you, Mr. Wolfe."

He nodded, hoping she would continue.

"But I can't tell you these things. Rose must. It is her story to tell. If she chooses to remain silent, then I must abide by her wishes."

"Even if she's in danger?"

Bea nodded. "Besides, I don't think there is anything you could do to help her, Mr. Wolfe. This is between the Bastyrs and us."

"So I just stand by and watch?"

"Believe me, Mr. Wolfe, if you get involved, you could very well lose your life."

"Why? What kind of family are we talking about here?"

"A strange family. And that's all I'm going to say." She raised her chin and pressed her lips together.

Taylor limped to the door. "So where is she—upstairs in the workroom?"

"Yes."

Edgar squawked when Taylor entered the workroom, ruining Taylor's chance to catch Rose unaware, the best time to see her aura in its purest form. Taylor was confident now that he could see her aura simply by concentrating and shifting his vision. When he didn't want to see auras he kept his vision from going out of focus. Knowing he had some power over his ailment seemed to give him control over the sounds he heard, as well. What had once been cacophony became delightful musical tones when heard individually. Only the unexpected pipe-organ sound could still overwhelm him.

He would have studied her aura earlier in the morning, when she lay in his bed, except the dark background of green and burgundy in his bedroom was a poor backdrop for the purpose. Here in the workroom, with its white walls and tarnished gilt trim, he would be able to see her aura clearly.

As a test, Taylor glanced at Edgar and shifted his vision. The raven's head and wings were crowned by an indigo

sheen that emitted a faint hum, much like a note drawn from
the string of a cello. Edgar cawed again, as if in protest at
the survey, and Taylor shifted his sight to Rose.

She sat in a chair, the scarf draped over her knees, holding a needle with its tail of thread trailing to the silk in her
hand. Rose was dressed in a deep apricot skirt and blouse
trimmed with swirls of tiny rust-colored braid on the bodice. Interlocked figures of birds were painted along the hem
of the skirt and the sleeves of the blouse, in the same color
of her hair, which was loosely braided and draped over her
shoulder. The end of the braid hung along the inside curve
of her arm, drawing his eyes to the shapely mounds of her
breasts. She wore a chunk of carnelian nestled among a
clutch of foreign coins on a thong around her neck and another at her wrist. Rose had never looked more beautiful,
and for a moment all he could do was stare at her.

Rose regarded him coolly, aloof and beautiful, but with
a small muscle trembling at the corner of her mouth, as if
she were holding back a flood of emotion.

"Yes?" she asked.

"I've come to study your aura," he answered, stepping
closer.

"Why?" She sat back in her chair, as if to distance herself from him.

"To get a better look at that black spot."

She bent over her work and took a stitch. "I told you I
didn't want your help."

"It will only take a minute."

"I don't mean to be rude," she said tersely, "but I'm under a strict deadline, Taylor. I don't have a minute to spare."

"Just keep doing what you're doing, and I'll look at
you."

"I would prefer that you leave." She frowned at her work,
obviously displeased with the last few stitches. "I don't like
it when you stare at me."

"Why?"

"Because it makes me nervous." She shot a glare at him.
"And then my stitches go awry."

"Well, at least I elicit some kind of emotion from you."

Rose jumped up and held the silk to her breast. "I want you to leave. Now."

"Just a minute—"

"Now, Taylor."

He frowned, unaccustomed to taking orders from anyone. Yet he didn't want to offend her any more than he already had by coming on too strong with her.

"I will. Just humor me for a minute and stand still."

She sighed and shifted her weight impatiently. "Is this another one of your ploys, like the brandy?"

"Hardly," he retorted. "Last night I saw someone or something turn into a cloud of smoke and go into that spot in your aura. And I want to know who the hell it is."

"You saw something go into my aura?"

"Yes. The pipe-organ noise woke me up, and I saw someone standing by the bed."

"What did it . . . he look like?"

"I couldn't tell in the dark. When I called out, he simply dissipated and funneled into your aura. And that's why I want to look at the black spot—to find out if he has a face."

"That's preposterous!" She turned away. "I've got better things to do than listen to such—"

"And I've got better things to do than second-guess you, Rose. So why don't you tell me about the Bastyr family?"

"I don't want you involved."

He looked at the back of her russet head, the slope of her shoulder, the curve of her hips, wanting more than anything to draw her back to him. She had felt so right against him last night. Yet if he reached for her, he was sure that she would pull away. He couldn't bear the humiliation and the pain that would cause.

Instead of responding, he shifted his vision and let his gaze drift to the side of her head, allowing her hair to go out of focus. Her rainbow-colored aura shimmered with an outer layer of green, accompanied by a light buzzing sound, like the whir of hummingbird wings. The black spot came into view, and Taylor carefully concentrated on it, hoping she wouldn't move until he could inspect the inky blotch.

In the black spot glowed the oval of a man's face with a waxen complexion and dark eyes, nearly as dark as his own.

But the eyes of the face in the aura were simianlike, lacking visible whites and deeply set in shadow. Below a hooked nose was a stern, thin-lipped mouth that turned down in cruelty. Taylor couldn't tell the man's age, but he was once again struck by the evil emanating from him.

"Taylor!" Rose whirled, realizing that he was staring at her.

Taylor blinked back to reality. His lips felt tight and dry, and his heart pounded in his chest.

"What's wrong?" she demanded.

"There's a man's face in your aura. Someone evil."

That got her attention. She lowered the scarf. "What does he look like?"

"He's got a narrow face. Dark hair, dark eyes. He looks like he could be a real bastard. Know him?"

Rose draped a hand at the base of her throat. He noticed that her emerald ring was still missing. Then he glanced at her face. She had paled and looked as shocked as he felt.

"Do you know anyone who might fit that description, Rose?"

She shook her head too emphatically for Taylor to believe her.

"Rose, don't run from me."

She swallowed, and for a moment her eyes locked with his as if she were about to weaken. Then her expression hardened, and she motioned toward the door.

"You saw what you wanted, now leave."

Taylor sighed in frustration, aching to crush her in his arms and kiss away her disbelief. He balled his fist and then released it, fighting off the urge to overpower her with his sheer physical size. Once he kissed her, he knew she would surrender to him again. Then he could talk some sense into her and convince her to confide in him. But instead of overpowering her and taking the chance of losing her forever, he squeezed the handle of his cane and left the workroom.

Taylor spent the rest of the day sequestered in the drawing room downstairs, poring over his books, trying to find out more about auras, certain now that his only hope in

dealing with the dark figure would depend on his knowledge of his special sight. He practiced shifting his vision so
he could do it with ease. When Bea walked down the hall
with a feather duster, he caught sight of her aura in the brief
time it took her to pass the open doorway. Heartened by his
success, Taylor tried more difficult subjects, such as the
flitting sparrows outside the window. While he was staring
out the window he noticed four black shapes under the
rhododendrons by the herb garden, but before he could
switch back to his normal vision, he was interrupted by Bea
coming in to announce dinner. When he looked back at the
rhododendrons he couldn't see anything but curled dried
leaves on the ground.

Shrugging off the incident, Taylor followed Bea out to the
dining room. No matter what she thought of him, she still
cooked delicious meals for him, and he knew he would miss
her cooking once he left Brierwood.

Just as he finished his after-dinner coffee, he heard the
doorbell ring. Taylor turned in his chair, listening intently
for the sound of voices, curious to know the nature of
Rose's client but aware that his presence would not be appreciated during the transaction. Still, he had to get a look
at the man and make sure that Rose received a fair price for
her wonderful workmanship.

"Come into the parlor," Bea's voice echoed from the
foyer. "And I'll get Miss Quennel."

Taylor hobbled to the door of the dining room, holding
his cane off the floor to keep from making his telltale tapping noise. He poked his head around the doorway of the
dining room just in time to see the tall figure of a man
walking behind Bea. The man wore a long black overcoat,
black pants and well-polished shoes, and cut quite an elegant figure. Taylor moved down the hall, wishing he had
seen the man's face, and wondered why anyone would wear
an overcoat on a warm summer night.

Taylor heard Bea returning and ducked into the shadow
of the stair as she passed by him on her quest to locate Rose.
Taylor expected that she was upstairs, taking great pains
with her appearance for her influential client. He decided to
wait at the foot of the stairs so he could watch her descend.

There was no way she would turn back, even if he was the one standing at the bottom.

He didn't usually care what kind of clothes he wore. Jeans and T-shirts were his usual garb. On the job at Jensen's Quality Boats he wore slacks, a tie and a sports jacket, hating every moment the tie cinched his neck. But now, waiting for Rose and knowing how elegant her visitor appeared, he wished he had changed into something more attractive than his well-worn jeans and black polo shirt. For some reason he felt in competition with the man who had just entered Brierwood, and he didn't want to come up lacking in Rose's estimation.

Above him, he heard Bea's excited chatter and the softer tones of Rose's voice as she answered. He heard her step on the stair, looked up and felt heat waft up around his ears.

Rose was attired in a dark green dress that draped in soft folds nearly to her ankles. Around her willowy waist she had tied an exotic-looking belt made of copper and gilded cording shot with green beads. Her hair hung loose, a glorious nimbus of dancing reds and golds. Her neck and ears flashed with more copper and green, and her feet were bare except for a pair of delicate sandals. Taylor was aware that he held his breath until she reached the last stair.

Her eyes met his with a cool level gaze.

"Good luck," he said.

"Thanks." She held a white cardboard box in her arms, probably for the safe transport of the scarf.

"Don't let him get away without paying full price for that."

"I don't intend to."

"Come along, Rose," Bea urged, taking her elbow and giving Taylor a dark glance. "We don't want to keep him waiting."

Taylor moved backward, allowing them to pass. He watched Rose walk away with graceful steps. She looked capable and in control, and he had no doubt that she would get top dollar for the scarf. Then she slipped into the parlor, and he heard her greet her client while Bea remained in the hallway. Taylor ran a hand over his chin, battling the urge to eavesdrop and wishing Bea would clear out and let him see what was going on. But she didn't seem eager to return to the kitchen, and he certainly wasn't going to stand there with her like some mismatched cheering section, so he gave up and retired to the drawing room and his book.

But the words in the green book faded as he listened to the voices that carried across the foyer through the open door of the drawing room. Once he even heard Rose laugh—a lovely sound he had never heard her make. Scowling at his own jealousy, he forced himself to ignore the activity in the parlor and trained his attention on the open book in his lap.

His glance fell on a strange subhead—"Auric Vampires." He scanned the ensuing paragraphs, first in doubt and then in earnest. According to the book there were beings that fed off the energy of other people, just as vampires in the horror movies of his childhood fed off the blood of their victims. Auric vampires were not immortal monsters but merely everyday people who either didn't have enough of their own energy or grew addicted to a higher level of energy than normal. Their "bite" left a wound in the aura, which allowed energy to drain out. Auric wounds rarely healed on their own, and if a person wasn't aware of their wound, they might spend a lifetime in an altered, debilitated state.

Shaking his head in disbelief, Taylor shut the door, surprised to find Edgar sitting on the back of his wing chair. He hadn't even heard the bird come into the room.

Edgar cocked his head and hopped closer. Taylor wondered if the raven was thinking about pecking his head.

"Watch it, buster," he warned.

Edgar hopped down and rubbed the sides of his beak on the walnut claw that decorated the arm of the chair. Taylor kept a wary eye on the bird, surprised that the creature would come so close to him.

The bird eyed him and then hopped onto his wrist. Edgar's claws were clammy and soft, and he was careful not to grasp Taylor's flesh too tightly.

Slowly Taylor lifted the raven to eye level, amazed that the bird trusted him enough to make contact.

Then Edgar squawked so loudly that Taylor wrenched back in surprise, flinging the raven into the air. The bird flapped out of the room, cawing raucously.

Taylor jumped to his feet and followed him out to the foyer just as Rose and her client emerged from the parlor. Taylor paused at the bottom of the stairs and watched in disgust as the man slowly drew Rose's hand to his lips and kissed the back of it. He was wearing gloves, which Taylor considered as ridiculous as the overcoat.

Then the elegant man turned and looked at Taylor. For a moment his stare bore into Taylor's, and Taylor felt as if his entire body were being traced by a hot flashlight beam. He had never felt anything like it before. He forced himself to ignore the way the hair rose on his arms and legs and the back of his neck, and concentrated on the man's face. He froze as he recognized the simian eyes, the waxen pallor and the widow's peak in the man's dark hair. This was the man from Rose's aura.

CHAPTER ELEVEN

Taylor couldn't move, and his calf started to throb. He saw the man walk to the door with Rose flowing beside him. Taylor wanted to shout at her to get away, to run, but his mouth wouldn't open.

As Rose's client came abreast of Taylor, he nodded slightly. "Good evening," he said, his voice dry and his words tinged with an accent Taylor couldn't place.

Taylor stood mute, unable to reply. The simian eyes inspected his face with a gaze so intense that he felt as if the man were looking beneath his skin. Taylor was sure he could read amusement in the man's eyes, the same condescending smirk that cats displayed to their prey. Taylor wanted to punch the sneer from his face, but his arms were like wooden boards.

He shifted his vision and saw the man's aura streaking all the way to the third-floor balcony in shafts of black—the color of evil, the mark of a psychopath bereft of human feelings, the badge of a demon. With the black aura came the blast of the pipe organ, so loud that Taylor couldn't hear what Rose and her client were saying to him. He could see their mouths moving, but their voices blurred together. With a great effort he shifted his vision back to normal.

"Are you ill, Mr. Wolfe?" the man asked. "You look pale."

How did the man know his name? Had Rose been introducing them a moment ago?

Rose glanced at Taylor, her brows drawn together in concern. "Taylor?"

He shook his head, trying to warn her with his eyes, but she didn't pick up on his expression.

"Well, I must be going," the man said.

"Thank you so much." Rose opened the door. "I hope your lady likes the scarf."

"Oh, I know she will." He stepped out on the front porch and turned. "She will adore it. Goodbye, Miss Quennel, Mr. Wolfe."

"Goodbye," she answered. "And watch out on the way to your car. We've seen some dogs on the property."

"I'm sure they won't bother me." He nodded and walked down the front steps, looking neither right nor left, as if totally unconcerned about the pack of dogs.

Rose closed the door and locked it. When she turned to face Taylor, her eyes were hard with displeasure.

"Why did you have to be so rude!" she sputtered. "That man can make or break my career."

The organ sound dissipated enough to allow Taylor to think and move. He wiped his forehead with the back of his hand. "Rose," he gasped. "That client of yours is the man I saw in your aura!"

"I hardly think so."

"I'm certain." He hobbled to the window and looked out into the dusk, but he saw only the circular drive and the gardens beyond. "Where did he park?"

"I don't know. I didn't hear him drive up."

"Neither did I. I bet he's not going anywhere. I bet he's staying right here at Brierwood." He shut the drapes and turned. "Rose, he did something to me just by looking at me. I couldn't move or speak."

Rose crossed her arms, thinking back to the times in the night when she had felt hypnotized and immobile. Could Taylor be right?

"He *is* the man in your aura!"

The possibility that her client and Seth Bastyr were one and the same was too shocking to contemplate. Unsure of what she thought, she lashed out. "Why shouldn't he be in my aura? He's been significant to me, especially since I've been working so hard to get the scarf done. Didn't you say that images of significant people could exist in a person's aura?"

"Yes, but have you ever met him before?"

"I've talked to him on the phone a few times."

"Ever seen him in person, Rose?"

"No, not until tonight."

"The figure in your aura was a perfect facial representation of him. How could you know what he looks like if you'd never seen him?"

"How do you explain his presence in my aura, then?"

"I think he's put himself there without your consent, like a brand, to mark you or control you."

Rose stared at him. Her eyes went as wide as the coins on her necklace. "A brand? No," she replied, her voice fading as if she were preoccupied. "No, that isn't possible."

"He's evil, Rose. His aura is black, totally black."

She seemed to hover on the brink of a decision, then rushed to the stairs as Edgar soared upward in front of her. Taylor followed her to the foot of the stairs and put a hand on the newel post.

"Rose, there are steps you can take. I've been reading about them."

She paused at the first landing and looked down. "I *am* going to take a step. I'm leaving Brierwood in the morning."

Before he could reply, she hurried up to the second floor and disappeared down the hall. Taylor sighed. He didn't think running would do her any good, since the man resided in her aura and would go anywhere she went, no matter how far from Brierwood she ran.

One thing he did know for sure—he wasn't going to sleep tonight, not when that man was roaming around the grounds. Taylor followed her up the stairs, determined to keep her in sight in case the man returned and tried to seep back into her aura. He didn't know exactly what he would do if the man did appear, other than blocking him physically, but he would deal with that problem when the time came. As for now, he had to come up with a reason to spend time with Rose and convince her to pass the night in his room. As he gained the landing, his calf hurt, providing him with an excuse to remain in her company. In spite of the pain, he smiled. He would ask Rose to doctor his leg. She would jump at the chance to practice her healing arts on his wound.

Rose spent the rest of the evening packing her belongings. She hated the thought of leaving all her fabric paints and supplies behind, but it would be impossible to take them with her, at least not now. She consoled herself with the fact that if she survived her birthday tomorrow she could always come back and get the rest of her things. She glanced at Edgar and wondered if the raven would follow her. She had nothing in which to transport him and knew he would fight being caged, anyway. If Edgar had to be left behind she would be devastated.

Just as she decided to turn in for the night, she heard a knock on her door.

"Yes?"

"It's Taylor."

Rose's heart flopped painfully. She longed to confide in him and feel the strength of his arms around her, but she had to keep him safe. And the only way she knew how to do that was to deny her love for him by holding him at arm's length.

Brushing a wisp of hair off her forehead, she walked to the door and opened it. "Yes?" she asked, wishing her voice wouldn't tremble so much.

Taylor looked around her. "All packed?"

"Yes. Bea and I will be leaving bright and early tomorrow."

"Is there a place where we can forward her paycheck?"

"No. I don't know where we're going just yet." She wondered why he had come to her door to make small talk. Such behavior didn't seem appropriate for him.

Taylor shifted his weight. "Can I come in for a minute?"

How could she deny him? Even with his scars, his face was so compelling that she felt a flush of fever wash over her. How would she ever purge that face from her thoughts?

"Just for a minute."

Taylor limped into the center of the bedroom and turned to face her. Next to his tall, broad-shouldered form, her lacy bed seemed fragile and ethereal, as if it floated above the floor. She couldn't imagine him in her bed and wondered if it would hold up beneath his masculine weight. Thinking of the bed, Rose left the door open, hoping he would take it as a sign that she wanted nothing physical to go on between them. To reinforce her resolve, she remained near the door.

"I was hoping you'd do something for me before you left Brierwood," he ventured.

"Such as?"

"Putting that stuff on my leg. You know that plant you told me about?"

"Plantain?"

"Yes. That's right."

"Why now?"

"My leg's been bothering me more the past few days. And I thought maybe I'd give your herbs a try."

Rose crossed her arms. His request sounded suspiciously like a ploy. Yet she could not deny a plea for help—or her own heart's desire to spend the last few hours at Brierwood with the man she loved.

"I'll have to go down to the kitchen and prepare a poultice."

"Will that take long?"

"Fifteen minutes or so."

"Do you have time to do it?"

"Well, yes...." She stared at him, wondering why he had suddenly changed his mind about herbal remedies, all the while hopelessly awash in the glint of his pirate's eyes.

"Good. Can I watch you make it? See how you do it?"

"If you want to."

"Are you finished packing?"

"Yes. We could go down now, if you'd like."

"I'll change into some shorts so it will be easier for you."

"All right."

Taylor brushed past her into the hall. She followed him and closed the door, wondering how she would ever keep from confiding her fears to him. If he so much as touched her, she knew she would crack and spill everything in a flood of aching need.

While Rose lingered in his doorway, Taylor slipped into a pair of black shorts and transferred his keys, lighter and Swiss army knife to its pockets. Years of sailing alone had trained him to carry those three items at all times. He stood near his closet, wishing he had something to give her in appreciation and also in celebration of her sale. Without the chilled champagne on the deck of the *Jamaican Lady,* he didn't know how to make a woman feel special, other than making love to her. He had never been the type to give flowers or candy, and he would feel like an idiot if he tried to write a poem or letter to convey his love. Yet he longed to do something to make the evening special.

Still feeling at a loss, he walked with Rose down the hall to the stairs in companionable silence. In the kitchen they were met by Bea, who was cleaning up the dinner dishes. Taylor made a pretense of watching Rose prepare the plantain leaves, all the while thinking of something he could give her in return. He decided to brave the danger of the wild dogs and look around in the garden for a perfect flower, a blossom that reminded him of Rose's own perfection.

Surely she would be safe while she bustled around the kitchen in Bea's company. Excusing himself for a moment, ostensibly to use the bathroom, he slipped out the rear door, hoping the two women couldn't hear him from the kitchen. Before he left the safety of the house, he surveyed the gardens ahead, paying close attention to the rhododendrons where he had spotted the black shapes earlier that evening. The garden appeared peaceful and deserted. He limped across the flagstones and past the sundial to an overgrown patch of lilies and forsythia. Taking out the lighter, he flicked it on and held it close to the lilies. One stood out among all the others—a beautiful peach-colored tiger lily with a crimson heart. Taylor flicked off the lighter and carefully plucked the flower. He sniffed it and discovered the appearance of the lily far surpassed its fragrance.

Just as he was rising to return to the house, he heard a strange noise, like the sounds of a string quartet warming up with none of the instruments playing the same note. Alarmed, Taylor glanced in the direction of the sound, near the sundial. He could see nothing but the fronds of poppies moving slightly in the breeze. He whirled around, searching for the dogs Rose had seen, wondering if they were surrounding him. Still he saw nothing. A sheen of sweat broke out on his skin as he let his vision shift to search for hidden shapes and colors. Sure enough, when he turned back to the sundial, he saw four black writhing shapes moving around the stone, as if in a slow dance. The shapes were indistinguishable—neither human nor canine. What were they? And what kind of beings had auras, but no physical shapes?

Taylor didn't know what to do He had to go past the sundial to get back to the house. Would they attack him if they saw him go by? How could they attack, however, if they didn't possess physical forms? What if they could funnel into his aura, just as the evil man had entered Rose's? Taylor's heart hammered in his chest as he stood in the garden holding the lily in one hand, his cane in the other, damning more than ever the fact that he had a lame leg. He could never hope to outrun anyone or anything.

Suddenly the back door opened and Bea's ample figure appeared in silhouette. "Who's out there?" she demanded.

The black shapes around the sundial vanished.

Taylor had never been so happy to see Bea.

"It's me. Taylor!" He stumbled forward, skipping on his good leg and hardly touching the ground with his bad one.

She backed up as he burst into the pool of light from the house.

"Mr. Wolfe! What are you doing outside?"

"Just getting some air." He tried to hide the flower, embarrassed to be caught holding it.

"I saw a strange light out in the garden and thought someone was poking around where they shouldn't be."

"That was my lighter you saw."

She shut the door after him. "You shouldn't be out here, Mr. Wolfe. What if those dogs happen to come back?"

"It seemed safe enough." He kept close to the wall, holding the lily between his thigh and the wainscoting.

Rose appeared at the end of the hall. "What's going on?" she called.

"Mr. Wolfe was outside. I thought he was an intruder."

Rose came closer. Taylor tried to move the flower behind him but stopped when he realized Bea would spy it then. One way or another, he was going to be found out. He could see the romantic moment he had envisioned—presenting the flower to Rose—fizzling before his eyes. He should have known better than to step out of his element. Frustrated, he let his arm drop to his side.

The slight movement caught Rose's attention.

"What's that you have in your hand, Taylor?"

"A flower." He wrenched his arm up. "A damn flower."

She stared at him in shock as he pushed it toward her. "For me?"

"For finishing your scarf. Congratulations." He shoved it into her hands and hobbled up the hall so she couldn't see his flaming face. He knew he was blushing. Even his ears were hot. He could hear complete quiet behind him, as if both women had been shocked into silence. He had never felt more like an idiot in his entire life. What had come over him?

Though he had asked Rose to tend to his leg, Taylor stormed up the stairs to his bedroom instead, too chagrined to face her. He was sure she wouldn't come to his room, not after the way he had come on to her the night before. He flung off his clothes, not bothering to put on his pajama bottoms, and crawled into bed. Why stay up all night to protect Rose? Who was he kidding? He couldn't even pick a damn flower for her without botching it.

A few minutes later, he heard a light rap on his door.

"Go away," he croaked.

"Taylor, I just want to come in for one minute."

"I'm tired."

"I'm coming in."

Taylor heard the door swing open and peered over his shoulder as Rose entered his room, carrying a tray. The lily was perched in a slender vase, a bright flag to remind him of his folly. Taylor grimaced at the sight and sat up.

Rose put the tray on the nightstand and straightened. He saw her gaze flit across his bare chest, then land on his face. "Thanks for the flower," she began. "I've never received flowers from anyone before."

"It's just a lily from the garden."

"But it's about the prettiest lily I've ever seen. Thank you." She reached down and placed her delicate hand on his rough cheek. Then, before he could resist, she leaned over and pressed her warm lips to his. Her hair tumbled forward in a silken wave that lapped at the side of his face and shoulder, tempting him beyond endurance. With a groan, he opened his mouth to take her in and raised his hands to grip the tops of her fragile white arms, but she immediately pulled away, defeating his efforts. He sank back to the pillows, realizing that she had offered only a chaste kiss and wanted nothing more from him. Choking back his disappointment, he willed his senses into submission and hoped she didn't notice the telltale sign of his reaction to her beneath the thin blanket and sheet draped across his midriff and legs.

"I thought you wanted me to see about your leg," she remarked.

"I changed my mind."

"You're wasting a poultice, Taylor, not to mention my time. I could apply it right now. I brought it with me."

Taylor glanced at the bowl of steaming green leaves, the pads of gauze and the metal teapot crowded around the lily. He had asked her to make the poultice. Only a jerk would make her go to all that trouble for nothing.

"Well, all right."

"You'll have to turn down the bedclothes."

"I'm buck naked." He glanced up, challenging her.

She flushed, which increased her allure. He could barely keep from pulling her down on him and forcing her to make love with him. He could still feel the touch of her hair on his skin, and the memory made him swell tighter with desire.

"Well, then..." She blinked rapidly. "Why don't you just expose your injured leg?"

"I'd like to expose more."

"Taylor, don't...."

Her blue eyes swam with a pleading emotion and something that looked very much like hurt. He felt ashamed for teasing her.

"All right." He slid his leg to the side until it was free of the covers.

His leg was well formed, with a strong calf, and his foot was slender, his toes long and straight. Except for his wounded leg, Taylor was a perfect male specimen, whose attributes were not lost on Rose. She had to force herself to work and not think about what other attributes lay beneath the covers.

Gently Rose removed the clumsy bandage he had applied earlier that day, all the while highly conscious of his gaze on her profile, and then carefully pulled back the dressing.

Rose stepped aside to allow the light from the lamp on the nightstand to illuminate Taylor's wound. The gash was still red and inflamed, as if it had been recently inflicted. Fresh blood spotted the bandage.

"How's it look, Doc?" he asked.

She glanced at him, avoiding the sight of his naked torso. "It doesn't seem to be healing."

"I know. And it has been throbbing lately."

"That isn't a good sign." She leaned closer. "It doesn't smell as if it's festering, though." She stood up and gazed at his leg. "This is the strangest thing I've ever seen."

Taylor shifted onto his elbows and raised himself up. "Put on the poultice, then, and see if it helps."

Rose reached for the warm plantain leaves. "This might smart for a minute," she warned.

"I can take it."

Gingerly, so as not to touch the wound with her fingers, she layered the plantain over his leg. He grimaced and narrowed his eyes, but he didn't make a sound, much to her admiration. Hot poultices on open wounds could be excruciatingly painful. After she finished applying the leaves, she soaked gauze in hot water from the teapot and draped it over the leaves.

"How are you doing?" she asked, glancing at his face.

"Fine." The terseness of his words spoke of the pain he was enduring.

"It will feel better soon, Taylor."

She touched his hand in a gesture of reassurance and smiled at him. He closed his eyes and lay back upon the pillows.

"You know a lot for someone so young," he remarked. "How old are you, anyway?"

"Twenty. I'm going to be twenty-one tomorrow."

"It's your birthday tomorrow?"

"Yes." She looked away, toward the shadows of his bathroom, wondering what the day would bring.

"You're trembling," he said. "What's wrong?"

"I'm tired, that's all."

He didn't press her further, and she was thankful that he accepted her explanation.

"How is your leg doing now?"

"It's tingling. Feels okay."

Rose lingered at his bedside, unwilling to cut short their conversation. She was reluctant to climb into her own bed, afraid that the nightmares of the past three evenings would return. But if she stayed with Taylor, she knew she would weaken and end up in his arms, giving him the fatal gift of her virginity. She inspected the sharp lines of his profile, wishing she could afford the luxury of kissing his lips again. But the temptation to do more would be too great.

"Rose," Taylor began, slipping his hand over hers. She allowed her palm to remain trapped beneath his. "We need to talk."

"About what?" Instantly she was on her guard and tried to pull away, but he held her fingers. She glanced up to find his black eyes boring into her.

"Don't pull away from me, Rose. Just listen for once."

She glared at him.

"Listen to me, for God's sake!"

Slowly she acquiesced and made her hand relax beneath his.

"Now, I know you don't put much stock in the aura stuff I've been telling you. I know you think you can escape the danger here by running away. But listen to me, Rose." He squeezed her hand. "You can't run away from this thing in your aura. He's there. And he'll be there wherever you go."

"How do you know?"

"Because I think he's like a leech clinging to a host. I believe he's what is called a vampire. An auric vampire."

"What's an auric vampire?"

"A creature that feeds off the energy force of another human being."

"I still have my energy."

"But for how long?"

"That's ridiculous!"

"Do you think I'd tell you something ridiculous? I'm a no-nonsense guy, Rose. I always have been and always will be. And when it comes right down to it, you've got to make a decision. Whom do you trust—a straightforward man like me, or that namby-pamby guy with gloves on who kisses your hand and wears an overcoat in the middle of summer? That's what it comes down to. Who do you trust?"

"You think my client is a vampire?"

"Yes. You've talked about a man coming to you at night. That was him—your client. He's even kissed you, hasn't he?"

Rose looked down, ashamed to admit what she'd let him do to her.

"He's already started to put his spell on you, just like old Count Dracula, by coming to you at night. Little by little he'll take you over to the dark side."

A chill passed over her. Taylor's words sounded preposterous, but they did offer an explanation for her nocturnal visitor and the supposed dark spot in her aura.

"I can't let him do that to you, Rose."

She felt the tug of his hand as he drew her down against his chest. Confused and frightened, she let herself collapse on top of him as his arms came around her. Rose clung to him tightly, nestling her cheek against the side of his neck.

"Don't you understand, Taylor?" she whispered. "He'll kill you just because you're involved with me."

"How do you know?" He ran his hand up and down her back, giving her a wonderful sense of security.

"It's part of the family tradition."

Taylor stopped caressing her. "This guy's part of your family?"

"Yes."

Taylor held her back so he could see her face. "Who is he? What's his name?"

"Seth Bastyr. He's my—" She averted her gaze and sat up. She couldn't tell him the truth—that Seth was both grandfather and great-grandfather, that he might even have been her father had her mother not escaped the charmed state of the ritual bride. What would he think of her once he found out about her family?

"Tell me, Rose!"

"I can't!" She pulled away, but he grabbed her wrist.

"I deserve to know. I *need* to know."

She looked down at her wrist and didn't struggle. Taylor's grip was too strong, and her will to resist was eroding. Taylor seemed to sense the change in her, and his hand loosened to slide down to her fingers.

"Rose, why can't you trust me?" His low, warm tone nearly broke her heart.

Rose lifted her gaze to his face. His black eyes glistened, full of care and concern. She swallowed and looked back down. "I do trust you, Taylor."

"Then why can't you tell me about your family?"

"Because I'm too ashamed!"

"Why? What's wrong with them?"

"They're strange." She raised her chin and shut her eyes, forcing back the urge to break into tears. "Please, I can't tell you any more."

He let go of her hand and sighed. "You don't have the corner on strange families, Rose. We all have our burdens of shame," he commented. "Every one of us."

"You do?" She didn't step away from the bed.

"Yeah." He lay back on the pillows, wove his fingers behind his head and smiled grimly, looking up at the high ceiling where the light couldn't reach. "But I guess I've never told anyone, either."

The way his arms angled outward made his chest look incredibly wide. Rose crossed her arms, as if to fend off the male magnetism of his exposed chest and the possibility that he would divulge his secret and expect her to do the same. Yet such a trade would not be fair, for she doubted the magnitude of his shame could ever approach hers.

"If you never tell anyone, it just eats you up inside, Rose."

"You don't appear to be eaten up inside."

"No?" He switched his attention from the ceiling to her face. "Maybe you just don't know me well enough. I've been called everything from a heartless bastard to an ungrateful cad.''

''You don't seem that way to me—not anymore.''

''That's because—well, with you it's different. *I'm* different.'' He quickly looked away. She studied him, wondering what he was trying to say. She thought of the lily he had thrust at her, almost as if he were ashamed of being gentle and giving. Perhaps Taylor didn't know how to behave in that way. She wondered what had made him become hard-hearted and gruff, but she wouldn't dare ask in case he demanded the truth from her in return.

''That's one of the reasons why I want to help you,'' he said. ''If I could keep that bastard from dragging you down, I just might be able to find some peace with myself.''

''Atonement?''

''In a way.'' He swallowed and glanced back at her. ''But more importantly, to save you, Rose. I can't let that bastard have you.''

''Even if it means your death?''

''Yeah. I'll put myself on the line.'' He clenched his jaw and closed his eyes. ''There's a first time for everything, isn't there, Brier Rose?''

''I can't ask that of you.''

''It has nothing to do with asking. I'm giving.''

''Why?''

CHAPTER TWELVE

"Why? Because when I was sixteen, an acquaintance of mine raped a girl from the wrong side of town. She took him to trial. I was to have been the key witness, but my father forbade me to say a word against the guy because it would have soured a deal my father was making with the kid's dad. So I kept quiet and lost my honor. The boy was cleared, but the girl was made the laughingstock of the town, and I heard later that she had a child by my so-called friend." He sighed. "The Wolfe fortune was built on lies and misery, Rose, and I was part of it. I could have done something about it. I *should* have done something about it, but I didn't."

He fell silent and lay with his eyes closed while Rose looked down at him. She couldn't believe that he would let something from so long ago haunt him. He hadn't been more than a boy when it happened. Surely he could forgive himself for that.

"You were a boy, Taylor. You were just trying to obey your father."

"I knew right from wrong, Rose. And what my father and I did was wrong. I still feel ashamed."

"Have you ever tried to contact the girl, to explain yourself?"

"Why? So she could slam the door in my face? What good would that do?" His eyes opened, and he looked directly up at her. "She'd call me a bastard. And she'd be right."

"It might be worth a try. She might surprise you."

"I doubt it." He sighed. "So that's my family, Rose. And that's who I am." He paused and looked up at her, as if waiting for her to speak.

What did she expect from her—to be told about the Bastyrs? She could never divulge the heinous practices of her family. Taylor thought the Wolfes were bad. He would be shocked to hear about the Bastyrs. Rose felt heat on her face, as if Taylor already knew the thoughts that shadowed her mind.

"So who are you, Rose?" he asked, enclosing her fingers in his warm grip.

She hesitated. Taylor deserved something in return for his confession, but what could she say? She wet her lips and decided to tell him the barest of facts. "Until a few days ago, I didn't know who I was, Taylor. But I've been told I come from a family called the Bastyrs."

"And what are they like?"

"The Bastyr family is very old, from what I've learned. They've always been different, ruled by a patriarch with peculiar tastes."

"What kind of peculiar tastes?"

"He—he—takes the females of the family."

"Takes them? What do you mean?"

Rose felt her cheeks flaming, but she plunged onward. "He makes them his bride, to keep the Bastyr line pure and strong."

"You mean he marries his distant relatives?" Taylor sat up and clutched her more tightly.

"Worse." Rose slipped her hand from his and turned away. "Your poultice needs to come off now."

"To hell with the poultice, Rose. What about the patriarch?"

Rose lifted the gauze strips. Her hands shook, and a muscle in her eyelid twitched uncontrollably, but she forced herself to attend to his leg and ignore his questions.

"Rose, don't do this to me!"

"I don't want to tell you any more." She threw the limp plantain leaves in the metal bowl.

"Is Seth the patriarch?"

"Yes."

"And you're turning twenty-one?"

"Yes."

"My God, he's come to make you his bride, hasn't he?"

She stared at him, her eyes burning with fear and loathing. "Yes."

Taylor returned the stare, obviously stunned by her revelations.

Grimly she returned to her task and wrapped Taylor's leg in a new bandage. He watched every movement she made while he lay upon the pillows, as if he were deep in thought.

When she finished, she clasped her hands in front of her.

"Well, that's it for the poultice. I'll check it before I go tomorrow and see if it's done any good."

"Rose, I don't give a damn about my leg."

She studied the edge of the cotton comforter, afraid to look him in the eyes. His voice sounded far too ragged.

"I'm more concerned about what we're going to do about Seth Bastyr."

"We?" She shook her head. "No, Taylor. This is my fight. My family. I don't want you fighting my battles."

"At least stay here for the night, so I can keep my eye on you."

Rose's heart skipped a beat, and she backed up a step to keep him from grabbing her wrist.

"Come on, Rose. I'm serious. I don't want you alone tonight, in case Seth shows up. I won't touch you, I promise."

"What if Seth does show up? What will you do, Taylor?"

"I don't know yet. There must be some way to keep him from entering your aura."

"How? With a wooden stake? Maybe I should wear a necklace of garlic."

"This is no joking matter, Rose. I've felt the evil of that man."

So have I, she wanted to say, but she remained silent.

"I don't want you out of my sight," he urged. "I'd feel safer if you stayed here, just in case he comes back tonight."

"No, Taylor, I couldn't."

"I insist. I'll keep my hands off you."

"You won't get a decent night's sleep on that couch."

"I'm not going to be on the couch."

"You're not?" She backed up another step.

"No. If Seth comes back, I want to be right next to you, not halfway across the room like last time."

Rose hesitated. She did want to stay. Perhaps if she spent the night with Taylor, she wouldn't have another bad dream. Yet could she trust herself or Taylor to remain apart during the night?

"I'll throw on some clothes, Rose. I won't touch you, believe me."

She inspected his face, paying close attention to his eyes to make certain he was telling the truth. Taylor seemed sincere, and she decided to trust him. After all, he hadn't made a move the last time she slept in his room.

"All right." The decision left her with a feeling of relief, as if she were doing the right thing.

"Good. I'll pull on my jeans, and we can go down the hall and get your nightclothes."

"I can do it."

"No. Like I told you—I don't want you out of my sight tonight, Rose."

Rose snuggled into the familiar security of Taylor's bed and pulled the cover up to her chin. She was highly aware of Taylor stretched out beside her, and she longed for the warm expanse of his chest and his strong arms to take the edge of the chill and fear off the evening. But he remained true to his word and didn't let so much as his foot graze hers. In fact, he slept on top of the counterpane with a separate blanket thrown across him for warmth. Rose sighed and shut her eyes. If she and Taylor could just survive tomorrow, perhaps they would spend a night together and know the miracle of exploring each other's bodies. She knew he wanted her, and she more than wanted him.

Rose closed her eyes, thinking of the way it would feel to make love with Taylor. But she had nothing to draw upon for her fantasy except for movies and books, which fell far short of how she imagined it would be between them. She fell asleep still trying to picture the way Taylor would pull her against him and show her how a man and a woman became one being.

Later that night she felt a hand stroking her hair.

Taylor?

"Ah, it's Taylor, now is it? Not Mr. Wolfe?"

Rose froze. The voice belonged to Seth Bastyr.

She felt Seth's hand venture down the side of her face and throat, but try as she might, she couldn't open her eyes. Where was Taylor? Didn't he know Seth had returned? Hadn't he heard the pipe-organ sound?

"You have become attached to Mr. Wolfe these past few days, haven't you, Roselyn?"

No. He means nothing. I'm—I'm just using him.

"For what?" The dry voice chuckled. "You don't fool me, Roselyn Bastyr. You love Mr. Wolfe, don't you?"

No. He's heartless. He's only out for himself.

"You are not much of a liar, my dear. How precious you are."

I am a liar. You've said so yourself.

"At one time, dearest Roselyn. But you learned your lessons well, didn't you? You were always such a quick child. To think of the things I could have taught you if your mother hadn't sent you away from me. And the things I still can teach you. Ah, Roselyn, you have no idea."

I don't want to learn. I want you to go away.

"Dear child. You cut me to the quick. I'm only here to reacquaint you with your heritage."

I don't want to be reacquainted. I like my life the way it is.

"That's because you haven't known anything else. But believe me, Roselyn, there is much more to the world than meets the eye, much more than Mr. Wolfe will ever show you. He is but a child himself."

Rose felt his hand upon her breast. This time the sensation filled her with a sense of disgust, now that she knew her own flesh and blood was touching her, and that the man who stroked her was probably centuries old.

How did you find me?

"It took many years, but my patience is vast. I tracked you by the mark you carry."

The mark in my aura?

"Why yes." His hand quit stroking her breast, as if he was surprised at her knowledge. "My dear, you continue to delight me."

Not my intent.

"Still, I have much to teach you, sweet Roselyn. And to-morrow we will begin a whole new life together."

I would rather die than become yours.

"Sweet liar. You've ached for my touch, as I have ached for yours."

You delude yourself.

"I suffer no delusion, Roselyn. I know you as I know myself. Your passions run deep, deep enough to match my own. Your passion and this place remind me of one I had so long ago—Constance. I will take you on the sundial in the garden, just as I took Constance."

Constance was the name she had been called during her strange dream the previous night. Was Seth referring to that same Constance? And if so, was she somehow connected to the past of three hundred years ago and to Seth? The possibility scared and repulsed her.

You'll never have me, Seth Bastyr. I loathe you.

"Not when you learn what I have to offer. Of all the brides I have taken, you—sweet beautiful Roselyn—will be premier, the mate I have awaited all these years. You shall make me young again. And I shall make you my queen.

I don't want to be your queen. I just want to be left alone.

"That, my dear, is not a possibility. You were born to become mine. However..." He stroked her midriff, running his hand down her belly. Rose tried to move away, hoping he wouldn't invade her any further, but she had little command over her body. "I can spare your Mr. Wolfe."

Spare him?

"Surely you realize he is destined to die when you become my bride." He caressed her thigh. "You won't believe the passion you will feel when we make love, Roselyn. It will be like a thunderbolt, a—"

I have no interest in that moment.

"That is because you don't know what it is like. But once you feel it, my dear, you will live for the instant the energy courses through every fiber of your being."

At the expense of someone else? No thanks.

"You will change your mind, my dear, once you have tasted the fruit of our union. And tomorrow will be like no other consummation. It will be a triumph, the zenith of the Bastyr tradition."

Rose loathed his touch, felt dirty wherever his fingers drifted. She couldn't fathom a lifetime chained to the bed of this man. She had to get away.

"There is nowhere to hide, Roselyn. You shall be mine."

What about Taylor? You said you would spare him.

"Mr. Wolfe? Yes, I could be persuaded to bargain for him."

What kind of bargain?

"I will give you his life if you will tell me where the emerald is—the one your mother stole from me."

The emerald?

"Yes. A large stone. Surely you know where it is."

Rose thought of the emerald in the wooden box and of Bea, who had said she'd kept the box hidden under her bed for fifteen years. If she revealed the secret location of the emerald, she might be jeopardizing Bea's safety. Yet if she didn't tell, she would send Taylor to his death.

"Thank you, my dear. That wasn't hard, was it?"

What do you mean? I told you nothing.

"Ah, but you did. You don't need to form words with those beautiful lips of yours, Roselyn. Those are for kissing, not for speaking."

You—you read my mind!

"Of course. We are on a similar—how do they say it these days?—a similar wavelength, you and I." He chuckled and caressed the side of her face. "Until tomorrow evening, my dearest Roselyn, when I return to make you mine."

He pressed an impassioned kiss on her lips. Rose cringed and willed herself to float away from him, somewhere far away where his mind couldn't follow.

Taylor woke up just as dawn sent a herald of light through a crack in the gauzy curtains. He pushed the hair off his forehead and sat up, wondering what time it was. As he tilted his watch to the light, he glanced over at the bed to see if Rose still slept. The bed was empty.

Taylor leapt to his feet, crushed by the possibility that she might have left at first light. Surely she would have said goodbye to him, wouldn't she? Last night he had felt a growing bond between them, as if they could work through this madness together and come out with something substantial.

He grabbed his cane and hurried out to the hall.

"Rose?" he called at the threshold of her bedroom. When he received no response, he opened the door and spied her bags still clustered near the closet.

"Rose?" he ventured farther into the room and checked the bath. She wasn't there, either. Perhaps she and Bea were downstairs eating a quick breakfast.

Taylor walked to the stairs and descended, noticing with every step that the pain in his leg was not as severe as it had been yesterday. Maybe the plantain had done more good than he had expected it would. Maybe the secret lay in tender loving care, the kind of attention he had received from Rose.

The kitchen was bare and showed no evidence of breakfast. Where could Rose be? He wandered out to the foyer, uncertain in which section of the house he should look.

Suddenly Edgar soared down from the chandelier and landed on the settee.

"Edgar," Taylor greeted the bird. "Where's Rose?"

The raven cocked his head. Taylor could have sworn the bird was listening to what he said. Then Edgar cawed, bobbing forward with the effort, and flapped down the hallway toward the back of the house.

Intrigued, Taylor followed him to the rear entry. He unlatched the door and looked out at the misty garden. The rear grounds had been transformed by morning fog into an alien world of drooping greenery and unrecognizable lumps and shapes. Through the fog he caught sight of something white fluttering near the sundial and an occasional splash of gray green where the shrubbery and clumps of flowers appeared and disappeared in the roiling mist.

Taylor stepped out and cautiously peered into the fog, wondering if the creatures he had seen the night before were still around. He let his vision slide out of focus in the hopes that he might see a clearer version in the hidden auric world, but the fog obstructed his special vision, as well.

"Rose?" he called, returning his gaze to the sundial. He didn't recall there being anything white near the stone-and-metal timepiece, and he wasn't about to venture into the garden without a damn good reason.

A muffled moan drifted his way.

Taylor stiffened. He took a step toward the sundial and paused, listening intently. The moan came again.

He limped across the flagstones, guided by the soft moan into the claustrophobic gray world of mist.

When he got within a few feet of the sundial he could see the outline of Rose's body where she lay, sprawled faceup on the hard, cold surface of rock, her white nightgown draped over the edge, her flaming hair in wild profusion around her ivory face. What in the hell was she doing out here? Had she walked in her sleep without him even knowing? What kind of protector was he?

"Rose!" he exclaimed.

She moaned and drew her arm over her forehead.

Taylor placed his palm on her elbow and gently squeezed. "Rose, wake up."

Her eyelids fluttered, and for a moment she gazed skyward until she realized she was not in his bed any longer. Shocked, she scrambled to a sitting position, leaning on one hand while she raked her fingers through her mane of rippling hair. Taylor watched the movement, wishing he had thought of brushing her hair from her face, for he longed to caress her.

"Taylor, what am I doing out here?"

"I was just about to ask you the same question."

"I—I must have walked in my sleep."

"Are you all right?"

"Yes. I'm just a bit cold."

"I can fix that." Taylor smiled and put down his cane. "Come here." He put his hands around her delicate waist and helped her to the ground. Then he pulled her against him and wrapped his arms around her. She didn't protest and instead held him tightly around his neck. He ran his hand over her hair, surprised to find it touched with dew. She must have been outside for quite a while.

"Did Seth come to you last night?"

"Yes," she remarked, dragging her hands down to rest on his chest. "But he didn't take me out here. I don't understand how I got out here."

"Never mind that. You're frozen. We'd better get you to the house."

Suddenly she pulled back. "Listen!"

"What?"

"I hear them!"

"Hear who?"

"The dogs! They're coming!" She grabbed his arm. "Taylor!"

Then he heard it, too, a snarling, growling sound coming from the herb garden. Taylor glanced in that direction and caught a glimpse of four black shapes in the fog.

He needed no further entreaty. Swooping down for his cane, he clutched Rose's hand and dashed for the back door, ignoring the screams of protest from his leg. The dogs pounded behind them and were close on their heels as they gained the flagstones of the patio. Taylor could hear their jaws snapping and their labored breathing mere inches from his feet. He pushed Rose ahead of him and whipped around, brandishing his cane. The four rottweilers bared their fangs and growled, pacing around him as if waiting for an opportunity to strike.

"Taylor!" Rose cried.

"Get in the house!" he shouted over his shoulder. One of the dogs leapt for his throat. He swung the cane and caught the dog in the rib cage. It fell, howling in pain, while the other three charged. Taylor staggered back, lashing out with the cane, and managed to hit a second dog in the head. By that time, however, the first dog had recovered. He grabbed the leg of Taylor's jeans and jerked his head, nearly toppling Taylor to the ground. If he went down, his throat would be ripped out in a second by the dogs. Frantically, he jabbed the rottweiler in the chest with the end of his cane while he half dragged the animal to the door.

Then Rose appeared at his elbow and bashed a wrought-iron chair across the dog's back. The rottweiler rolled away, yelping in agony. Taylor managed to pull open the door while he fended off another dog, and Rose threw another chair in the path of the remaining animals. Then Taylor pushed her into the house and fell in backward, hanging on to the handle of the door for dear life. If the dogs got in the house, he and Rose wouldn't stand a chance of surviving an assault in the hallway

Taylor threw his weight against the door and locked it and immediately the dogs fell silent. Shaken, he looked out the window beside the door and watched the dogs pacing the flagstones. Taylor remained at the window, his heart pounding like a jackhammer, until he saw the dogs take off toward the herb garden. Then he turned.

Rose was standing near the kitchen doorway, her face white, a knuckle to her lips. He tried to smile in reassurance, but his leg was a column of fire that consumed the grin before it made it to his mouth.

"Taylor, are you all right?" She ran to his side and took his upper arm.

"Yeah," he panted and put his arm around her shoulders. "Whose dogs are those?"

"I don't know. I think they're wild."

"God." He looked down at his tattered pant leg. "I hope they're not rabid."

"Did you get bitten?"

"Amazingly enough, no."

She squeezed his arm and he felt a warm feeling flood his senses.

"You throw a mean chair," he commented, heading toward the kitchen with her still tucked under his wing.

"Don't joke around, Taylor. They could have killed you!"

"But for some reason they didn't. Beats me why."

"I'm going to call the dogcatcher as soon as they're open. We've got to get rid of those dogs before they really hurt somebody."

"In the meantime, I'm going to make you a cup of coffee."

"I'll make it. You look as if you're in pain."

"I am. This damn leg of mine is like a curse."

"Sit down, Taylor," she urged.

He complied, grateful to take the weight off his leg. He sighed and eased his leg out straight in front of him. He ignored the throbbing in his calf and watched Rose as she reached up to the cupboard for a coffee filter and ground a handful of beans. "I might as well make enough for Bea," she commented with a smile, but the grin was only a shaky imitation. "After all that racket, I'm sure she'll be down, wondering what the fuss was about."

Taylor nodded, enjoying the sight of her puttering around the kitchen in the faint glow of the light above the sink. There was something intimate about sharing the kitchen so early with Rose, and he fervently hoped that Bea wouldn't come down too soon and break the spell. He wished he could spend more mornings smelling the earthy fragrance of brewing coffee and watching Rose arrange cups and saucers in her careful, quiet fashion. Yet if he didn't do something to stop Seth Bastyr, this would surely be the last day he ever spent with her.

"I forgot to wish you happy birthday," he remarked as she carried the cups to the table.

"Thanks," she replied. She slid his coffee in front of him, and her hands shook enough to rattle the china.

"Are you going to be okay?" He touched her wrist.

She sank to the chair nearby without breaking eye contact. "I'm scared."

Taylor curled his hand around hers. "So am I. But we'll get over this."

"Those dogs," she swallowed. "When they attack, I can hear them calling my name."

"Your name?"

"Yes. Roselyn, Roselyn, Roselyn. When they snarl I can hear my name."

"I didn't hear it."

"Maybe I'm just imagining it." She wrapped her long fingers around the base of the cup. "But I wonder if they're normal dogs, or if they're—"

"Part of the Bastyr curse?"

"Yes. I know it sounds crazy, Taylor." She shook her head and looked down. "I feel as if I'm losing my mind."

"You're not. There's a reasonable explanation. We just haven't found it."

"Bea told me that the Bastyrs have weird powers and that Seth is the most powerful one of all. But what is he? A man? A hypnotist? Or a vampire, like you've said?"

"If Seth Bastyr is a man, Rose, he's the embodiment of evil. His aura is black." Taylor took a drink of the steaming coffee. "Come to think of it, maybe the dogs are connected to him, because they have black auras, too."

"I don't think they're normal dogs. I've never had an animal attack me or even nip me. Never." Rose sipped her coffee and glanced at the doorway to the morning room. "And something else is odd."

"What?"

"It isn't like Bea to sleep through so much noise. I thought she'd be down by now."

"I was hoping she'd take her time." He stroked Rose's wrist, but she remained looking at the door.

"Maybe I'd better go see if she's all right."

"She's probably sleeping, Rose. Just relax for a minute."

"I can't." She stood up. "I have an awful feeling, Taylor, that this day is going to be filled with trouble. Starting with those dogs."

He rose. "I'll come with you, then."

CHAPTER THIRTEEN

Edgar swooped down and alighted on Rose's forearm as she and Taylor walked up the stairs. Though Rose stroked the raven, her eyes were focused on the floor above, and Taylor could tell that her thoughts were with Bea. When they reached the top of the stairs, she paused and sniffed.

"What's that smell?" she asked.

She had heard the dogs before he had. And now she smelled something. Apparently her senses were much more acute than his. Taylor inhaled but didn't notice anything different.

"Smoke!" she cried. "Down there!" Rose pointed to the end of the hall, where a puff of gray billowed from under Bea's door. "Bea's apartment!"

She broke into a run as Edgar flapped away squawking and headed in the opposite direction from the smoke. Taylor sprinted down the hall behind her, sure now that Rose's feeling of doom was an accurate forecast for the day. She gained the door before he did and reached for the knob.

"Wait!" Taylor cried. "Feel the door first."

She tested the wood with the palm of her left hand as Taylor came up behind her.

"Is it hot?"

"No."

"Okay. You can open it."

She turned the knob, but it rotated only halfway. "The door's locked," she exclaimed in a shrill voice full of panic.

"Stand back." Taylor dropped his cane and then threw his shoulder against the door, but it remained tightly shut. "Damn," he gasped, holding his bare arm. "I'll have to try kicking it down."

"But your leg—"

He ignored her words and the pain in his leg and backed up a pace, turning sidelong to the door. Then, standing on his bad leg, he kicked to the side, hitting the door near the latch. It burst open onto a room full of rolling smoke.

"Bea!" Rose cried, stumbling into the cloud. "Bea!"

Taylor coughed and held his hand over his nose. His eyes stung as he strained to see Bea's parlor through the smoke. He bumped into a chair and knocked over an end table, sending something that sounded like china crashing to the floor.

"Bea!" Taylor yelled. Neither of them got a response.

A strange sound crackled in the kitchen up ahead. Taylor grabbed Rose's hand. "The fire's in the kitchen! I'll go look there. Any other rooms on this side?"

"A bedroom."

"Check it!" He coughed and peered to the side. He had to get some kind of protection for his bare skin. A wet blanket would be ideal, but he would have to make do with the objects in the parlor, and the only available fabric was the long drapes near his elbow. He yanked the heavy curtains, pulling the fixtures out of the woodwork, and slid the rod out of the rings. While Rose headed off in the direction of the bedroom, he swirled the fabric over his head and shoulders and plunged through the smoke toward the kitchen.

Taylor groped his way across the parlor, stubbing his toes and knocking over furniture until he reached the kitchen. Flames licked the floor of the kitchen and leapt from a tall wastebasket to the towel hanging on the door of the refrigerator, but the fire seemed to be confined to a small area. Whatever was in the wastebasket burned like rubber tires, filling the apartment with a stench that made him feel lightheaded and nauseated. Then he caught sight of Bea in her blue housecoat, tied to a chair on the other side of the room. She was slumped in her bonds, her head hanging and her feet and legs lashed to the chair.

Taylor felt a dark shaft of dread at the thought that she might already have succumbed to smoke inhalation. For Rose's sake, he prayed that Bea was still alive.

"Bea!" he gasped, hunching beneath his fabric cloak as he hurried to her side. He picked her up, chair and all, and retraced his steps, straining with the weight of her ample body. The curtain dropped from his shoulders as he passed the wastebasket, and he felt heat from the fire on his bare back.

Ignoring his cramping muscles, he hobbled into the parlor.

"Rose!" he yelled. "I found her!" His voice came out hoarse and ragged from the smoke, and the words burned in his throat. He ran his tongue over his lips and struggled across the room to the door and out to the hall, where he set down Bea and the chair.

Gasping for breath, he leaned closer and eased back Bea's head, all the while wondering if Rose would soon find her way out of the apartment, or if she had even heard him. What if she had collapsed from the smoke? He couldn't think about it for a moment, not until he saw to Bea.

With tender fingers he felt the side of her neck and sensed a faint pulse. Heartened, he gently patted her cheek. "Bea, Bea! Wake up!"

He fumbled with the clothesline that was wrapped tightly about her torso, hands and legs, all the while throwing glances over his shoulder to see if Rose had found her way out of the smoke yet. He caught sight of Bea's eyelids fluttering open and felt a rush of relief. She would be alright.

Then Rose burst from the apartment, holding the skirt of her nightgown to her face. Her eyes streamed with tears. "You found her!"

"Yes. She's breathing. But just barely."

Rose sneezed and coughed as she stumbled forward.

"Here, Rose." Taylor held up an end of the rope. "Take over. I'm going back in to put out that fire."

"No, Taylor. I'll call the fire department."

"It might be a while before they can get out here. I'll see what I can do."

"No, Taylor!"

"Mr. Wolfe." Bea moaned, which caught Rose's attention and gave him enough time to slip away.

Rose blinked her watering eyes as she tried to untie the clothesline, but she could hardly see through the bleariness caused by the smoke. Her hands shook, and she kept stopping to encourage Bea, who coughed and sputtered and closed her eyes as if exhausted. The woman's face was unnaturally flushed from the fire, as were her hands and knees, and Rose only hoped that she hadn't been seriously burned.

At last the rope came free from around Bea's torso. Rose unwound it, dropping it to the floor, and then knelt at Bea's feet to unfasten the bonds at her knees and ankles. Whoever had tied Bea had made certain she would not wriggle free on her own. And that whoever was most likely Seth Bastyr.

Rose rebuked herself as she struggled with the knot. Why hadn't she listened to Bea's fears and left Brierwood when they still had time? Why had it taken so long for her to accept her past and believe in the dangerous power of the Bastyr family? This was all her fault. If it hadn't been for Taylor, Bea would surely have died in the fire. What if she still didn't make it?"

"Hang on, Bea," Rose urged, finally freeing the older woman's legs. She jumped to her feet and looked down at her grandmother.

Bea panted and opened her eyes.

"Rose," she croaked. "The emerald—"

"Never mind that. Can you walk?" Gently she took Bea's left arm. "We've got to get you out of this smoky hallway."

As if in answer, Bea held out a hand and clutched Rose's forearm. With great effort, Rose managed to hoist Bea out of the chair.

"All right so far, Bea?" Rose asked.

Bea nodded, her eyelids fluttering. Though her skin was tinged with ruddiness from the fire, Rose was not fooled by the appearance of color. Bea was on the verge of collapse from shock and lack of oxygen, and she had to get her some fresh air as quickly as possible. Rose drew Bea's arm across her shoulder and stooped slightly to support her, in case Bea suddenly lost consciousness. She only hoped she could withstand Bea's weight should she succumb.

Together they staggered down the hall to Rose's room. Rose pushed opened the door with her foot and urged Bea to the bed, where she helped her lie down on the comforter. Carefully she lifted Bea's legs and straightened her housecoat. Then she rushed to the bathroom to get a glass of water and cool wet towels, denying her own parched throat until she saw to Bea's care.

"Bea, drink this," Rose said, helping her sit up. Bea opened her eyes and tried to reach for the glass, but her arms sank to the counterpane, too weak and trembling to function.

Rose held the glass to her mouth. Bea gulped down the water and sighed. At least her breathing was less labored now. Rose eased her back against the pillows and then draped the hand towels on Bea's pink arms and legs, and covered her flushed face. She could see Bea relax beneath the soothing terry cloth.

Rose leaned closer. "Bea, I've got to call the fire department. I'll be right back."

"Okay, Rose." Bea's voice was reedy and weak, not at all like her.

Rose hurried to her writing desk and picked up the receiver of the phone. She dialed 911 and held the plastic handset to her ear, and only then noticed that the line sounded dead. Frowning, she depressed the button and waited for a dial tone. Nothing happened. Frustrated, she depressed it again and again. Nothing.

"Bea, my phone isn't working. I'll be right back."

Unnerved, Rose sprinted down the hall, her bare feet chilled and tender. She fled to Taylor's room and dashed to the side of his bed, to the phone on the nightstand. She grabbed the handset and listened. His phone had no dial tone, either. All the phones were out. Had the fire caused a short in the wiring? Or had someone cut the line? Rose felt the bottom of her stomach curl with fear. What should she do now?

Bea needed medical attention. Taylor might, too. And what if he couldn't get the blaze under control? Would Brierwood burn to the ground?

Frantic, Rose ran back to her room to check on Bea. She lay in the bed, still covered by the damp towels.

"How are you doing, Bea?" Rose queried, peeling back the cloth on her face.

"Better." Bea opened her eyes. They were dark with worry. "Much better."

"Shall I refresh the towels?"

"They're fine, Rose." She lifted the fingers on her right hand in an effort to touch Rose's hand in reassurance, but she was still too weak to move. She sighed and then looked up at Rose. "Mr. Wolfe saved my life," she said in wonder.

"Yes, he did. He's trying to put out the fire now. The phones are down, Bea, so I can't call the fire department."

"Oh, dear!"

"Rest, Bea." Rose straightened. "I'm going to see if Taylor is all right. Then I'll be back."

"But the emerald—" Bea put in.

"Later, Bea." Rose left the room, hoping she would find the box and the emerald unharmed by the fire. If Taylor had managed to put out the blaze, she would search the apartment for the emerald until she found it, just to ease Bea's fears.

A haze hung in the parlor as she entered the apartment, but at least the heavy, rolling smoke had dissipated to reveal a war zone of debris. Furniture lay upended and one of the windows was hung with half a curtain. Shards of Bea's prized china figurines littered the floor. But Taylor must have made some headway, if she could see this much of the parlor. Heartened, Rose walked across the floor, careful not to step on any of the broken china, while her eyes watered anew, for the acrid odor still permeated the air. She could hear Taylor banging around in the kitchen and continued in that direction.

The kitchen was in worse shape than the parlor. Taylor had dumped flour into the blackened wastebasket and poured it over the tile floor, creating a weird fallout effect. He had flung water on the now-steaming refrigerator and counter, making a sticky paste of the flour and ash, and was standing at the sink with his back to her as he filled another bucket. The stove and refrigerator were streaked with soot, as were Taylor's bare back and tattered jeans.

Before she could speak, he turned with the bucket and hurled the water against the counter near her, unable to stop in time when he saw her standing in the doorway.

She cried out, more surprised than anything, as the water splashed over her. She froze, holding her arms up in the air as her filmy nightgown was instantly sealed to her skin by the cold water.

"Rose!" Taylor gasped, horrified that he had drenched her.

For a moment they gaped at each other. She probably looked like a drowned rat and she was sure that Taylor could see the outline of every part of her body beneath her sopping nightgown. He, on the other hand, looked like a clown, with his face smudged by soot and his hair and lashes dusted in flour. His lips appeared cherry red in contrast to the flour. Suddenly those lips turned up in a grin.

He dropped the bucket, and it rolled around the floor, unheeded, as he began to chuckle. Rose grinned in return, crazy with relief that the fire was out and Bea and Taylor would survive. Taylor waded across the debris on the floor and swept her into his arms, laughing hysterically as he held her. She clung to him, the wet cotton of her clothing sticking to his dusty coat of flour and making a terrible mess. She couldn't have cared less, however. Taylor was safe. The fire was out. For the time being, everything was going to be all right.

"Sorry, Rose!" he gasped, shaking with laughter. "Oh, God!"

She pressed against him, her laughter abating as quickly as it had begun. She could have lost Taylor and Bea. She might have come into the kitchen and found him sprawled on the floor, dead. The thought doused the chuckle immediately.

"Taylor!" she exclaimed. "Oh, Taylor, you're all right!" Desperate and shaken she clutched his neck and stood on tiptoe to reach his lips, yearning for a kiss to reassure herself.

''Rose!'' He gathered her still closer. She could feel her limbs and torso molding to his touch as he brought his mouth down on hers. She kissed him, not in gentle surrender, but in harsh desperation, as if the kiss had to encompass everything she felt at that moment—fear, glory, love, relief and a great shattering need brought on by the calamity they had just survived. She felt as if this was their first real kiss and might very well be the last one she would ever share with him. She had to tell him everything with her lips—everything that burned in her heart and lit up her soul for him. Everything.

Taylor's hands spread across her back as his tongue entwined with hers. She could feel need and fear in both his kiss and the rigid way he held her, as if he, too, realized how close they had come to losing each other and how soon they would be tested again. His chin and nose grazed hers, branding her with dust and smoke as his lips claimed her. She wanted to be claimed. She wanted to be his. Forever and ever. But tonight, if she didn't find a way to escape, she would be lost to Taylor, never to know his touch again.

She longed to tell him how she felt about him. *I love you, Taylor.* The words ached in her heart and threatened to crawl up her throat. But how could she reveal her feelings now? It wouldn't be right. Her love would only bind him closer, make him even more determined to help her fight Seth Bastyr. She knew now that Taylor's sense of honor and duty would never let him turn his back on her. And if love were involved, he would probably sacrifice himself to save her. She couldn't take that chance. She swallowed back the words she yearned to say and squeezed her eyelids shut, pressing out tears of frustration and sorrow. What could she do? How could she save the life of this man who had become so precious to her?

The only way to save him was to run from Brierwood. If she left, she would take the Bastyr curse with her, allowing Bea and Taylor to resume their normal lives. The trick was in leaving. She couldn't call a cab. The phones were down. She would have to make a run for the carriage house, where the Jacobys' car was parked, and hope to escape the wild dogs. She knew her chances of succeeding were almost nil, but she had to try. And if the dogs killed her, she would still succeed in a way, for certainly with her death both Taylor and Bea would be released from danger.

Resolved to leave Brierwood as soon as possible, Rose gave Taylor an extra hug, knowing the embrace would have to last her forever. He squeezed her back and then looked down at her. All laughter had died in his eyes as well, and his mouth was set in a grim, straight line.

"Rose, do you have to be a virgin to become a bride of the patriarch?"

"Yes."

"What would happen if lost your virginity before to-night?"

She felt a hot shaft of desire course through her at the mere mention of making love. "I—I don't know."

"If you weren't a virgin, old Seth Bastyr would probably reject you."

"Yes, but—"

"And if he's some kind of vampire, he only comes out at night, right?"

"Yes."

Taylor brushed a strand of hair from the side of her face. "If you lost your virginity today, Rose, when Seth wasn't around, we might just save you yet."

She stared at him, longing to tell him to ravish her, to tear off her nightgown and take her on the floor right now, regardless of the flour and ash. But she recalled the warning in her mother's letter and was afraid to take the chance. So far, her mother's information had been correct. If she had heeded the advice in the first place, she might have avoided much of the trouble they'd experienced. She glanced away, distraught.

"Unless," his voice lowered, "you don't want to go to bed with me."

His words hung in the air, awkward and challenging.

Rose met his smoldering gaze and saw two patches of red blossom beneath the dust on his cheekbones.

"I have been warned not to," she put in. "Something terrible might happen."

"Like what?" He cupped her elbows. "Don't you think it sounds like an empty threat, the kind a worried parent makes?"

"I don't know. I just shouldn't do it. What if you get hurt! Or killed?"

"I've never suffered any damage from a woman yet. And neither have they. In fact, we rather enjoyed ourselves."

Rose blushed. "But I'm not your run-of-the-mill woman, either."

"That's right," he replied softly. "You aren't. But, Rose—"

"I've got to check on Bea," she interrupted, afraid that he would press her further. She knew she should leave immediately, before she changed her mind. When she pulled away from him, he reluctantly let her go. She headed for the parlor.

"Rose?"

She paused and looked back at him. He sighed and gazed at her as if he wanted to say something. Then he seemed to think better of it and stuffed his hands in the pockets of his jeans. "The virginity idea—it wasn't just a ploy to get you into bed."

"I know." She smiled sadly and hurried out of the apartment, promising to look for the emerald after Taylor was finished.

Rose saw to Bea's comfort and then stood near the bed, deep in thought as she considered Taylor's offer. No one really knew what would happen if Seth found out she had lost her virginity. So far, all the Bastyr women had been maidens when taken during the ritual. Of course, Seth would be enraged to find her virginity stolen from him, but why should she care? At that point, her life would mean nothing to her. Her memory would be wiped out, Taylor would be lost to her, and she would be Seth's prisoner for the rest of her life. If Seth killed her out of spite and rage, it really wouldn't matter.

Rose crossed her arms and looked out the window at the sundial in the back garden. What if she ran to the carriage house and the dogs attacked her and killed her? She would never know Taylor's love. To die before knowing him intimately was too painful to think about. What if she did give herself to Taylor? Would Seth reject her? If he did, she would be free to live her own life. If he didn't reject her and chose to punish her or kill her, at least she would have had the opportunity of knowing what it was like to make love with Taylor. Any way she looked at it, she wanted to give herself to him.

With her decision came a sudden piquancy, a compelling need she had never felt. She had to seek him out immediately and ask him to make love to her. A rush of heat passed through her as she slipped out of her room. What would she say to Taylor? How would she ask him to take her? Would she simply disrobe and offer herself? How did one ask such a thing of a man? Her mouth went dry as she hurried down the hall to Bea's room. She walked through the smoky apartment, searching for Taylor, but he wasn't there.

Next she tried his room. She could hear his shower going as she approached the door. Her first thought was to knock. Then she reconsidered and quietly pulled it open. He didn't call out to her. Obviously he hadn't heard her come in over the spray of the water.

Still in bare feet and wet nightgown, she padded across the floor to the bathroom, which was roiling with steam. The Boston fern fronds trembled in the wafting air currents. Rose paused at the threshold and glanced at Taylor's indistinct form through the frosted glass of the shower door. She realized she smelled of smoke and remembered that her nightgown was plastered with flour and water. Why hadn't she thought of bathing first before coming to him? How desirable would she appear to him? She was crazy to have come into his room like this.

Before she could turn and flee back down the hall, she saw the shower door slide open slightly.

"Rose?" Taylor's tanned face appeared in the opening. His raven hair was slicked back, and beads of water hung in his lashes.

"I—I just came to—" She flushed hotly, losing her nerve altogether.

He scanned her bedraggled nightgown and her face. Then he tilted his head and slowly smiled. "To scrub my back?"

"Taylor, I—" She backed up a step, wondering how she would ever extricate herself from this situation with any semblance of grace. What had possessed her to come to his room?

"Shut the door and come in, Rose. All the heat's going out."

Thankful that he hadn't asked the reason for her presence, she pulled the door shut.

"Come here," he continued.

She ventured closer, stepping onto the plush bath mat. Swallowing her embarrassment, she looked up at him. "Taylor, I—I changed my mind."

For a moment he stared at her, as if disbelieving the words she had just uttered. For an awful moment more, she was afraid that he might ask her to explain what she meant, and she wasn't quite certain if she could come right out and say what she wanted of him.

"Then take off that nightgown," he finally replied. "And come on in."

He winked at her and left the door slightly open, as if expecting her to obey him.

Rose hesitated. She hadn't anticipated joining Taylor in the shower. She had visualized the act of love as taking place in a bed, with a low lighting and plenty of blankets to shield her nakedness from his gaze. She wasn't anxious to step into the lighted cubicle of the shower and meet him face-to-face with nothing to hide behind but a washcloth or a bar of soap.

"Rose?" he called above the thunder of the shower.

Rose frowned. What kind of coward was she, to want to hide from him? He'd already seen her breasts. And what did she have to hide from him, anyway? She wanted to give him everything—her heart and soul. No holds barred. This was not the time to hang back.

Yet, what would he look like naked? She had never seen a naked man before. She glanced at his blurred shape and fought down the clamoring of her heart. She had to carry this through. She *wanted* to carry it through. She wanted to see him bare and beautiful, as beautiful as she'd dreamed he would be. And she wanted to offer her own nakedness without reservation. With trembling hands she pulled her damp nightgown over her head and slipped out of her panties. Then she eased open the shower door and stepped in.

She looked up immediately, not daring to take in his full figure. Taylor stood facing her, his back to the spray. His powerful body appeared to fill up the small enclosure. He looked incredibly dark and tall against the white tile. Drops of water clustered on his chest and accentuated the streak of hair that feathered down the center of his firm abdomen. He stood there gazing at her, with his intense, inscrutable expression darkening his eyes.

"Rose," he murmured, struck by the sight of her.

She flushed. Then he reached out for her, cupping her shoulders and slowly sliding his hands down the backs of her arms until her chilled fingers rested in his hot palms. Without breaking eye contact, he drew her toward him as if leading her in a dance. Mesmerized, she let him pull her closer until their bodies touched—first her nipples to his warm chest and then her belly to his hips. The sensation of his hard wet body against hers was like a bolt of electricity that sent her heart hammering out of control. She gasped and reached up, linking her arms around his neck to keep from collapsing out of sheer shock.

Taylor surrounded her in a warm embrace, one hand at her back and one in her hair. Slowly he slid both hands down her back to her rump and lifted her slightly against him.

"Rose," he whispered, his mouth near her ear. "Are you sure of this?"

"Yes." Her voice wavered, but her body knew a conviction more solid than anything she had ever experienced. She wanted Taylor. Every cell in her body wanted Taylor. Her mouth wanted to kiss him, her breasts ached for his hands and lips, and deep inside she longed for him, even though she had no way of knowing what it would feel like to encompass him.

Between them she felt the strange and wonderful length of him grow and harden. She started to say something, but he bent down to kiss her, and the shower spray broke over the top of his head to splash her face and hair. Water drenched her upturned face and streamed down her cheeks, but she was hardly aware of it. All she could feel was the way his naked skin burned against hers and the way his lips took possession of hers. The inside of his mouth was even warmer than the water that drenched them, and his kiss harder than the relentless pounding streams. He crushed her tightly, nearly lifting her off her feet. He had never kissed her this way before, with such dominating strength, and she had never kissed him back with such needful abandon.

Taylor pressed feverish kisses on her lips, her cheeks, her eyelids and her temples while the water sprayed around them, and Rose let herself melt into him, feeling as if the water consecrated them, as if she were being born again in the spray. In that instant she knew that this moment with Taylor would sustain her to the end of time, that she would never need more than this to know heaven on earth. Closing her eyes, she lifted her face to him and moaned his name as if chanting a prayer.

The water thundered in her ears as he turned and backed her against the wet wall of the shower. She was lost—lost to the noise, to his hot demanding mouth, to the way he took possession of her, and the way his long hands splayed over her derriere.

"Ah, Rose!" he exclaimed, lifting her up and pinning her against the tile. She felt his rigid shaft between her thighs and knew the moment of truth had arrived. In a few seconds she would be his. Another electric shock zapped through her. She cried out and lolled her head back. She felt the tip of him against her and wrapped her legs around his hips.

"Damn—" Taylor gasped, surging against her. He dropped his head to the small of her shoulder and crushed her to the tile. She felt the rigid length of him pass across the unbelievably sensitive part of her. When she tried to adjust to accommodate him, he squeezed her rump with both hands and lowered his mouth to her breasts.

"No," he breathed. "Not yet!"

As he bent down to suckle her, the shower hit her full force. She looked down at his raven head, taking the spray as if being anointed, writhing in ecstasy as he drove her crazy with longing. She wanted him so much, that she almost cried out in supplication. Slowly Taylor raised his head, kissing her exposed throat and her lips, while his hips moved against hers.

"Taylor!" she pleaded. She couldn't stand much more.

"We've got to get out of this shower," he replied. "This is your first time—"

"Taylor!" She raked her nails down his back, arching against him with a hunger that was about to overwhelm her.

"Rose, this isn't the place to—"

She ran her hands down his slick muscular back to hold him against her. Her breath came fast and hard as she felt him at the entrance of her most private opening. She shifted her hips to guide him closer, and he groaned.

"Turn it off," he said. "Turn off the damn shower!"

She fumbled for the handle of the shower and pressed it down as Taylor reached back and yanked open the door. The next thing she knew, he had lifted her out of the tub. She straddled his hips as he sank to his knees on the floor of the bathroom. She felt the soft plush fabric of the bath mat as he laid her upon it.

"It might hurt," he said against her lips.

"No," she murmured, running her hands into his glossy wet hair. "Not with you. I want you, Taylor." All she was aware of was the way her body screamed for him. She didn't think of the pain, of the consequences, of the moment after. All she wanted was to take him inside of her and complete herself by engulfing him.

"Taylor!" she urged. "Just—oh, Taylor! Please!"

He knelt above her, taut and dripping wet. Then he bent his elbows and lowered himself to her, probing her with gentle urgency. He seemed incredibly big, unbelievably blunt, uncompromisingly male.

"Don't move," he warned, pulling back. "Just don't move for a minute."

She closed her eyes and reached for his shoulders, lost in the blind bliss of anticipation. She felt his hand on her, making certain she was ready for him. Even the touch of his finger was enough to make her arch upward.

His breath blew on her face, hard and strident.

"Tell me if I hurt you."

"Taylor, just—just do it!" She clutched his hard shoulders. His arms were like columns of marble.

Rose heard him suck in a breath while he pushed into her. She lifted her hips. He leaned closer and clutched her hips in his big hands. The pressure of his manhood against her delicate flesh increased as he pulsed against her. Rose opened her legs to allow him more room. And suddenly he was partially inside her. She gasped at the strange invasion. Then he pulled away. Why was he leaving? Desperately, she clutched his back, afraid that he wouldn't keep going.

"Don't stop!" she cried in a hoarse voice.

"Don't worry. I won't. I can't!"

With a grunt, he shoved into her, hard and insistent this time. She felt a twinge of discomfort as his shaft came up against her maidenhead. She gasped as he pushed further into her, all the way into the very depths of her. For a moment he remained motionless, as if trying to gain control over himself. She glanced up at him and saw that his eyes were tightly closed, his mouth set in a grim, determined line, almost as if he were suffering. That she could make him lose control gave her an awe-inspiring sense of power.

Then his mouth sank upon hers, and she met his kiss in a glorious melding of body and soul. A rapturous fulfilling sensation obliterated the slight pain as he moved back and forth, letting her get accustomed to him. He twined his fingers in her wet tresses, while his tongue plunged into her mouth. For a long moment he lay atop her, gently undulating against her. Finally, his lips broke from hers.

"Okay so far?" His voice was husky.

"Yes!" she gasped. "Oh, Taylor, yes!"

She squeezed his arms as he drew back and pushed in again, this time more forcefully, and again and again until the surface of his skin broke out in a sweat. Rose held on for dear life, surprised that the act of lovemaking could be so violent.

"Rose. Oh, Rose!" He sank his head to the small of her shoulder. His damp hair tickled her neck, sending a layer of chills across her feverish skin. She stroked his hair and moved beneath him, smiling and gasping with each new sensation.

And soon he was plunging into her, completely uncontrolled. She wrapped her legs around his waist.

"Don't move!" he cried. "Don't move, Rose!"

"I'm not!"

"Ah, sweetheart!" he gasped. He thrust against her again and again.

Suddenly, he pulled out.

"No!" she wailed. She grabbed his arms.

"We've got to go to the bed. Not here! This is your first time—"

"I don't care!"

She felt devastated, desperate against the burning flame of need that flared deep inside her. If he didn't return to her, she would die of wanting him. She reached down and surrounded his shaft with her hand, urging it back toward her.

He moaned.

Ignoring his protests, she guided him to her, amazed at his silken firmness. "Stay, Taylor, please!"

With a growl of passion, he yielded to her demands. He drove into her, flattening her against the bath mat, pummeling her mercilessly, a slave to his desire for her.

"Oh!" she exclaimed. Something new was happening to her. She could feel a wave of something she could only describe as anxiety building deep within. She writhed, feeling as if she would crawl out of her skin, or shatter into oblivion.

He pinned her wrists to the mat and ground into her, his abdomen rubbing against hers in a frenetic rhythm. She reached for his mouth and arched into him, taking each assault with a thrust of her own. Just when she thought she would go mad with need, she felt him burst deep inside her, filling her with a molten warmth that matched her own. Rose cried out, astonished by the uncontrollable spasms that rocked her. He let go of her wrist and braced himself on his palms while she clutched his wide shoulders. Then she filled her hands with the muscles of his buttocks and her mouth with the strong wedge of his tongue, and for a long while refused to release him.

They hung there, both lost to rapture, barely coherent of the time or place. Then Taylor collapsed on top of her, raggedly sighing in exhausted completion.

She tried to think of a way to tell him how he had made her body sing, but words failed her. And after a moment, she was glad she had kept silent, for the time they lay quietly together, fused into one being, was more precious than anything she could have said. She lay back, vaguely aware of the cold tile beneath her head, and tried to catch her breath.

After a few minutes Taylor rose up on one elbow and looked down at her. His eyes glistened a deep brown, their usual hard blackness softened by such newfound intimacy. His hand slid up her torso and caressed her breast. He kissed the rigid nipple. "That was incredible," he murmured in his understated way.

"Yes," she replied and looked into his eyes. "Taylor, whatever happens, I'm glad I lost my virginity to you."

"So am I." He caressed her cheek, pushing back the hair at her temple.

"And, Taylor?"

"Yes?"

"Would it be possible for you to do it one more time before I go?"

Taylor smiled down at her. "Brier Rose, I'm your man."

Later, Rose slipped back into her damp nightgown and pattered down the hall to her bedroom. She could feel a warm flush over her entire body—the aftereffect of Taylor's lovemaking—and hoped that Bea wouldn't notice and ask questions. Luckily, Bea was lying on the bed with her eyes closed, and Rose was able to hurry past to the bathroom and take another shower. She wished she could have spent the rest of the day in Taylor's arms. She hated to wash away the scent of him, as if sloughing off his memory. But

Bea needed her, and they had too much to worry about for her to spend the day making love.

As she turned on the water, she thought of being in the spray with Taylor. She would never take another shower without thinking of him.

Taylor knocked on the door of her bedroom twenty minutes later. He had showered again and was dressed in a pair of jeans and a white shirt that set off the blue highlights in his hair. For an instant they simply stared at one another, savoring the secret they shared. Rose felt a blush spread over her skin as he gave her a low smile full of warmth and intimacy.

Though she had seen him many times, she was struck anew by his good looks whenever he entered a room. She wondered if the reaction would ever wear off with time. She doubted that it would—and longed for the opportunity to prove her theory correct.

She had changed into a simple blue cotton smock. She resumed braiding her wet hair as Taylor walked across the floor toward her.

"How are you doing, Bea?" he asked, looking down at the older woman.

Bea actually smiled at him. "Much better, Mr. Wolfe, thanks to you."

"What happened to you this morning? Who tied you up?"

"Why, that Mr. Bridges—Rose's client!"

"Taylor thinks Mr. Bridges and Seth Bastyr are one and the same," Rose put in.

Bea glanced from Taylor to Rose and back again. "He does?"

"Yes."

"Oh my!" Bea fingered the collar of her robe. "Oh my, that would explain it, then. I thought he had just come to rob us!"

"Rob us of what?"

Bea's hand spread out at the base of her throat. "Of the emerald."

"What emerald?" Taylor questioned, sitting on the edge of the mattress to ease the weight off his leg.

"An emerald Rose's mother entrusted to me to keep Rose safe. We both wear emerald rings as a talisman against the Bastyrs. We don't dare take them off for fear of becoming overpowered by that awful family."

Taylor glanced at Rose. He had noticed the absence of her ring yesterday morning. "Why have you taken yours off, then, Rose?"

Rose's gaze darted to her own hand, as if in surprise. Bea sat up in horror. "Don't tell me you aren't wearing your ring, Rose!"

"I didn't notice it was gone." She held out her hand and stared at her fingers. "I wear it so much that I rarely think about it." She frowned. "I don't remember taking it off."

Bea hung her head in defeat. "That's it. First Donald's. Now yours. All they need is mine now."

"Your husband had an emerald, too, Mrs. Jacoby?" Taylor asked.

"Yes. But when the setting fell out, he became vulnerable and they killed him."

Taylor saw Rose's head rise in surprise, as if she hadn't known.

"The Bastyrs killed your husband?" Taylor went on, trying to get more information to use against Seth.

"Yes."

"But I thought he died of a heart attack or something," Rose countered, her face blanching. "Natural causes...."

"No, Rose. Didn't you notice that the plants all around him were withered and dried up, as if something had sucked the life out of them?"

Rose ran her fingers through her hair. "Yes. But what could have done that?"

"Seth could have." She set her jaw in determination. "He killed my son and my husband. I'll die before he gets to you."

"But what about my mother's emerald, the big one?"

"He's got it, as well. That's what I've been trying to tell you, Rose. Seth Bastyr came into my room last night, and I thought he was Mr. Bridges."

"What did he do?" Taylor asked.

"He asked me for the emerald. When I refused to give it to him, he told me I'd be sorry. Then he tied me up and said he'd take it himself. He seemed to know right where to look for it."

Rose rubbed the bare finger of her hand where the ring should have been. Seth had read her mind during the night and then had gone to Bea's room to steal the stone. Once again she was reminded that the danger Bea had been subjected to was the result of her own bullheaded foolishness. She put a knuckle to her lip and knew what she had to do.

She could hear Bea and Taylor still talking, but they sounded as if they were far away.

"Why didn't Seth just kill you?" he asked.

"He couldn't, not when I was wearing the emerald ring. But he probably thought I'd die in the fire."

Rose swallowed and stood up. There could be no more death, no more killing. It was time for her to leave Brierwood, time to make her run for the carriage house.

CHAPTER FOURTEEN

Her only obstacle was Taylor's concern for her safety. She had to invent an excuse to get away from him. Rose brushed out the wrinkles of her dress and adopted a casual tone. "Since you're here, Taylor, would you stay with Bea for a minute? I need to get something from the kitchen."

"I don't want you going off by yourself."

"Bea really shouldn't be left alone yet. Besides, I'll only be a moment."

He surveyed her. "I don't think it's safe, Rose."

"You said yourself that Seth is a vampire. If he is, he won't be out and about in the daylight. I'll be perfectly safe."

"A vampire?" Bea screeched in surprise. "What are you talking about?"

"Why don't you fill her in on your theory, Taylor, while I go downstairs?"

"Mrs. Jacoby might not want me to stay with her—"

"I don't mind." Bea pushed up her glasses. "I misjudged you, Mr. Wolfe, thinking you were a Bastyr, and for that I'm sorry. I was just so afraid for Rose, you understand."

"I understand, Mrs. Jacoby. Seth Bastyr is a dangerous man."

"I'd like to hear more of your theory about him." Bea glanced at Rose. "But I still don't think you should be going off alone, Rose."

"I'll come right back. I need to get some medicine." She hurried to the door.

"Then hurry right back, dear."

"I will," Rose lied, knowing that she wouldn't see Bea or Taylor again. She wished she could look at both of them one last time, to imprint their images on her mind, but she couldn't allow herself the luxury of a final gaze for fear that one of them might suspect her motives.

She slipped out of the room and down to the kitchen to get the car keys, which Bea kept on a rack by the pantry door. Edgar soared through the doorway and landed on the back of a kitchen chair.

"No, Edgar," she said, slipping the keys into the pocket of her dress. "You can't come this time. Not where I'm going."

A tear slipped down her cheek as she crossed the floor to him. She knelt on the floor beside the chair and reached out to stroke his back.

"Dear Edgar," she crooned. "I'll miss you."

He gazed at her sideways, in his peculiar fashion, and angled his head, reminding her of the way Taylor tilted his head when he studied her. Tears streaked down her cheeks as she thought of Taylor. She wished she could have embraced him one last time and told him how much she would miss him, how much she had come to love him.

"I've got to leave you all here," she whispered, scratching Edgar's head. His eyes closed in hedonistic appreciation, as if he were heedless of her trouble. "It's the only thing I can do." His form shimmered through her tears. "I've got to face my problem alone."

He half opened a lid and looked at her.

"Be good, Edgar, my friend," she murmured. Then she slowly got up and heaved a sigh. Nothing stood in her way now. She would open the back door and run for the carriage house. Grimly, she wiped away her tears with the backs of her hands while she walked to the utility room near the rear entry. She got her running shoes, pulled them on and laced them, trying not to think about what lay ahead. Then she padded to the back door and looked out. The garden stretched outward, bathed in morning sunshine, with dew twinkling on the leaf tips of the rhododendrons, and the faces of the poppies and lilies opening to the brilliant blue June sky. The fir trees beyond the sundial stood unmoving, their dark green branches tipped with new buds. Nothing disturbed the peaceful green of the garden, and it was hard to imagine that anything evil at all existed at Brierwood.

But Rose knew the truth. Beneath the flowers and the sunshine of Brierwood was a network of secrets and debauchery, a network as finely woven and deadly as a spider-web. And she was the hapless fly.

She unlatched the door and warily poked out her head, glancing down both sides of the house. The overturned patio furniture reminded her of their narrow escape from the dogs earlier that morning, and a shudder coursed through her. Carefully, she surveyed the few shadows at the edge of the foundation plants and along the herb-garden wall. The rottweilers were nowhere in sight. She listened intently for the sound of their panting or their strange chant of *Roselyn, Roselyn, Roselyn.*

No noise broke the stillness of the garden, not even the song of a bird.

Senses straining for the slightest sound or movement, Rose ventured out to the patio and silently closed the door behind her. She had a nearly overwhelming urge to leave the door ajar, but she was afraid that, should the dogs attack, they would get into the house and endanger Bea and Taylor. She couldn't allow her fate to jeopardize the others any longer.

The carriage house was about a hundred feet from the main house, accessible by both the drive in front and a walkway from the patio in back. All she had to do was run along the path between two buildings and unlock the side door of the carriage house. A hundred feet wasn't a great distance, especially for a healthy young person. Yet her heart pounded as if a chasm thousands of feet deep stretched between her and the outbuilding, and she had to run across a felled log to reach the other side.

Glancing right and left again to make sure the dogs weren't around, Rose stepped onto the narrow cement pathway bounded by lavender impatiens. The moment her tennis shoe came in contact with the walk, she heard a familiar, dreaded snarl.

Roselyn, Roselyn, Roselyn.

For a moment she stood poised in midair, undecided what to do. If she turned back, she would be sentencing Taylor and Bea to certain death. If she ran for the carriage house, the dogs would rip her to shreds.

"No!" she cried, unwilling to choose and angry that she had to make a choice at all.

The dogs bolted around the carriage house, heading right for her, as if they knew her plan of escape. The instant she saw them charging at her, Rose whirled around and fled back to the house, skittering across the flagstones of the patio, and flinging herself toward the door.

She pulled it open just as the rottweilers scrambled around the toppled wrought-iron chairs. Only a few strides ahead of them, she dashed into the house, slamming the door behind her. Once again, as soon as she returned to the house, she heard no more of the dogs. She slumped against the wall.

She had failed. In the split second when she had been forced to choose between life and death, she had chosen her own life over those of Bea and Taylor. How could she have been so weak, so selfish? Damning herself for being a coward, Rose backed into the hall, never taking her eyes off the door. Behind her, she heard Taylor thundering down the stairs.

"Rose!" he called. "Rose!"

"I'm here," she answered, anguish hanging in her voice like an old curtain.

Taylor trotted down the hall, using his cane to aid his injured leg. "What happened?"

"The dogs!" she replied. "They came back."

"You didn't try to go out, did you?" He took her shoulders.

Rose hung her head. "I tried to get away, to see if Seth would go with me and leave Brierwood alone."

"Rose—"

"But it's like the dogs can read my mind, Taylor." She looked up in distress at him. "It's as if they knew what I was going to do!"

"Read your mind? How?"

"I don't know. Last night Seth read my mind about Bea's emerald. That's how he knew where to find it. Perhaps the dogs are connected to him."

She tried to pull away, but Taylor only wrapped his arms around her and drew her against his chest.

"So you thought you'd just leave me, Brier Rose?" He looked down at her, his brown eyes glowing with concern and reproach.

"I thought I could save you and Bea."

"You could have been killed." He entwined his left hand in the hair at the nape of her neck. "Don't try that again. You hear me?"

She gazed up at him and nodded, feeling as if she were the biggest failure in the entire world. Now she would never leave Brierwood. Taylor would make sure of that. Because of her cowardice, Taylor would face death, and she would meet with dishonor and who knew what else at the hands of Seth Bastyr. Against her will Rose began to sob, clutching the front of his white shirt as if it were her only anchor to reality.

"He must know everything I think," she said. "Everything! Now that he's been in my aura, he must be able to read my mind."

Taylor wiped away a tear with his thumb, unaware of how the gesture made her heart swell with love for him.

"And *you* can't leave either, Taylor—not with those dogs out there and the phones down."

"I don't plan to leave."

"Even if it's the only way to save yourself?"

"That's kind of a moot question now, Rose." He urged her head back by gently tugging on the fistful of red hair. "So let's forget it, all right?"

For a moment his eyes glittered at her, and then his mouth lowered to hers and he kissed her. Their lips clung to each other as his hand kept her pressed against him. She released the front of his shirt and slid her hands up the sides of his neck, then wrapped her arms around him, succumbing to the wonderful sensation that spread over her when she was in his arms, as if everything would turn out all right. She pressed desperate kisses on his cheek and jaw.

"Oh, Taylor," she breathed, her lips near the underside of his strong jaw. "How will we ever fight Seth?"

"For starters, I'll get that pistol of Bea's," he answered, stroking her hair. "And then we're going to go hunting for a vampire."

"But how can you hunt him down when he's in my aura?"

"He's not in your aura. I checked."

While Taylor cleaned the gun, Rose and Bea sorted through the jumbled mess in Bea's apartment, searching for the box that had held the emerald and list of instructions. Bea found it shoved beneath her bed, the lid ripped off its hinges, as if Seth had been in a hurry or a maniacal rage.

Bea held up the bottom of the box and shook her head as Rose joined her by the bed.

"What about the list of instructions?" Rose asked, taking the empty box in her hands.

"They're gone, too."

"I never really read them thoroughly," Rose put in. "I should have, when I had the chance."

"I've gone over them again and again, dear, worrying about the day you would turn twenty-one. I think I can remember most of the words."

"But what good will that do us without the my mother's emerald?"

"Maybe if you wore my emerald ring—"

Bea started to twist the band off her finger, but Rose put out a hand to stop her.

"No, Bea. You keep it. If you take that off, there's no telling what Seth will do to you. At least we know he wants me alive for tonight."

"But there must be something I can do to help."

"You can't help me if Seth gets to you," Rose reasoned. "Keep it on for now."

Reluctantly Bea nodded in agreement and looked about her disorderly apartment. Rose glanced at her, aware of the lines of tiredness around Bea's mouth, the smudges under her eyes and the telltale way she stroked her temple to alleviate the onset of a headache. She shouldn't even be up and about after having narrowly escaped death earlier that morning. There was nothing she could do, either, to prepare for the night to come, other than be fully rested in case a chance to save herself should arise.

Rose put the box on the bed and slipped her arm around Bea's shoulders. "Bea, why don't you go back to my room and take a nap?"

"But there's so much to do—"

"This mess can wait. And there's nothing we can really do until tonight, anyway, other than try to find Seth and the emerald."

"So we just sit here and wait?"

Rose squeezed her shoulders. "What else can we do?"

"I feel so helpless. Like a sitting duck." Bea clutched Rose's hands. "And I'm frightened, Rose."

"So am I." Rose straightened and looked down at her grandmother. "I only hope you will forgive me."

"Whatever for?"

"For not believing. For not leaving when you asked."

Bea gave her a tremulous smile. "Dear Rose. Don't worry about me. I'll be all right. It's you—"

"We should have left days ago, Bea. I'm so sorry I refused to go."

"You couldn't have known the consequences, child." Tenderly, Bea patted her cheek. "And none of us could have predicted the dogs and the phone."

Rose gazed down at her. "I love you, Bea. I just wanted you to know."

Bea's eyes glistened. "And I love you, dear. You've been the best grandchild a grandmother could have." She reached up, and Rose bent to embrace her. Before her emotions could get the best of her again, however, she drew away, just as Taylor appeared in the doorway of the bedroom.

"I'm ready when you are," he said, tucking the pistol in the waistband of his jeans. "Let's go find that sonofabitch."

"I'm going with you," Bea put in, shuffling toward Taylor.

Rose put out a restraining hand. "Bea, you're exhausted."

"I'm not staying behind," she countered. "Seth Bastyr killed my son and my husband. And now he wants you. Do you think I can take a nap when I know Seth's somewhere at Brierwood? Not a chance. I'm going with you. And that's final.''

"Come on, then." Taylor looked at his watch. "It's four o'clock. We have about six hours until dark."

As they left Bea's room, Rose realized just how monstrous a job lay before them. And that was assuming Seth lay sleeping somewhere in the house and not out in the extensive grounds, where they were prevented from going by the rottweilers. Brierwood was a huge, rambling house with three full floors of nooks and crannies, topped by a shadowy attic and built over a dark labyrinth of cellars that Rose had always made a point of avoiding. If they could have split up and conducted individual searches their task would have been considerably easier. But Taylor insisted that they stay together for safety's sake, and she had to agree with his decision. If Seth showed up unexpectedly, or if the dogs managed to break into the house, she would feel much safer with Taylor by her side.

Rose suggested searching the house from attic to basement, going methodically from one wing of the house to the other, so they wouldn't miss a single room. She and Bea carried flashlights. Taylor kept the gun as well as a light.

Taylor led the way to the attic by ascending a short flight of wooden stairs and opening a small door onto a long, narrow room lit by a pair of dormers and two high windows at either end. The windows were dusty and festooned with thick cobwebs, which blocked most of the light. Rose didn't relish the idea of searching through the contents of the attic, but she knew she couldn't turn back. Her glance darted around the attic, which was crowded with trunks and boxes that cast strange, distorted shadows on the floor. What if Seth was somewhere in this creaking, musty place, pressed against the wall like an earwig in the crack of a fence, waiting until nightfall, when he could surge to life? If she came upon him like that, she would absolutely faint.

With her heart pounding in her ears, Rose eased farther into the room, too proud to admit how scared she felt. The rhythmic tapping of Taylor's cane on the wooden floor as he searched the room only served to remind her that time was quickly ticking away.

"What will we do if we find him?" Rose asked, gingerly lifting the clasp on a large, dusty chest. What if Seth were curled inside the box waiting to leap to life? With fingers that were frozen and stiff, she lifted the lid slightly, wishing she had a stick in her hand so she could perform the task and still keep her distance from the box. She peered into the murky depths of the chest and let out a relieved breath. The chest was filled with old linens.

"We kill him!" Bea replied vehemently.

"How, though? With a gun?"

Taylor moved a drapery aside with the tip of his cane. "I don't think vampires can be killed by a gun—at least, not the vampires I've ever read about." He let the drapery fall back into position and turned to look at Rose. "Vampires are killed with wooden stakes and wolfsbane, aren't they?"

"What about auric vampires?" Rose asked, trying to keep her voice from cracking with fear. "What did the book say about getting rid of them?"

"Nothing. That's the problem. The book only mentioned how a person could avoid auric vampires or heal auric wounds. Perhaps the author of the book never encountered an auric vampire as powerful as Seth."

"And without the emerald, we're helpless," Bea put in, pushing up her glasses. "Your mother's instructions depended on the emerald."

"If we find him while he's resting, we might be able to get the emerald back." Taylor knelt on one knee and aimed a flashlight into the crawl space under the eaves of the roof. Then he stood up and switched off the light. "I'm hoping he'll be in a weakened state then, and that he'll have hidden the emerald somewhere on his person."

Rose sneezed from the dust particles that wafted into the air with every step she took and every trunk and carton she dislodged. She rubbed the tip of her nose. "So we'll body-search him?"

"That's right."

Rose hated the thought—dreaded the prospect, as a matter of fact—and from the look on Taylor's face, she knew he felt the same way.

The afternoon flew by, as if fate guessed they were pressed for time and was playing a cruel joke on them by hurrying the sun toward the horizon. After they completed their search of the second and third floors, they trudged down the stairs to the main floor just as the grandfather clock near the stairs struck the half hour, chiming its mournful tune through the house. Seven-thirty. Rose shuddered involuntarily. They had only two hours until dusk. After a search of the main floor, they returned to the stair hall.

Bea took the opportunity to sink to the bottom step and lean her head against a lathed baluster. She sighed and closed her eyes in exhaustion. Rose let her rest for a moment and looked out the window, dismayed to see the sun melting behind the trees. She sensed every tick of the clock in her own rapid pulse. If they didn't find Seth soon, within the next hour or so, all hope would be lost for saving themselves.

She looked down at Bea, who sat on the stair in silent exhaustion, her hands curved together in her lap, and then at Taylor, who stood leaning on his cane and staring out the window, his sharp features outlined by the golden glow of sunset. Dust motes danced in the rays that streamed through the window by the door, lending a vibrant note to an otherwise weary stillness. Even Edgar was uncharacteristically quiet, content to sit on the newel post near Taylor's elbow. Rose surveyed all three of them, her heart heavy with dread and despair.

Soon, however, Taylor sensed her gaze and slowly turned to look at her. She didn't avert her eyes, and for a long time they simply stared at each other, aware that this could be their last quiet moment together. Rose could feel her love for him streaming through the air, as real and warm as the light rays that beamed around him. She did nothing to disguise her feelings for him and hoped he could read her mind as easily as Seth picked up her thoughts.

I love you, Taylor. I love you. I love you.

He gazed back with an inscrutable expression on his face, his mouth an unbending line, his eyes a glittering black. Yet across his cheekbones crept the rosy patches she had seen once before, and she wondered if he had guessed what she so desperately wished to tell him. And did he love her in return? She didn't know. He wasn't the kind of person to let down his guard, not even with his eyes. Perhaps he had stayed to help her as a way of seeking atonement for his past, as he had said, and not because he cared about her. She couldn't bear the thought that he might be helping her for reasons of duty instead of love.

As if to validate her doubts, he suddenly broke eye contact and in his brusque fashion issued a command. "Let's hit the basement."

Bea pushed herself to her feet with a sigh. Rose watched her, worried about the tired way Bea straightened her spine and looked up at the ceiling.

"Bea, perhaps you should stay up here. Taylor and I can look downstairs."

Bea straightened her shoulders. "You're not leaving me here." She picked up her flashlight and smoothed back her hair. "I'm ready."

"How about you, Rose?" Taylor asked, crossing the floor to her. She longed to reach for him, to kiss him and tell him everything in her heart. But he barely glanced at her as he went by. Perhaps he couldn't accept the way she felt about him. Perhaps all he had wanted was to explore her body and nothing more.

"Yes, I'm ready," she replied, turning the flashlight in her hand. She hoped the batteries were still good, for she knew the basement was full of shadows and dark corners.

"I'll go first," she said, hurrying toward the door near the servants' stairwell. She hated the idea of leading the way into the gloomy, dank cellar, but she wouldn't allow Bea to guide them, and Taylor wouldn't be aware of the myriad twists and turns in the basement. "I know where the lights are."

"All right." Taylor held the door open for her, and Rose stepped across the threshold.

The cellar beneath Brierwood mansion was like the room in a house where everything was tossed and visitors were never allowed to wander. The rest of the house, though old and outdated, was a showpiece of craftsmanship and expensive materials. Not so the cellar. It was the abandoned project, the poor relative, a raw ugly cavern hacked out of dirt and stone.

Rose flipped on the light switch, which illuminated a bare bulb hanging from a twist of wire at the bottom of the wooden stairs. Beyond the stairs was a curtain of darkness, hiding a series of other bare bulbs that had to be turned on one by one.

Taylor and Bea creaked down the stairs behind her. The gloom below was almost too opaque to be penetrated by her flashlight.

"Paradise lost," Taylor murmured sarcastically.

"Really lost," Rose replied. She gained the cellar floor and waited for Taylor and Bea to reach the bottom. She rubbed her nose again, hating to take a single breath of the close, musty air.

Taylor scanned the perimeter of the room with his flashlight. "What's down here, anyway?"

"Everything," Rose replied. "Canning supplies. Jars of preserves that no one ever eats. Newspapers your aunt saved since the time she first came here—the twenties, I believe."

"Good God."

"Then there's the furnace room. And a place that was walled-in after being used as a garage. Only no one bothered to take out the car."

"What's the dripping noise?"

"The wall leaks under the west wing," Bea explained, rubbing the backs of her arms. "There's a sump pump that takes care of most of the groundwater. But some of the cellar just stays wet all year round."

Rose remained at Taylor's elbow, longing to wrap her hands around his arm and seek the protection of his body. Instead, she took a resolute step toward the next light.

"Come on," she said. "Let's get this over with."

They turned on the next light and did a systematic search of the area, poking into dark alcoves and inspecting shelves and cupboards. All Rose wanted to do was turn tail and run up the stairs, but she forced herself to continue, knowing they had to exhaust every possible hiding place.

One by one she turned on the lights, and little by little they crept through the cellar, a pitiful reluctant parade, sinking their feeble beams of light into the blackness. Once she took time to glance at her watch and saw that it was already nine o'clock. Her stomach rumbled with hunger, but in the next heartbeat she felt a burning twist of anxiety sear through the emptiness. Only by concentrating could she keep her flashlight from shaking and betraying her terror.

Somewhere beneath the closed-off east wing, Taylor aimed his light at the wall.

"What's that?" he asked.

Rose turned and followed the light beam. "A boulder."

"What's a boulder doing in the cellar?"

Bea walked up to stand at Taylor's elbow and added her flashlight beam to his. "The builders came across the rock during construction. When they couldn't move it, they simply built the foundation around it."

"Incredible." Taylor walked closer. The rock was chest-high and protruded into the chamber a good three feet. "Looks like the foundation is cracked."

"Old houses shift," Bea put in, trailing after him. "Plus, we've had some fairly strong earthquakes over the years."

"There's a sizable crack above the boulder."

Reluctantly, Rose followed them. She had no desire to get any closer. Once, when she was younger, she had approached the stone, only to feel a blast of fetid wind blow out of the crack. The thought of a hidden cavity behind the moldering wall, not to mention what might lie beyond it, had been enough to fuel her adolescent nightmares for years.

"I wouldn't think the foundation is stable, with a crack like that," Taylor continued, walking to the boulder. "It must be two feet wide."

"Taylor," Rose implored. "Let's go. I don't like it here."

He glanced at her over his shoulder. "I've got to check this first, Rose. Eliminate all possibilities."

She held her breath and shivered as he angled his flashlight for a better look.

For a moment Taylor froze, holding the light above his head as he stared into the gash above the rock. Rose knew something was wrong by the way his body stiffened, but she couldn't see his face to read his expression. Then he motioned for them to stand back.

"He's here," Taylor gasped.

CHAPTER FIFTEEN

To Rose's horror, Taylor dropped his cane, pulled himself on top of the rock and wedged his body through the crack in the wall. She dashed forward, ignoring his command to stay away, and saw the bottoms of his feet disappear into the gloom.

"Taylor!" she cried. Her heart thundered in her ears as she craned her neck to see where he had gone. With a shaking hand she trained her light into the abyss and spied Taylor crouching over a figure wrapped in a shroud. She moved the light over the figure and saw the scarf on which she had slaved so many hours serving as a barrier between Seth and the damp earth. Beyond the two men was a chamber that wormed far back into the earth, too far for her light to penetrate.

"Be careful!" she whispered as she watched Taylor slowly pull away the scarf from Seth's torso. Seth lay near the opening, hands crossed over his chest, his profile in full view of her light. His eyes were closed, his mouth slightly open, his cheeks gaunt and pale in the darkness. His body lay motionless, as if he weren't breathing.

"Has Taylor found the emerald yet?" Bea asked behind her. She was too short to see anything through the crack above the rock.

"No." Stale air wafted from the chamber, and Rose held her hand over her nose. "Hurry, Taylor! Please hurry!"

He gave no indication that he'd heard her. With calm, deliberate movements he slipped his hand into the strange black robe Seth wore, searching for the emerald, but without success. Rose marveled that he could retain his composure under such stressful conditions. Next he tried the sides of the robe, looking for a pocket or pouch. Taylor let out a frustrated sigh and leaned over to pull the scarf down, enough to allow him to check the other side of Seth's body.

Suddenly, outside in the garden, a dog howled mournfully, sending a wave of shivers across Rose's scalp. As if cued by the sound, Seth's eyes blinked open.

In that moment Rose knew pure, heart-shriveling terror.

"Taylor!" Rose cried, knowing he was intent on unveiling Seth and wasn't looking at the vampire's face. "Taylor! He's awake!"

Before Taylor had a chance to scramble backward, Seth sat up and flung off the scarf. He looked right at her, his odd sunken eyes locking with hers.

Rose thought her heart would stop, thought her knees would buckle and she would drop into a dead faint. But her worry for Taylor kept her on her feet. She forced her mind to go blank, knowing that Seth could delve into her thoughts and find out what they were after. She concentrated on the silver swirls of the scarf and thought of galaxies, of the Milky Way and the end of the universe, all the while hoping Taylor might get away.

Taylor whipped the gun out of his jeans. "Hold it right there, Seth," he warned, aiming the weapon at Seth's chest.

Seth began to snicker. Then he tipped back his head and laughed, filling the chamber with the unholy sound of his amusement. It echoed off the stone walls of the cellar, traveling through the labyrinth like a maelstrom. Rose clamped her palms over her ears, trying to block out the noise, but she could still hear his laughter through her flesh and in her blood.

Taylor held firm, refusing to give in to Seth's ridicule. Never once did his hand waver. Rose wondered if the discordant blast no longer affected Taylor of if he had learned to overcome the effect of the noise.

"Go ahead," Seth growled, abruptly biting off his laughter. "Shoot me."

He stood up, taking the scarf with him.

Taylor clenched his jaw as he considered his options.

"Shoot me, Mr. Wolfe. Go ahead." As if to test Taylor, Seth lunged at him.

In reflex, Taylor squeezed the trigger. The bullet passed through Seth's chest without spilling a drop of blood. Seth didn't even flinch.

"Again?" he taunted, smiling his small, mirthless smirk.

Taylor squeezed off two more shots, hitting his mark, but without consequence.

"Finished, Mr. Wolfe?" Seth purred.

Rose gaped at him, shocked by Seth's invulnerability and distrustful of his ominous civility, for she knew how quickly he could burst into a rage.

Taylor let his arm swing down to his side, still holding the useless gun. He waited in grim silence as Seth folded the silk scarf and tucked it into his robe.

Seth brushed off his clothing, taking all the time he needed, and then straightened. "You could have saved yourself the trouble," he commented, stepping toward the rock as if he weren't in the lest concerned that Taylor might attack from the rear. "The emerald can't save you."

Rose heard Bea's intake of breath as she caught sight of Seth in the fissure above the boulder.

"And now, dear Roselyn. The time draws nigh for our wedding ceremony."

"No!" Taylor yelled. He burst through the opening, toppling Seth to the floor of the cellar. For a moment they struggled on the ground, but Taylor was no match for the other man's superhuman strength. Seth stood up, yanked Taylor to his feet and threw him across the room. Taylor hit a shelf lined with cans of who knew what and crumpled to the dirt, while nails and screws rained down upon him. An old coffee can rolled in circles at Rose's feet. She was barely conscious of the spiraling tin, so great was her fear for Taylor.

"You told me you'd spare him!" she blurted.

Seth turned his glowing eyes upon her. "Did I?"

"Yes. You wouldn't go back on your word, would you? That isn't the Bastyr way."

His upper lip curled into a sneer. "Precious, precious Roselyn. How quick to learn, how flawless a memory. You are the ultimate of the Bastyr offspring."

"So you won't hurt him?"

"Of course not." Seth fussed with his gloves. "If he promises to leave Brierwood."

"No way, you bastard!" Taylor retorted. He stood up and wiped the blood from his mouth. "I'll see you in hell first!"

"Such language," Seth remarked. "I can't see what Roselyn finds so attractive about you."

Rose was too upset to blush. She darted forward to give her support to Taylor, but Seth reached out and arrested her by grasping her braid. Pain seared her scalp, and she lurched to a stop, tilting her head backward.

"Not so fast, my dear," he murmured, pulling her against his chest. His robe reeked of nightshade and the pungent aroma of moist earth. She thought she would retch if she took a deep breath.

"Please, Taylor," Rose implored. "Go while you have the chance."

"No!"

"There's nothing you can do now."

"Listen to the lady," Seth put in. "She's being sensible."

"I'm not leaving you alone with him, Rose."

Bea skittered to Taylor's side, all the while keeping a fearful eye on Seth. She held out her hand to display her emerald ring. "Don't you dare try to hurt Mr. Wolfe," she warned in a quivering voice. "I've still got my ring, and I'm not afraid to use it."

Seth only chuckled at Bea's trembling display of courage. "And how will you use it, old woman? Do you know the secret of the emeralds?"

Proudly, Bea raised her chin, but Rose guessed that she was ignorant of the power of the gem. Rose gazed at her through a sheen of tears. She had never loved Bea more than at that moment, as she stood up to the vampire in the only way she knew how.

"Well, if you do know the secret, then work your magic." Seth laughed and pulled Rose toward the main hallway. "Try to stop me, old woman."

Bea stood helpless as Seth moved to the door. Rose dragged her feet as much as possible, until his grip on her hair forced her to move more quickly.

"I don't mean to be cruel, Roselyn, but you must cooperate."

"Never."

"Let go of her," Taylor demanded, striding after them. Seth only laughed.

Taylor grabbed his shoulder and pulled Seth around to face him. Seth released his hold on Rose's hair. She backed toward the wall, wondering what Seth would do to Taylor.

"You bastard! I said, let go of her!" Taylor drove his fist into Seth's face, knocking him against the wall. Seth shook his head, dispelling the impact of the blow, and smiled. Taylor lunged for him, intending to pummel him senseless. Instead, Seth lifted his leg and kicked Taylor in the stomach, hurling him across the room again. This time Taylor's head struck the boulder, and he collapsed to the floor in an unconscious heap.

"Taylor!" Rose cried.

"Silence!" Seth roared. "He's no concern of yours." He grabbed her arm and yanked her to the passageway.

"Taylor!" Rose cried again, peering over her shoulder as she was hauled away. She saw Bea run to his side and kneel down. Then Seth pulled her around a corner, and she lost sight of them. She quit fighting him, knowing she would never escape Seth now. And if Bea and Taylor stayed away long enough, perhaps Seth would remain true to his word and spare their lives. She brushed the hair out of her eyes and let herself be dragged out of the cellar.

"That's better, my dear," Seth murmured, opening the back door. "And don't worry so. It will all be worth it. Just you wait and see."

Rose hung in his grip, half-numb with trauma and fright, as she stared dully at the garden, so soft and peaceful in the twilight. She hoped the dogs would come and deliver her from Seth. Yet she knew in her heart that the rottweilers were somehow connected to Seth and probably did his bidding. If that were the case, the dogs would not appear, or if they did, Seth would bring them to heel. Either way, she would not escape her fate. Tonight she would become the ritual bride of Seth Bastyr and forget everything and everyone she had ever known. To lose her memory and her self-will would be like dying. Rose faltered, terrified at the thought, and Seth turned to glare at her.

"You'll never have me," she declared vehemently. "Not all the way. I'll fight you, just as my mother did."

"Your mother was a fool." He tightened his grip on her upper arm, watching to see if she would show any sign of pain. Rose kept her chin up and her shoulders straight, refusing to give him the satisfaction of seeing her wince. "She took her life when she had everything she could possibly want," Seth continued. "I gave her everything."

"You took two children from her."

"They were unworthy of carrying the Bastyr name."

"You took her life, her identity, her soul."

"To make her over, Roselyn, to make her better." He stroked her cheek. "Women are frail, my dear, in need of direction. And a strong hand such as mine molds a strong character."

"You had no right to try to change her." She twisted out of his grip. "And as God is my witness, you won't change me!"

"Oh?" He pushed her against the edge of the sundial. "We shall see about that, Roselyn." He drew the scarf from his jacket and placed it on the flattened stone. "We shall soon see the stuff of which you are made."

Taylor opened his eyes, blinded by Bea's flashlight and a halo of sparkles in the periphery of his vision, caused by the blow to his head. He moaned and tried to sit up. His stomach protested the movement, reminding him of Seth's excruciating kick to his diaphragm. He was exhausted, not only from fighting Seth, but from his efforts to block the overwhelming sound he heard in Seth's presence. He had succeeded admirably in repelling the discordant noise but had failed in the hand-to-hand-combat department.

He rolled onto his side and let a wave of nausea pass over him.

"Mr. Wolfe, are you going to be all right?"

"Yeah, Bea. Hold on a minute."

"We don't have much time. He's taken Rose."

"Bastard." Taylor coughed and managed to prop himself up on one elbow. "God, my head is ringing like St. Mark's."

"You hit it on the rock. You're lucky to be alive."

"I don't feel lucky. I feel like hell." He took another breath and sat all the way up. Another wave of nausea swept over him, and he closed his eyes, forcing it to subside. Then, using all his willpower, he rose to his feet. He swayed.

"Mr. Wolfe!" Bea clutched his arm while she held out his cane.

"I'll be all right in a minute. I'm dizzy, that's all."

Dizzy, hell. His leg was on fire, his abdomen felt as if a logging truck had run over him, and his head throbbed and pulsed with each beat of his heart. Any minute now he expected his skull to explode from the pressure. Yet he couldn't fall apart. He had to find Rose and get her away from Seth.

Taylor took the cane and leaned on it. One more beating from Seth and he would be in no condition to save anyone.

With his cane on one side and Bea on the other, Taylor managed to stumble through the cellar passageways until they reached the stairs. For a moment he had to rest and catch his breath before ascending. He couldn't believe he had lost so much physical strength that he had to lean on a seventy-year-old woman for support. Some heroic savior he was. Taylor frowned and slowly made his way up the steps.

Once in the hallway on the main floor, Taylor paused, unsure where to look for Rose.

"Where would Seth have taken her?" he asked, glancing down at Bea.

She fingered the edge of her collar. "I haven't the faintest idea, Mr. Wolfe."

The sounds of their voices must have alerted Edgar, for he hopped out of the kitchen and cawed.

"He's shown me where Rose was before," Taylor mused. "Maybe he can help us." Taylor held out his wrist in the position he had observed Rose take when she wanted the raven to perch on her arm. Edgar obliged by flapping up to him.

"Where's Rose?" Taylor asked, staring the bird in the eye.

Edgar cocked his head. Then he took off toward the rear of the house.

"Come on," Taylor said, hobbling in pursuit. Bea followed him to the back door.

"There they are!" she exclaimed, pointing to Seth's tall, dark figure and Rose's slender form standing by the sundial. She reached for the handle of the door.

"Wait. The dogs might be out there."

Bea pressed close to the window and looked out.

Taylor let his eyes go out focus, searching the grounds with his special vision. Just as before, he caught sight of four black wraiths slowly circling the huge sundial. Were the wraiths the spirit form of the four rottweilers? He had a hunch they were. Yet why didn't they dissipate at the appearance of Bea's emerald? Were they stronger now that Seth stood with them? And what would they do if Taylor and Bea stepped out of the house?

They had no choice but to continue toward the garden.

Taylor led the way out the back door onto the flagstones, half expecting the black wraiths to transform into vicious dogs and attack them again. But the dark shapes continued their slow circling around the sundial, as if unaware of the two strangers approaching.

Though Seth's back was turned to him, Taylor caught snatches of his voice as he spoke to Rose. She seemed to be in a trance, standing in the fading light as he loosened the braid of her hair and spread her fiery tresses around her shoulders. He had removed his gloves, obviously to relish the texture of her hair, a fact that caused a hot flare of jealousy to flash through Taylor. He didn't want Seth to touch Rose—not her hair, not her body, not any part of her.

"Let her go, Seth," Taylor demanded, brandishing his cane.

"Ah, Mr. Wolfe." Seth turned, not in the least concerned about the cane. "We have been waiting for you."

He motioned toward the wraiths, which shimmered and roiled, gradually taking the shapes of figures dressed in black robes.

Taylor stared at them, hardly believing his eyes. What kind of magic was this? What kind of creatures were they? Humans? Spirits? Seth seemed to possess a fairly normal human body, except for the fact that he was impervious to bullets and could turn into a smoky haze and enter Rose's aura. But these wraiths were part dog, part shadow, part human. Were they members of the Bastyr family, too? And if so, what other powers did they possess?

He glanced at Rose, who was watching the robed figures, her expression white with shock. The wind blew tendrils of her hair across her face, but she did nothing except stand motionless beside the sundial. What had Seth done to silence her? Had he hypnotized her? Threatened her into submission?

He had to keep her from the Bastyrs. Taylor held the cane in both hands, ready to strike, while two robed figures stepped away from the sundial and flowed over the flagstones toward him. He knew only one way to defend Rose—with brute force. But would it be enough?

"Take Mr. Wolfe to that tree and tie him," Seth instructed.

"You'll have to fight me first!" Taylor tapped the wooden cane on his palm and planted his feet.

"You are tiresome, Mr. Wolfe." With amazing speed and strength, Seth whipped out his arm, grabbed the cane and flung it to the far side of the garden. Taylor fell in a clump of poppies from the force and speed of Seth's attack and for an instant sat there dazed. He hadn't even seen Seth turn for the attack. He hadn't struck even a single blow in return. And before he could scramble to his feet, he was grabbed by his arms and hauled to a fir tree by the robed figures. They tied him to the trunk with a length of rope, pinning his upper arms to his sides. Taylor pulled at the bindings until they gouged into the flesh at his elbows, but he couldn't break free.

"The old woman, too," Seth commanded, pointing at Bea.

She turned to run, but the robed figures quickly outdistanced her and tied her to the tree next to Taylor. Edgar flapped to a branch near her head.

"You'll pay for this in hell, Seth Bastyr!" Bea shouted.

"Hell holds no threat for me, old woman." Seth smiled at her and then returned his attention to Rose. "Now then," he announced. "Let the ceremony begin."

Without another word he reached out and tore Rose's dress, popping the buttons down the front. Taylor caught glimpses of her slip and bra straps as Seth pulled off the blue cotton fabric. Taylor yanked his arms, jerking like a wild animal to free himself, but he remained lashed to the fir tree, helpless, watching as Seth continued to disrobe Rose.

In moments she stood completely nude in the deepening twilight, her ivory skin glowing in the darkness, her hair an undulating diaphanous cloak. Even in the dusk he could see the rosy tips of her breasts, the creamy curves of her slender hips and the hidden womanly place he had thought would be his alone.

"No!" Taylor bellowed. How could Seth humiliate her like this? How could he let them see her like that, exposed to everyone's eyes? And what did the ritual entail that she had to be naked? Wasn't this supposed to be a wedding ceremony?

Slowly Seth turned around to face him, his hand draped across Rose's right shoulder.

"Look upon her, Mr. Wolfe. Does she not arouse you?"

"Let her go, you bastard!"

"Is she not beautiful?"

"You're insane!"

"You love her, don't you, Mr. Wolfe? Admit it." He drew back Rose's hair to provide Taylor with a clear view of her breasts. "You'd cut off your arm to save her, wouldn't you?"

"Is that what you want—my arm?" Taylor retorted, pulling at his bonds.

"Oh, no, Mr. Wolfe. I want something much more precious, much more rare and so much more subtle than self-mutilation." He stroked Rose's cheek. "I want to feel how much you love this young woman."

"Bastard!" Taylor strained with every fiber of his being in an effort to break free of the rope. The sight of Seth stroking Rose's skin sent him into a paroxysm of rage so great, he thought he would burst. He could feel his heart thundering in his ears, his neck and his chest, as if huge clots of anger pulsed in his veins. "Sonofabitch!"

"Excellent, Mr. Wolfe. Simply excellent!" Seth turned back to the remaining robed figures, who had climbed up on the giant sundial. "Lift her up," he instructed.

The figures pulled Rose up to the surface of the rock.

"Kneel," Seth barked. Rose sank to her knees and hung her head in shame.

Taylor leaned his head against the tree and panted in frustration, gritting his teeth with the effort it took not to scream. What could he do? Somehow he had to get hold of his emotions and try to think logically. His blind rage was doing nothing but fueling Seth's passion, which wasn't helping Rose at all. Desperate, Taylor pulled at his bonds again. This time, when his hand brushed the pocket of his jeans, he felt the outline of his Swiss army knife.

His anger shrank to cool calculation.

"Distract him, Bea," he said out of the corner of his mouth.

Bea tilted her head. "How?"

"Ask him questions."

"All right." Bea paused to marshal her thoughts and then cleared her throat. "Mr. Bastyr, I just want to know one thing, before you go on."

Seth hesitated in the process of removing his robe. "And what is that?"

"I want to know why. Why the ritual?"

Taylor half listened as he strained to push the bump of the knife upward, moving in such a way as not to draw attention to himself. He forced his expression to remain blank and his eyes focused on Seth, as if hanging on his every word.

"It is a ritual of renewal, old woman." He pushed back the hood of his robe. "Roselyn's purity shall renew us. She is a symbol of the mother earth, of fertility, of birth. Without her, we grow old. Without her, we die."

"But why can't you have someone else? Why a Bastyr?"

"Because she keeps us untainted, pure, a race apart from the rest of the world. The people of this world are a race of mongrels, old woman. They have lost their strengths through the breakdown of their bloodlines.''

Taylor eased the knife out of his pocket. Straining with concentration, he held it between his fingers and wedged open the blade with his thumbnail. Then he curved his hand backward, struggling to saw the rope that imprisoned his arms.

''We Bastyrs have kept our bloodline pure for centuries, for millennia. That is the secret of our special powers and our supreme intellect.''

''But what if Rose isn't a full-blooded Bastyr?''

''That is impossible.'' Seth unfastened a clasp near his neck. ''Roselyn is the embodiment of the best of the Bastyr genes. She shall be a glorious bride. Glorious.''

''She isn't your daughter, Seth Bastyr.''

''Lies shall get you nowhere.''

One strand free! Taylor felt the slight release of his bindings and centered his attention on the remaining rope. The muscles of his wrist burned in protest, but he continued to saw the rope, aware that if he failed, Roselyn would be lost to him.

''It isn't a lie. Rose's father was my son, Will Anderson.''

''Impossible.''

''Impossible?'' Bea leaned forward, as if to break from her bonds. ''All you could create with Deborah were monsters—pitiful twisted little creatures. My Will gave her a perfect child, Rose.''

''No, Roselyn is a Bastyr through and through. I can tell just by looking at her.''

The last strand free! Taylor caught the rope between his fingers, so it wouldn't drape to the ground and betray him. Then he forced himself to remain calm and think about his actions. Physically, he was no match for Seth. If he approached him again, Seth would probably kill him. He had to think, had to use his head, for time was running out. In his heart he knew what he needed—the emerald. But how could he get his hands on it? And where was it?

As if in answer, a thought struck him. Bea had an emerald on her finger. Why not look at it with his special vision and find out what type of aura it emitted? Then, using the color as a guide, he could look at Seth to see if a similar aura existed somewhere on his body or in his clothing. If he could find the emerald and somehow get his hands on it, he might have a chance to save Rose after all.

Taylor shifted his vision and glanced at Bea's hand. The emerald glowed with a shimmering tan color outlined with green.

"If you take Rose, you will be tainting the Bastyr line," Bea warned. "I know she's Will's child. Deborah had herself tested."

"It is of no matter, even so. Roselyn is the last female of the line. She is Deborah's daughter, and she must carry on the tradition." Seth let his black robe fall to the ground and heaved in a great breath of air. His bare chest rose in the twilight, accentuating his narrow shoulders and thin arms and legs. He seemed unconcerned with his nakedness.

Taylor stared at him, loathing the thought that this man intended to take Rose as his bride. Taylor wanted to break his neck. Instead, he searched Seth for the telltale aura of tan and green, starting at his shoulders and traveling down his lean body. No sign of the aura glowed in the darkness.

Seth held out both arms. "Prudence, bring the robe."

One of the hooded figures lifted the scarf from the sundial and carried it to Seth, offering it up like a sacred object.

"This scarf shall bind you to me, Roselyn," Seth said, as the hooded figure draped it over his shoulders. "When I wrap you in it, you become one with me, never to be separated through all eternity."

"That's not true, Rose," Bea taunted. "Deborah broke away from him."

"Deborah did not weave the scarf as instructed. She was a headstrong fool!" Seth wrapped himself in the magical scarf, and the silver pigment glinted with every move he made.

Frantic to find the emerald, Taylor inspected the ground and Seth's discarded clothing. For a moment he saw nothing, and then he caught a faint tan shade glowing in Seth's cast-off robe. The emerald was there, probably in a pocket he hadn't had enough time to find.

"Deborah was too strong for you, Seth Bastyr," Bea continued, seemingly heedless of Seth's darkening expression. "Rose will break away, too!"

"Silence!" Seth whirled to face her, lowering his head as if he were a bull preparing to charge. Yet he didn't move but stood his ground and balled his hands into fists. Taylor saw a black shaft shoot out of Seth's aura and whir straight for Bea's head. The spear pierced Bea's yellow aura, which out of fear had contracted into the barest shell of color. To Taylor's horror, he saw a black mark appear against the yellow, like an ink stain. Bea gasped, her knees buckled, and she slumped in her bindings, unconscious or dead.

Choking back a cry of rage, Taylor burst into action, flinging away the rope. He lunged from the tree and dashed across the flagstones to Seth's robe, hoping to grab the emerald in time.

CHAPTER SIXTEEN

He knelt down to recover the discarded robe just as Seth kicked him in the side and sent him sprawling across the flagstones. Taylor was so intent on finding the emerald that he ignored the agony in his side. As Seth strode toward him, Taylor plunged his hand into the pocket of the robe and pulled out a velvet bag. His fingers could feel a slick, heavy object inside the bag. Without seeing it, Taylor knew he had found the emerald.

But before he could get the gem out of the pouch, he looked up to see Seth looming above him, his eyes wild with anger.

"Give me that emerald!" Seth demanded. "Or I will crush the very life from you."

"Like hell," Taylor retorted, struggling to his feet. Before he stood all the way up, Seth kicked him again, this time in his injured calf. A fire of agony shot up his leg, and Taylor felt white-hot pain pour over him. He nearly blacked out. Nauseated, he fell backward, and his hand struck the stone, which knocked the pouch out of his grip. The bag slid across the ground, out of reach. He lay on the ground, panting, his shin throbbing. He could feel the leg of his jeans wet with blood.

"Meddler," Seth growled. "I would have spared you, had you not interfered."

Taylor glowered at him, knowing it would be useless to try to get back up. He could see the velvet pouch out of the corner of his eye. He had held the emerald in his hand. How could he have managed to lose it so quickly?

"I grow impatient with your attempts at heroics."

Taylor saw Seth's hands tightening into fists and guessed he was about to become a victim of Seth's auric spear, just as Bea had been. He shifted his vision, waiting until the very last minute, until the spear emerged above Seth's head. Then Taylor rolled to the side, barely avoiding being struck. He heard a deep tone behind him on the flagstones as the spear hit the ground. Ignoring the fire in his shin, he scrambled to his feet as Seth swung around to try again. Unfortunately, Taylor had managed to roll even farther from the emerald and realized that he would have to run around the sundial in order to gain possession of the gem.

He lunged toward a figure in black, running into him with his shoulder lowered for a tackle. The figure toppled to the ground. Behind him, Taylor caught a glimpse of Seth moving to get a clearer path for his auric ray. Taylor ducked behind the granite sundial as the ebony spear shot toward him. The lilies at his feet shriveled, and the grass beyond bore a streak of brown, as if burned by the shaft of energy. A cold wave of dread washed over Taylor as he realized that he would have been killed by now, had he not been blessed with his auric vision. In that moment he knew that his special vision was not the curse he had considered it to be but a gift given to him by the lady in his dream. He had been sent back to earth to save Rose Quennel, to break the chain of ritual. He was her champion, the champion of the Bastyr women. Though crippled and weak, he was their only hope.

Perhaps Seth had never encountered a man who could see auras. Perhaps Taylor had the power to overcome the Bastyrs, after all. Taylor jumped to his feet, only to see Rose raise her head.

"Stay down!" he yelled.

But Rose didn't listen to him. She sat back on her heels, straining against the leather thong lashed around her wrists and tied to the gnomon of the sundial.

"Edgar!" she called. "Get the emerald!"

Just as Taylor saw the raven glide down from the fir tree, he was attacked from behind by a hooded figure. Then all hell broke loose. Seth shot another bolt of energy at him, while the remaining hooded figures transformed into rottweilers. One of them jumped for Taylor's throat. With his last burst of energy, Taylor bent forward, flipped the robed figure over his shoulder and threw him onto the attacking dog. Then Taylor leapt onto the sundial, stuffing his hand in his pocket for his knife. The rottweilers ran around the base of the sundial, snarling and snapping, jumping up with their huge paws on the edge of the slab. He was sure that any moment one of the dogs would make it onto the sundial.

"Taylor!" Rose cried. "Catch!"

Taylor looked up just in time to see Edgar fly overhead and release the velvet pouch. He caught the sack in his hand and dropped to his knees, keeping an eye on Seth, who balled his fists for another attack. With trembling hands Taylor shook out the emerald, which fell with a thud into his palm. The emerald was his! But how could he use it against the Bastyrs? He had no knowledge of the power of the gem.

He glanced at Seth and saw another auric shaft hurling through the darkness toward him. In the split second it took to see the shaft, Taylor knew his efforts were in vain. There was no time to roll away, no time to tell Rose to duck. In a purely instinctive reaction, he sprang forward, hand in the air as if to ward off the spear and keep it from hitting Rose. The bolt hit the emerald with such an impact that his hand whipped back and he nearly lost his grip on the stone. But he held on, though the emerald vibrated and burned with heat, and never once took his attention from Seth, who stood below him. To Taylor's amazement, he saw Seth turn to smoke and head straight for the emerald, as if being sucked toward the gem.

Rose watched Taylor holding out the emerald, as if signaling Seth to halt. She couldn't imagine what he thought he was doing. Surely he had lost his mind. She couldn't blame him. She had suffered a weird sort of mental apathy herself since being tied to the sundial. Yet during the time that Seth had been occupied with containing Taylor, the fog of her trance had gradually lifted. All she could conclude was that Taylor, in a last-ditch attempt, was offering himself as the ultimate sacrifice, hoping to save her.

"No!" she cried, just as Taylor froze, his hand outstretched.

Suddenly she heard the discordant sound, so loud that it shook the ground beneath the granite on which she crouched. Rose winced, squinting from the onslaught of noise. Above her Taylor was literally glowing. She could see a red cloud wafting up his arm and surrounding the hand that held the emerald. A red cloud enveloped his head and shoulders, and soon it encompassed his entire body. He looked as if he were glowing with heat, as if at any moment he would burst into flame.

The hand that held the emerald shook as the cloud turned from red to black. The sound of the organ whirled into a cacophony of tones, as if hundreds of music boxes and circus calliopes were being played at the same time. Tears welled up in her eyes at the force of the sound, and she squeezed her lids together, unable to cover her ears with her bound hands. For what seemed like hours the sound whirred around her in painful, throbbing waves. Then, suddenly, the noise broke off.

Gasping, Rose looked up at Taylor. His upraised hand was glowing a pale red. For an instant he stood as if turned to stone, and then he crumpled to a heap beside her. She couldn't see his face, only the back of his tousled black head. His left hand hung over the edge of the sundial. What if the rottweilers saw it? They would pull him off the slab and tear him to pieces.

Wildly, Rose glanced around, amazed to find herself alone. The dogs had vanished. Seth was nowhere in sight. All that remained of him were his discarded robe and the puddle of the silk scarf a few feet away. An oppressive quiet hung over the garden as she stared into the darkness, but she was too afraid after all she had been through to trust the silence.

"Taylor?" she called. He didn't respond. He lay still—too still.

"Bea!" she cried. She could just make out Bea's slumped figure hanging from the tree on the edge of the flagstones.

Edgar flapped to her side and landed ignominiously on Taylor's motionless shoulder.

"Edgar!" Rose exclaimed. "Oh, Edgar, you wonderful bird!"

He cocked his head and stared at something on the granite slab. Rose followed his glance. A red pocketknife shone in the moonlight. She strained to reach it with the tips of her fingers and slid it toward her. After a few moments of struggling to open it, she sliced through her bindings and pulled free. She dropped the knife and immediately leaned over to check Taylor's condition.

His eyes were closed, and his mouth was slightly parted. She glanced down at his hand, where his fingers were wrapped around emerald. The edges of his fingers still glowed red, as if he held a bright light in his fist. She touched his neck, searching for his pulse. His skin was unnaturally cold, just as Donald Jacoby's had been when she had found him in the herb garden. Frantically, she moved two fingers down his neck, trying to pick up the beat of his heart. Finally she found a pulse, a dangerously weak thrum.

"Oh, Taylor!" she cried softly. He was barely alive. She had to get him to a doctor immediately, before Seth returned to finish the job. Rose looked up. The garden had been plunged into darkness. She was virtually alone, and she was terrified. If she were to help Taylor, she must brave the darkness on her own—something she hadn't done since she was five years old. The thought of running through the night seized her with terror. But she had to do it. Every second counted. She had to face her fears to save Taylor.

Rose grabbed the knife, jumped off the sundial and ran to Bea to determine her condition. Bea was alive, but unconscious. Swiftly Rose cut her down and laid her on the grass at the foot of the tree. Then she retrieved the scarf, wrapped it around her naked body and fled to the house. There she pulled on some clothes and grabbed her purse, running down the stairs as the clock chimed the midnight hour. Unnerved by the sonorous bongs, she stuffed the scarf in the side compartment of her bag while she flew out the back door, anxious to put the sound behind her. Through the dark she dashed to the carriage house, then drove the sedan across the yard to the sundial, ignoring the flower beds she ruined and the shrubbery she demolished. Any minute she expected Seth to show up, laughing and mocking her.

But Rose pressed on. She had to get away as soon as possible and obtain medical attention for Taylor and Bea. She could feel perspiration beading on her forehead as she ran to Taylor.

Somehow she found the strength to lug him off the sundial and into the back seat of the car. Then she strained with Bea's heavy shape, positioning her in the passenger seat. Glancing around at the dark garden to see if any shadowy shapes lingered, Rose ran around the car and slid into the driver's side. She slammed the door and locked it. Her hand shook as she turned the key and tore out of the yard.

Bea recovered soon after their arrival at the hospital, but Taylor's condition was much more serious. He lay near death, his nose and mouth sprouting tubes, his arm hooked to an intravenous drip, his condition closely monitored by a nurse down the hall at the nurses' station. His breathing came in shallow, uneven puffs, and his eyes rolled wildly beneath this lids, as if his dreams were as nightmarish as Rose's had been. The nearest the doctor could come to a diagnosis was that Taylor had suffered severe electrical trauma.

Rose kept a vigil at his side, half expecting Seth to show up at the hospital to kill Taylor and take her away.

Later that night, when the nurses changed shifts, a new nurse bustled into the room to check Taylor's vital signs and update his chart. She picked up his wrist and looked down at his hand, which still held the emerald.

"What's this?" she asked, pointing in disdain at the gem.

Rose got to her feet. "It's an . . . a crystal."

"Oh, for goodness sakes." The nurse put her hands on her ample hips. "It should never have been left in his hand."

Rose stepped forward, afraid of what might happen should Taylor be separated from the gem. "Wait—"

Before she could finish her sentence, she saw the nurse yank the emerald from Taylor's fingers. Instantly an alarm blared, shattering the stillness and frightening the nurse so thoroughly that she dropped the gem. It clunked to the floor.

"Cardiac arrest!" she shouted and lunged for a button near Taylor's bed. Then she rushed out of the room before Rose could ask any questions.

"Taylor!" she cried, running to his side. His breathing had stopped, along with the movement beneath his eyelids.

"Taylor!" she shrieked, her voice cracking in disbelief.

Within seconds a cardiac team dashed into the room, pushing a cart of equipment up to the bed. The nurse demanded that Rose leave immediately. She had just enough time to scoop up the emerald before she was ushered out to the hall. The door slammed behind her.

For a moment she stared at the door, listening for the muffled sounds of the cardiac team as they tried to revive Taylor but unable to make out any particulars. The tension was driving her crazy. To save her sanity, she turned her attention to the emerald in her hand. She held it up to the light, surprised to see that the clear green color had been replaced by a smoky haze that seemed to shift and change, as if something alive were trapped inside. It even felt warm to the touch. The sight and warmth of the emerald distressed her so much that she dropped it into the pocket of her dress, unable to think of an explanation for the transformation. She would leave it for another time, when she could think more clearly.

Her thoughts were interrupted by Bea, who had returned from the cafeteria.

"What's happening?" Bea asked, hurrying toward her.

"Taylor's heart has stopped!" The moment she uttered the phrase, she lost control of her emotions.

"Oh, dear God!"

Rose fell into Bea's warm embrace and wept, her heart breaking. She had expected Taylor to get better. All along she had thought that she and Taylor would have more time to spend together, had intuitively sensed that their lives were meant to cross and intertwine. But he had been part of her life for less than a week. And now he was gone. Gone forever.

"This is all because of me," Rose sobbed. "If it hadn't been for me, he would be all right."

"Don't say that, Rose," Bea replied, patting her back. "He chose to get involved. He wanted to help you."

"I never should have let him."

"You had no choice, Rose. He was a determined young man. He did what he wanted to do. He cared for you very much."

"But I'm responsible for this. And for Donald's death. And my own father's, as well. Why am I still alive?" She backed away and stared at Bea. "I'm the one who should be dead!"

"No, Rose. Those men died defending you. They had their roles to play, as you had yours."

"And what was my role?"

"To be the first woman ever to escape Seth's ritual—by breaking the chain and freeing yourself and all the others of Seth Bastyr. Without you, there will be no more Bastyrs."

"Have I freed myself, though?"

"You've passed your twenty-first birthday, haven't you?"

Rose brushed the tears from her cheeks. "I guess so. But what about Seth? Where did he go?"

"I don't know. And I don't care. All I'm concerned about is your future. You have a future now, Rose. Do you realize that?"

Rose gazed at the carpet, her vision swimming with tears. "I don't know if I want a future that doesn't include Taylor."

Bea stroked her back. "It might be heartless of me to say this, but Taylor isn't the only man in the world, dear. There will be others, believe me."

"Not for me. Taylor is special." She raised her head and crossed her arms, hugging her chest to hold back her tears. "He's just got to pull through!"

Twenty minutes later the attending physician emerged from Taylor's room. Rose watched his expression go blank as he closed the door and knew in an instant that Taylor was dead. She observed the doctor as he crossed the tile floor toward them, and it seemed to Rose that an hour passed before he stopped in front of them and put his hands in the pockets of his white coat. It seemed as if another hour passed before he opened his mouth and confirmed her fears. His words slurred together, bombarding her senses with snatches of sounds. Cardiac arrest. Blood clot. Electric shock. All they could do.

Rose felt herself go limp at the news. Taylor was dead. It wasn't possible! But Taylor *was* dead. Rose heard her own voice thanking the doctor for his help, heard Bea informing the doctor of Taylor's next of kin, heard the doctor asking if she would like to say goodbye to Taylor.

She dragged herself across the hall and over the threshold.

Rose closed the door behind her, never taking her gaze off the long, still shape in the bed. All the life-support equipment had been cleared from the room, and the tubes had been taken from his nose and wrists. He lay with his eyes and mouth closed, so peaceful that it appeared as if he were sleeping. They had removed the hospital gown when trying to revive him and had left it off, leaving his naked body exposed from his abdomen upward. The rest of him was covered with a sheet. Even in death his body appeared powerful, with his wide, muscular shoulders and well-developed arms in full view. Rose looked at him through a sheen of tears and wished that he were sleeping and that if she called to him he would awaken and turn at the sound of her voice. But Taylor would never move again. He had given his life to save her.

She put her purse on the table next to his bed and sank down on the mattress beside him.

"Oh, Taylor!" she whispered, wiping away the tears that streamed down her cheeks.

The familiar unruly strand of black hair fell over his forehead. With a trembling hand she lifted the strand and smoothed it back over the rest of his glossy hair. His hair and scalp were already cool to the touch. She drew her hand down the side of his face, following the scar that lined his left cheek.

How she longed to look into his eyes once more, to see the smoldering fire of his pirate's gaze, but his eyes were forever closed to her. She caressed the side of his face, unwilling to leave him and unable to say goodbye.

"I love you," she whispered, even though she knew he couldn't hear her. "Wherever you are now, Taylor, I love you."

Sobbing, she draped herself over his chest, pressing her cheek against the side of his neck, hugging him with all her strength. How would she live without him? How would she ever forget the way it had felt to melt from the inside out when Taylor held her? She tightened her arms around him, but the embrace gave her no comfort. Taylor's arms didn't surround her in warmth, his heart didn't beat against her skin. Everything that Taylor had been to her had vanished, leaving a shell that looked like him but wasn't him at all. Rose drew back, feeling empty and devastated, and wished she had never hugged him.

She gazed once more at him. She wouldn't say goodbye. She just couldn't say it. She still couldn't believe he was gone.

Her face was wet with tears, and a drop hung from the tip of her nose. She would have to pull herself together before she left the room. Rose fumbled in her purse for a tissue, and it was then that she saw the edge of the scarf protruding from the side pocket.

Seth had said the scarf would bind her to him for all eternity. Was it a magic scarf, as magic as the emeralds had been? Would the scarf bind any two people together, or just Seth and his bride? Could the scarf bind her to Taylor? It was worth trying. In fact, the scarf was her only hope. Sniffing, she reached out and pulled the scarf from her purse. It slipped out, falling in a shimmering indigo-and-silver cascade over her knees.

Rose looked at Taylor's body. Wherever he was, she wanted to be with him. If she couldn't be with him in life, she would follow him into death, since living would be meaningless without him. Without Taylor, all she could see ahead of her was a bleak existence filled with sorrow and numbness. Bea was wrong—no man would measure up to Taylor, and she would never be satisfied with anyone else.

All along she had been destined to be Taylor's bride, and she would follow that destiny, though it meant giving up her life on Earth. Slowly, Rose got to her feet. She would wrap herself and Taylor with the silk and give herself over to the magic of the scarf, be it good or bad. She would live with Taylor or die with him—but either way she would be together with him forever. The scarf draped nearly to the floor as she held it up with both hands.

Rose closed her eyes in concentration, trying to come up with a prayer powerful enough to invoke the magic of the

scarf. She decided to keep her prayer simple and sincere—
for what could be more potent than the truth in her heart?

"May this scarf bind us together—Taylor Wolfe and Rose
Bastyr—through all time and eternity."

She waited until the words died out and then lay down
beside Taylor, carefully pulling the shimmering silk over
them. A strange tingle passed through her. She closed the
spaces between her body and Taylor's by draping her arm
across his chest and snuggling into the small of his shoulder. It felt right to be with him like this. She slid her leg over
his.

Rose closed her eyes as a strange lassitude swept over her.
She felt as if she had been drugged. Was this the way death
came—creeping up on silent velvet feet? She lay beside
Taylor and languished in the sensation of utter peace and
love. The scent of the sea and wind wafted through her
consciousness. She felt her fears lifting, her memory of Seth
and Brierwood fading, as if blown away in a breeze. Slowly,
like the first flower of spring opening to the sunshine, joy
blossomed inside her, and she smiled.

EPILOGUE

Off the coast of California

Rose stood near the rail of the *Jamaican Lady* and pulled the silk scarf from the pocket of her skirt. The wind picked up a corner and unfurled it, snapping it nearly out of her hands. She held it aloft, watching as the warm California sun glimmered off the silver swirls. For a long moment she gazed at her handiwork, never more beautiful than when illuminated by the rays of sunset. Then, knowing she would never see the greatest work of her career again, she released her hold. The scarf billowed upward, caught on an air current just above the waves. The silk sailed through the air like a magic carpet, never touching the water, glinting in the dying sun, until it disappeared from view.

Rose sighed and felt Taylor's warm arms come around her. She leaned back against his chest, still marveling that he was here with her. After covering him with the scarf in the hospital, he had miraculously revived. The doctors had labeled it a misdiagnosis. But Rose was convinced that it had been a miracle, brought on by the enchanted silk scarf and her love for Taylor.

Even more miraculous, he had emerged from death without a wound on his leg or the scars on his face, as if he had been released from a curse brought about by his mysterious connection to the Bastyrs. She wondered if he had been part of the cycle of the ritual in another lifetime, perhaps a lifetime during which she had loved him. It would explain the sensation of déjà vu and his strange familiarity. It would explain the strange dream in which he had called her Constance and she had called him Nathaniel. She still couldn't get over the way he appeared without his scars and limp. Now she was seeing him as the Taylor Wolfe he had always been—confident, capable and strong—and she didn't stand a chance against his physical beauty, even if she had wanted to fight her attraction to him.

She remembered her mother's letter and the explanation of the scarf, in which Deborah had claimed that Rose would forget everything once Seth draped her in the silk and made her his bride. Yet the scarf had not taken away her memory at all, perhaps because she had been the one to call upon the magic.

Slowly Taylor turned her around to face him. For a wonderfully long time he kissed her, languishing in the first privacy they had enjoyed since leaving the hospital. The days since his release had been spent traveling with Bea and his mother, and then in a short stint at the Wolfe mansion in San Francisco as the ship was readied for a trip to the Caribbean, where he and Rose would spend their honeymoon. They had been married only a few hours ago, standing before a judge in a quiet ceremony, with only Bea and Ruth in attendance. Ruth was disappointed by the quick, quiet wedding, but Taylor was adamantly against turning their nuptials into a social event. Besides, neither he nor Rose had wanted to put up with the time it would have taken for elaborate preparations to be made.

He remembered gazing at her before the ceremony and shifting his vision to check her aura once again. The black spot that had branded her aura had disappeared, just as Seth had vanished. Yet he still worried about her and knew he would keep on checking her aura each day in the years to come.

Finally he drew away and reached into the pocket of his shorts.

"It's my turn," he said.

Taylor held up the strange smoky jewel, which glinted in the light of the sunset.

"Time to get rid of Seth."

Rose linked her arms around Taylor's trim waist. She knew now that his embrace was a precious gift and one she would never take lightly. "So you think Seth is trapped inside the emerald?"

"Yeah. That was the power of the emerald all along. It could imprison Seth Bastyr's aura. I just happened to be in the right place at the right time to trap him."

"You mean to tell me there's a man inside that rock?"

"Man? No." Taylor shook his head. "Seth Bastyr was no man."

"What was he, then?"

Taylor gazed down at her. He tilted her chin upward and dropped a kiss on the tip of her nose. "Let's just say that Seth was a bad dream, Rose. Just a bad dream."

Then he released her and flung the emerald as hard as he could. It sailed through the air, flashing in the dying sun, and finally dropped into the waves, disappearing from sight. Taylor watched it without speaking.

Rose glanced up at him, honoring his grim silence with a silence of her own. She remained standing at the rail with her arms around Taylor and her head resting on his chest. She would never tire of his vibrant warmth.

"Well, that's the end of the Bastyrs," he murmured, stroking her hair.

"Not quite. There's still one left. Me."

"Not anymore." He smiled. "You're a Wolfe now." He urged her toward the hatch leading to the cabin below. "And if it's all right with you, Rose, I don't really want to hyphenate our last name."

"You don't?"

"No. I think Rose Wolfe sounds just fine."

"Rose Wolfe." She laid her head on his shoulder and smiled at the newness of the name, glowing at the mere concept of being his wife. "Yes. That sounds wonderful to me."

She let Taylor guide her to the cabin, which smelled pleasantly of teak and wood oil. As she flowed into the room, Edgar hopped onto her shoulder.

Taylor took exception to the raven's company.

"Uh-uh," he said, shooing Edgar away. "Three's a crowd."

"Taylor—"

"I'm not sharing you with anyone tonight," Taylor returned, running his hand over her rear. "Not even Edgar."

Cawing in protest, Edgar flapped down the hallway. Taylor shut the door and raised his black eyebrows. Rose felt a thrill course through her. She and Taylor had not made love since that first time, more from circumstance than choice. And now that the time had come to join together as man and wife, she felt a thrill of anticipation laced with apprehension. Rose backed up until her legs bumped into the bunk behind her.

Taylor grinned and took off his shirt.

"It's warm down here," he said.

"Oh?"

"I could use a cool drink. How about you?"

"Yes." She nodded, anxious to prolong the time until she had to face the moment of truth. "A cool drink sounds great."

Taylor strode to the side of the bed and pulled a bottle of champagne from a bucket of ice. She hadn't even seen it sitting there.

"Nervous?" he asked, handing her a tulip glass full of bubbling champagne.

"No." She sipped the drink and quickly broke eye contact.

"Liar."

She glanced up at his handsome face. He was smiling at her, and his black eyes sparkled with warmth.

"I never thought we'd make it, Rose," he said, sobering. "I never thought we'd live to see this day."

"You almost didn't."

"So I've heard."

"And I've never thanked you, Taylor, for saving my life."

"It was my pleasure." He cupped her cheek in his hand and looked so deeply into her eyes that she melted all the way to her toes. "I'd go to hell and back for you."

"You already have." She touched his lips with her fingertip. "What can I do to ever repay you?"

"As to that—" Taylor tilted his head and smiled down at her, his black eyes smoldering with love as he drew her against him "—I've got a few ideas, Brier Rose."

*   *   *   *   *